ABOUT THE AUTHOR

Susan Grossey graduated from Cambridge University in 1987 and since then has made her living from crime. She spent twenty-five years advising financial institutions and others on money laundering – how to spot criminal money, and what to do about it – and has written many non-fiction books on the subject.

Her first work of fiction was the inaugural book in the Sam Plank series, *Fatal Forgery*, set in London in the 1820s and narrated by magistrates' constable Sam Plank. This was followed in the series by *The Man in the Canary Waistcoat*, *Worm in the Blossom*, *Portraits of Pretence*, *Faith, Hope and Trickery*, *Heir Apparent*, and *Notes of Change* which was the seventh (and final) book in the Sam Plank series.

Whipster is the third book in Susan's new series, the Cambridge Hardiman Mysteries. The first in the series was *Ostler* and the second was *Sizar*. There will be two more books in this series, again set in the 1820s, but this time with Gregory Hardiman, a university constable in Cambridge, at the heart of them.

BY THE SAME AUTHOR

The Sam Plank Mysteries

Fatal Forgery
The Man in the Canary Waistcoat
Worm in the Blossom
Portraits of Pretence
Faith, Hope and Trickery
Heir Apparent
Notes of Change

Portraits of Pretence was given the "Book of the Year 2017" award by influential book review website Discovering Diamonds. And *Faith, Hope and Trickery* was shortlisted for the Selfies Award 2019.

The Cambridge Hardiman Mysteries

Ostler
Sizar

Ostler was shortlisted for the Selfies Book Award 2024. And *Sizar* was shortlisted for the Selfies Award 2025.

<u>Non-fiction books</u>

The Solo Squid: How to Run a Happy One-Person Business

Susan in the City: The Cambridge News Years

WHIPSTER

SUSAN GROSSEY

SUSAN GROSSEY PUBLISHER

Author contact details:

susangrosseyauthor@gmail.com

www.susangrossey.com

Sign up for my free monthly e-newsletter and receive your FREE complete e-book of *Fatal Forgery* (the first book in the Sam Plank Mysteries series)

www.susangrossey.com/insider-updates

Whipster / Susan Grossey -- 1st edition

ISBN 978-1-915491-04-6

*To my dear friend and former colleague Rowan,
for nurturing, encouraging and informing
my fascination with financial crime*

"The summer's flower is to the summer sweet
Though to itself it only live and die,
But if that flower with base infection meet,
The basest weed outbraves his dignity:
For sweetest things turn sourest by their deeds:
Lilies that fester smell far worse than weeds."

*From "Sonnet 94: They that have power to hurt and will do none"
by William Shakespeare (1609)*

Author's note

Any period of history has its own vocabulary, both standard and slang. The Regency was no different, and to capture the spirit of the time I have used words and phrases that may not be familiar to the modern reader. Moreover, Gregory is a Norfolk boy and sometimes uses words and phrases from his childhood. At the end of this book there is a glossary of these terms and their brief definitions. This glossary also contains an overview of the currency used at the time, and its equivalent modern spending power.

GREGORY
HARDIMAN'S
CAMBRIDGE
MDCC
CXXIV
N
Huntingdon road
Histon road
POUND GREEN
CASTLE GATE: County Gaol
CASTLE HILL
Haymarket
'THE BOROUGH'
Bandyleg Walk
St. Peter's Street
CASTLE HILL
Castle Inn
brick pits
CHESTERTON village
The FORT ST. GEORGE in ENGLAND
CAM
Pound Hill
White Horse Inn
BELL LANE
St. Neots road
'THE CAMBRIDGE WATERCOURSE'
CHESTERTON LANE
MAGDALENE
THE HYTHE
Ditch
JESUS LOCK
JESUS GREEN
Jesus Close
foot ferries
STOURBRIDGE COMMON and FAIR
BUTTS
barge basin
GREAT BRIDGE
Bin Brook
TRINITY AQUEDUCT
ST. JOHN'S
BRIDGE STREET
ST. CLEMENT'S COLLEGE
St. Sepulchre's Passage
The HOOP Inn
JESUS
JESUS-LANE
NELL

'S CAUSEWAY, Newmarket road

½ mile

SCALE

(new TOWN GAOL)

old orchards

Hadstock road

CHRIST'S PIECES

PARKER'S PIECE

NEW TOWN, ('NEW ZEALAND')

King

ST. ANDREW'S STREET

Spinning House

DOWNING PLACE

Town Gaol

Hobson's Brook

marsh

LENSFIELD ROAD

London road

the ... the ... leys.

EV. STREET

GREEN STREET

SUSS.

Nicholson, bookseller

MKT. ST.

MARKET HILL

Conduit

PETTYCURY

Fisher's Bank

Bene't Street

Botanic Gdn.

The Eagle

HOSPITAL

River Pot/Pem Brook

STREET

PETER HOUSE

TRUMPINGTON

King's

Bishops

Mills

St. Mary's Lane

Black Bull Inn

SILVER STREET

TRINITY

Senate House

'The Schools.

KINGS

TRINITY HALL

GARRET HOSTEL LANE

RIVER

MILL PIT

Sheeps Green

Coe Fen

river

upper

Parson's Brook

NEWNHAM MILL

WEST FIELD

CHAPTER ONE

PILLS

I woke at first light, as was my habit, winter and summer – and indeed, as now, in September. It was Sunday and there would be no stagecoaches at the Hoop. That said, seven gentlemen had booked a Saturday dinner and rooms and a young clergyman and his family had arrived unexpectedly with a wheel on their cart that only just made it to our yard before cracking through, so the stables were far from empty. I would need to be giving our four-legged guests their breakfast at eight o'clock, but I could have another hour in bed. I was just dozing off again when I heard a light knock at my door. "Mr Hardiman?" said a man's voice softly.

Myself aside, only two men live in the house: another lodger called Carey, and our landlady's new husband, George Chapman. Despite Mrs Jacobs telling me frequently that there was not a man in England who could measure up to her late husband, it seems that Chapman's dogged admiration for both her and her cooking had broken through her defences. And with only a little nudging from Mrs Jacobs herself, Chapman finally proposed earlier this year. He still works as a porter at St Clement's – I have my suspicions that his University connection was part of the attraction for Mrs Jacobs, who has great respect for that institution. But he has given up his own bachelor lodgings and moved in with his new wife – and, by extension, with me. Now, back to the quiet knocking at my door. Mr Carey was, as Mrs Jacobs – I beg your pardon, Mrs Chapman – never tired of reminding me, deaf as an adder. If he knocked and spoke, neither would be quiet.

"Yes, Mr Chapman?" I called back.

The door opened and the porter's head appeared around it. "I'm sorry to wake you, Mr Hardiman," he said, "but it's my wife. She's been taken bad."

I swung my legs out of bed, shoved my feet into my slippers and reached for the robe I had flung over the chair. Chapman was in similar attire, and his face was pale with tiredness and concern.

"She's been in and out of the privy all night," he said, holding the door open wider so that I could pass him.

"She won't thank you for telling me that," I said. "Something she ate, maybe."

"And she won't thank you for suggesting that," observed Chapman, following me down the stairs. "All she's had for days is her own cooking."

Mrs Chapman was an unadventurous cook, but she had never poisoned us, I had to admit.

We reached the door of the Chapmans' rooms. The porter put his hand on the knob and then paused. "She's in a foul mood – won't listen to anything I say, but she's a lot of respect for you. And you have a good, steady manner about you. But if she's, well, impolite, I am sorry for it."

We walked into the little sitting room. It smelt none too fresh, and as if noticing that for the first time, Chapman walked over to the window, pushed the curtain aside and opened the sash. Sitting in an armchair, her eyes closed, was Mrs Chapman. Her husband touched her on the shoulder and she groaned.

"I've fetched Mr Hardiman," he said to her.

She frowned but did not open her eyes.

"I am sorry you're unwell," I said. "Shall I fetch the doctor?"

"No need," she said, shaking her head but still not opening her eyes. "I have my own remedy."

"Your own remedy?" I asked. "From an apothecary?"

"A London apothecary," she clarified sharply, a note of pride in her voice. "As used by the gentry and royalty."

"She sent off for them," said her husband. He picked up a small box from the table next to the armchair and handed it to me. I walked over to the window and turned the box to the light. It was made of stiff paper, about three inches long and an inch wide, and shaped rather like a snuffbox, with black letters printed on it. "Morison's pills, number one," I read aloud. I shook the box: it seemed almost empty. "Why are you taking them, Mrs Chapman?"

My landlady said nothing.

"Women's troubles," said her husband to me, quietly.

"And are they helping?" I asked. I went over to the armchair and crouched down beside it. "Are they making you feel better, Mrs Chapman?" I asked again.

She opened her eyes slowly and shook her head. "Not yet," she said. "I just need to take more of them, like the advertisement said. Up to fifty a day, for some things. It takes time to clear the bad humours." She held out her hand for the box.

I stood up. "Fifty a day sounds a lot, Mrs Chapman," I said. "I think it would be best for you to rest today, catching up on your sleep. Perhaps Mr Chapman could fix you some broth." I looked at him and he nodded. "And if you don't mind," I continued, "I'll take these pills to my apothecary and see what he has to say."

"You do that, Mr Hardiman," said Mr Chapman. "You've not been right since you started with those pills, Mary, and Mr Relhan is a clever man."

I had been waiting outside his premises for a quarter hour and was just about to leave when I saw Richard Relhan coming round the corner into St Sepulchre's Passage. I raised my hand in greeting and he smiled.

"Good morning, Mr Hardiman," he said as he unlocked the door to his shop.

"Good morning to you," I replied. "I am sorry to disturb you on the Sabbath, but I am in urgent need of your sensible medical opinion."

The apothecary held the door open for me. "I have come home to change out of my church clothes and collect my drawing materials," he said. "I am keen to complete my sketches of Rose Crescent."

"Very fancy," I said.

"It is much easier to record the architectural detail while the shops are shut," said Relhan. "Now, what is bothering you, Mr Hardiman? Not the night terrors, I hope." His voice was full of concern.

"No, no," I said, shaking my head. "At least, no more than usual. No: my enquiry is on behalf of my landlady."

"Ah now, she has a new husband, if I recall," said Relhan. "Is she...?" he indicated a swelling belly with his hands.

I thought for a moment; it had not occurred to me, and I did a quick sum in my head. "Unlikely," I concluded. I took the paper box of pills from my pocket and put it on the counter.

The apothecary looked at it. "Morison's Universal Pills," he said. "Very popular."

"Do you sell them?" I asked.

"No: I believe Mr Wray in St Peter's Street is the agent for them here in Cambridge," replied Relhan, naming one of the other apothecaries in town. "I prefer to make my own remedies, and to be candid with my customers about what they contain and therefore what they can do – and what they cannot – do." He raised an eyebrow.

"And Mr Morison is not so honest?" I asked, picking up the box and looking at it more closely.

"Yes, and no," said the apothecary, sitting on the high stool behind his counter. "Mr Morison is admirably open – boastful, almost – about what is in his pills. But he makes astonishing claims for what they can cure. I can show you." He jumped off his stool and ducked down behind the counter, reappearing a few moments later with a leather portfolio. "My collection of interesting snippets," he explained. He untied the strings and opened the flaps. Inside were scraps of printed paper, a few handbills and some handwritten notes. He looked through them and pounced on one. "Here: an advertisement for Mr Morison's pills. From a London broadsheet, I believe."

He handed me the scrap of paper. It was a densely-worded advertisement, about four inches by three, with a line drawing of a box of pills in the middle of it. Above it was this enticing promise, which I read aloud: "'After thirty-five years' of inexpressible suffering, I have accomplished my own extraordinary cure. Now you too can benefit from my vegetable universal medicine!'" I looked up at Relhan.

"It gets better," he said. "Read on – you will be amazed."

I did so. "'Bad blood is the cause of all your ills. With these pills taken morning and night, you will soon find COMPLETE RELIEF from ALL DISEASES AND CONDITIONS, including dysentery, smallpox, fevers, pimples and general decay. Made of healthful innocuous ingredients that can be taken without the advice of a doctor.' How convenient, that you need not bother the doctor."

"Indeed," said Relhan. "Now read the ingredients – see, there, along the bottom of the advertisement." He pointed.

"'Aloe,'" I read, "'rhubarb, cream of tartar, myrrh and rare gamboge from Indo-China.' What on earth is gamboge?"

"A deep yellow pigment from a tree – used by artists," explained the apothecary. "But it is also a strong laxative. As are rhubarb, and cream of tartar."

"And myrrh?" I asked.

"An anodyne," he said. "To manage pain – which you would need, for the extreme cramping and constant diarrhoea brought on by the other ingredients."

"So these pills," I picked up the box again, "are just laxatives." Relhan nodded. "And people are encouraged to take more and more of them, all the while being reassured that they are simply cleansing their bad blood and do not need to take medical advice."

"It's worse than that," said Relhan, pawing again through his collection of snippets. "Look at this." He handed me a much larger piece of paper – a coloured handbill. "I was handed this when I last went to London. They were giving them away in the street."

"Giving them away," I repeated, raising an eyebrow. "And a coloured print like this is not cheap to make."

The handbill showed two pictures side by side. On the left was a drab, leafless tree, with words written on its bare branches: dropsy, asthma, white swelling and so on. Clambering over those branches were sinister men in dark clothes wielding saws, needles and probes – obviously surgeons and doctors. And beneath the dying tree was written *A tree under the organic or doctors' system – being undrained of corrupt matter, is in a state of decay throughout.* And on the right was a fine, thriving tree covered in bright green leaves, and no doctors in sight. This one was labelled *Tree under the Hygeian or Morisonian system, being drained of all impurities – is in a flourishing state!!*

"So Morison is not only claiming that his pills will cure everything," I said, "but also suggesting that doctors will make you ill.

And," I waved the handbill at Relhan, "paying a pretty penny to spread that message far and wide." I slapped the paper onto the counter.

"And people believe him," added the apothecary. "They would rather trust the clever words and pretty pictures paid for by Mr Morison than follow the advice of their apothecary. Do you know what I had to do in order to be able to set myself up as an apothecary, Mr Hardiman?" I shook my head. "I had to serve a five-year apprenticeship, during which time I had to undergo instruction in," he ticked them off on his fingers, "anatomy, botany, chemistry, *materia medica* and physic, as well as having six months' practical experience in a hospital. How much simpler to print some colourful caricatures." He glanced again at the handbill. "Irresponsible alarmism, that's what it is. Look at what is written on the building in the left-hand picture." He pointed at it.

"'A house for experiments on the poor'," I read, "'commonly called hospital or infirmary'."

I was sitting on the footstool in front of my landlady's armchair and looking up at her. She was as pale as I have ever seen her, her eyes sunken and her mouth drawn.

"Please, Mrs Chapman," I said. "You have to promise me – and George," I nodded towards her husband, "that you won't take any more of these pills. I know you have read all sorts of claims for them – I have seen the advertisements myself. But you must believe what Mr Relhan says."

"He's a good man, Mary," said Chapman urgently. "Mr Relhan's father was a clergyman, and his grandfather too – he's an honest, God-fearing man. We don't know this Morison from Adam, but Mr Relhan is one of us. Local."

"And he knows his remedies," I said. "He knows what's in these pills, and it's just a mixture of strong laxatives – purgatives, Mrs Chapman. Nothing more. No universal cure. If you keep taking them, you will keep, well, needing the pot. Whatever you are trying to cure with them, they are not working, are they?"

I looked at her and she slowly shook her head.

Chapman came over and knelt down by his wife's chair and took one of her hands in his. "Good girl," he said gently. "You let Mr Hardiman throw those pills in the stove, I'll fix you a nice pot of tea, and tomorrow we'll go to see Mr Relhan. You can tell him what's ailing you, and I'll pay for whatever proper remedy he suggests."

"That sounds like three very sensible ideas," I said.

Chapman clambered to his feet. He and I went into the kitchen and as he busied himself with the kettle I opened the door of the stove and threw the box of pills into it. They flared brightly for a few seconds and then disappeared into the ash.

Chapter Two

PROCLAMATION

"You should have seen the fair when I was a girl," said my landlady, pausing her stirring to look into the distance. "Stalls as far as the eye could see. Pottery, glass, perfumes, rugs – you've never seen the like. My brothers and me, we'd head straight for the toymen, with their painted puppets and dollies in pretty frocks." She sighed and reapplied herself to the soup.

"It's still a fine spectacle, Mrs Jacobs," I said. She turned and raised an eyebrow at me. "Mrs Chapman, I do beg your pardon," I corrected myself. I was relieved to see that a week off Morison's pills had done much to restore her strength and her colour.

She turned again to the stove. "If it's spectacle you want," she continued, "you should have seen the procession. The Mayor and all the Corporation riding in their finery from the Guildhall to the fair. Then the Vice-Chancellor and the other high-ups from the University would host a dinner at the Oyster House in Garlic Row, to celebrate the opening. But they stopped all that, oh, it must be forty years ago now." She shook her head. "Nothing's what it used to be, is it, Mr Hardiman?"

"Indeed, Mrs Chapman," I said, counting the church bells. "And now I must be off. Spectacle or no, I am thankful that I do not have to process all the way to Stourbridge in my constable's uniform in this warm weather. But if I am not waiting outside for the coach that the proctors have kindly arranged for us, I shall be in the suds." I stood and put on my coat. "Shall I see you and George at the fair later?"

"We shall be there, yes, but whether we shall see you is another matter," she said. "I want to visit the hatters and the silk-mercers while they still have their finest stock. I shall not buy, mind you," she waved her spoon at me, "but it is as well to keep up with the latest fashions. We're not joskins, after all."

The driver of the hired coach was just pulling his horses to a halt as I closed the front door behind me. George Swanney leaned out of the coach, smiling and beckoning.

"Come, Hardiman," he called. "We've one more space inside – Mr Gilbert and Mr Blake are meeting us by the Barnwell Theatre, so they will have to go outside."

He held open the door for me and I climbed in, carefully holding my cape to one side so that I did not tread on it, and settling myself between two fellow constables with our back to the horses, each of us putting our hat on our knees. I nodded a greeting to them as the coach lurched forward.

"It's not often we're all together," remarked my neighbour, a carpenter named George Wilson. "All eight of us."

"High days and holy days," said Swanney.

"I just wish they weren't all such hot days," I said. "Is that window down as low as it can go?"

The coach pulled to a halt again and we lurched around for a moment as Adam Gilbert and Tom Blake climbed aboard. I heard the driver encourage the horses and we set off again.

"He won't mind the discomfort," I said to no-one in particular, nodding towards the roof. "Mr Gilbert. I remember him telling me that he was trying to impress a young lady with his finery. The cloak and the hat."

"Ah well," said Swanney, smiling widely, "he might have impressed her a little too much. She's, well," he indicated a large belly with his hands, "and they're to marry in a fortnight."

"There's a warning there for us all," said George Wilson to my left, and we laughed, Swanney perhaps a little less heartily than the rest of us. He worked in Isaac Warwick's drapers' shop on Market Hill and had been courting Warwick's only child Ann for more than a year now. But Swanney worried what would happen to his sister Kate if he were to marry and so he delayed. I imagine that Ann's patience – or her papa's – might be wearing a bit thin.

The coach slowed as we went up the slight rise of Sun Street into Barnwell, past the ruin of the priory and on into George Street. We then slowed even more as of course we were not the only ones heading to the fair, and the road was busy with horses, coaches, carts and people on foot. After about ten more minutes we swung into Garlic Row and our coach moved carefully between the awnings jutting out over the stands selling the most luxurious goods at the fair – I thought of Mrs Chapman and her silk-mercers. As she had said, the days of the Vice-Chancellor hosting a grand banquet at the Oyster House were long gone, but that building was still at the centre of the fair, and provided a convenient meeting place for everyone involved in the proclamation. Our coach came to a halt and the two constables on the top jumped down and hauled open the doors for us.

"Gentlemen," said Gilbert, pretending to sweep his hat from his head and performing a deep bow while holding out a hand to help us from the coach.

"Fool," said George Wilson, but he was smiling.

Eventually all eight of us were lined up, checking each other's capes and collars, and careful to avoid kicking up dust onto our boots. The door of the Oyster House opened and out came Mr Tomkyns and Mr Pope, the Proctors, followed by the Vice-Chancellor Mr Wordsworth. With his long nose and piercing eyes, he brought unsmiling dignity to our group and we all stood a little straighter. The Proctors distributed the mace, the butter measure and the book of statutes amongst us – I carefully avoided the latter as it was very heavy and cumbersome, and instead took hold of the measure. We arranged ourselves carefully, one proctor and four constables on either side of the Vice-Chancellor, and waited for the crowd to fall silent. The last to be quiet were the party of officers from the Corporation, who had perhaps taken some refreshment already, but even they quailed when Mr Wordsworth fixed them with his gaze. The Senior Proctor handed the Vice-Chancellor a scroll; he unrolled it and began to read the proclamation. Despite his years in Cambridge and his stern demeanour, there was still a pleasing Cumbrian softness to Mr Wordsworth's voice.

"We charge and strictly command in the name of the King of England our Sovereign Lord, and in the name of my Lord Chancellor of the University of Cambridge," he began, "that all manner of scholars, scholars' servants and all other persons in this Fair and the precincts of the same keep the King's peace and make no fray, cry or tas, freaking or any other noise by which the insurrections, conventicles or gathering of people may be made in this Fair to the trouble, vexing and disquieting of the King's liege people or letting in the Officers of the University to exercise their offices under the pain of imprisonment, and further punishment as the offence shall require." At the word "imprisonment", Mr Wordsworth paused and let his eyes roam over the listening crowd.

"Also we charge and command that all manner of scholars and scholars' servants wear no weapon to make any fray upon any of the King's people neither in coming nor in going from this Fair under the pain of banishment." Another pause.

"Also we charge and command that all common women and misbehaving people avoid and withdraw themselves out of this Fair and the precincts of the same immediately after this cry, that the King's subjects may be the more quiet and good rule may be the better maintained under the pain of imprisonment.

"Also that no brewers sell into this Fair nor anywhere within the precincts of the University a barrel of good ale above two shillings, nor a barrel of hostel ale above twelve pence. No long ale, no red ale, no ropy ale but good and wholesome ale for a man's body, under the pain of forfeiture, and that every brewer have a mark upon his barrel whereby it may be known whose it is under the pain of imprisonment and fine at the discretion of Officers of the University." I knew it would be one of our duties during the fortnight of the fair, to visit the stalls of the brewers and check their barrel marks.

"Also we strictly charge and command that every potter and all other persons that bring pots to be sold in this Fair or precincts of the same that they all and all other from henceforth sell and buy true goods and lawful measures as gallons, pottles, quarts and half-pints, under the pain of imprisonment and there to remain 'til they have made fine at the will of the said Officers." We would also have to check the pot stalls, but oddly that duty was carried out with less enthusiasm than the visits to the brewers.

"Also if any brewer or beer-brewer be found faulty in any of the premises after that they have been in times immersed, then the said brewer shall be committed to prison there to remain 'til he hath fined at the pleasure of the Officers of the University."

The Vice-Chancellor rolled up the scroll and handed it back to the Senior Proctor. In unison, the Vice-Chancellor, the proctors and we constables all doffed our hats and made a small bow to the crowd. A few people applauded but most just stared and then turned away.

"Thank you, gentlemen," said the Vice-Chancellor. "Mr Tomkyns, Mr Pope." He nodded to the proctors and then went back into the Oyster House.

The Senior Proctor spoke. "Mr Pope and I will return to town with the Vice-Chancellor. Your coach will be leaving in an hour, constables. Please be mindful that you are in uniform and acting as representatives of the University, not as private citizens, and behave accordingly."

I could feel myself bristling at Tomkyns' tone. I looked sideways at George Swanney and he winked at me. The proctors held out their hands for the items of office to be returned, then followed the Vice-Chancellor into the Oyster House. We eight constables all looked at each other and burst out laughing.

"Well then, gentlemen," said Adam Gilbert, "I'm off to behave accordingly. I daresay there's a comely piece or two on these stalls who will bear closer inspection."

"Making the most of your last weeks of freedom, eh?" I asked, smiling.

Gilbert raised a hand in farewell as he walked off towards the ale stalls.

"Shall we head in this direction?" asked George Swanney, pointing. "I'd like to take a look at the drapers' stalls."

Swanney was discussing textiles with a manufacturer from Yorkshire and I was standing to one side when I heard my name called. I turned to see Francis Vaughan, the Master of St Clement's College.

"Mr Vaughan," I said. "I would not have expected to see you here."

The Master smiled. "And ordinarily you would be right, Mr Hardiman," he agreed. "I am rather long in the tooth for such," he gestured around him, "entertainments. But I am not here for my own amusement. Ah, here he is." A young man appeared at his side – an undergraduate, I assumed. "Mr Bendall, may I present Mr Gregory Hardiman, a constable of the University. Mr Hardiman, Mr Gerard Bendall." We shook hands. "Mr Bendall's older brother Edwin will be joining us at St Clement's in the Michaelmas term."

"I am sure he will make excellent use of his time," I said. "Are you hoping to come to the University yourself, Mr Bendall?"

Bendall shook his head. He was slight in build, with dark hair and eyes, ruddy cheeks and only the very beginnings of a beard. "I am not so fortunate, Mr Hardiman," he said. "I have recently come into an unexpected inheritance which takes all my time to manage. And what better way to spend some of that bounty than on the education and elevation of a beloved brother?"

"He is a lucky young man," I said.

"And St Clement's is lucky to have him," said Vaughan. "Edwin will be joining us as a fellow commoner." He looked at me. I knew, if Bendall did not, that St Clement's needed every penny from every undergraduate, and the five pounds a quarter paid by a fellow commoner would be most welcome.

Bendall had obviously caught the look between us. "I did consider the better-known colleges for Edwin," he said easily, "but with our background, I am not sure he would have settled amongst more... elevated society. I was struck at once by the more welcoming atmosphere of St Clement's."

"Your background?" I said without thinking. "Oh, forgive me, sir. I am far too curious for my own good. It comes with the job, I am afraid." I gestured at my uniform.

"I am a curious chap myself," said Bendall. "Indeed, I can attribute my good fortune almost entirely to my curiosity." He tipped his hat at Swanney who had finished his conversation and walked over to join us. "Another constable, if I am not mistaken." I introduced the two men to each other. "And you were curious about my background, Mr Hardiman. My father is a maltster – a tenant of a farmer near Bedford." He laughed. "Yes, that often surprises people."

"My father too was a farmer," I said. "In Norfolk."

"Then you will understand why I thought that Edwin might not feel quite at home among the nibs at Trinity or St John's," said Bendall. "Now, we must not keep you from your work, constables." He smiled again, and he and Vaughan moved off.

"So that's your Mr Vaughan," said Swanney. "He's certainly a sight more friendly than many University men, risking being seen conversing with a mere constable."

"He is," I agreed. "How was the merchandise? Does it put our Cambridge shops to shame?"

"There are some good colours," he said, "and some fancy ribbons from France." He reached into his pocket. "I bought this." He held out a length of emerald green ribbon. "I thought you might like to give it to someone. It's her favourite colour, and a pattern she won't have seen."

For about a year now, Swanney's sister Kate and I had been growing closer. I often spent the evening in the Swanneys' comfortable rooms in Silver Street, enjoying the lively discussions and companionable silences, and I hoped that they did not think me an intrusion. But Kate was used to her independence and I, well, you know my situation. I could not take on a new wife without telling her about my first wife and my daughter, and that would mean other revelations – about Spain and the rest. And I could not be certain that my friendship with the Swanneys would survive that.

George Swanney of course knew nothing of these deliberations and thought simply that I was being uncommonly slow in declaring myself to his sister. And he did everything he could to nudge me along, including spending his spare pennies on a fancy green ribbon. I took it from him with a smile and put it into my pocket.

Chapter Three

THEATRE

"Well!" said Mrs Chapman, coming into the kitchen and unpinning her hat and shaking the rain from it. When neither her husband nor I responded – he was snoring gently in his chair and I was lost in my book – she repeated herself a little louder. "Well! You'll never guess what Margaret Turner told me at church." She hung her hat on the hook along with her coat and turned to look at us. I nudged Chapman under the table with my foot and he jerked awake.

"Hello Mary," he said, smiling as he sat more upright and smoothed down his hair. "How was church? Good sermon?"

"You could come with me and find out," said his wife, lifting the lid from a pot on the stove and stirring its contents.

"I could," replied Chapman easily, "but as porter of St Clement's I think it is politic," he looked at me as he said the unfamiliar word and I nodded, "politic of me to attend chapel there." He winked at me; we both knew that he visited the college's chapel only when a porter was needed and not to tend to his immortal soul. Neither of us had much time for the Almighty.

Mrs Chapman replaced the lid on the pot and balanced the spoon on it. She touched her hand to the side of the kettle.

Her husband took his cue and stood up. "You sit down, my dear," he said, "and I will put the tea to brew."

"And you can tell us the news from Mrs Turner," I added.

All complaints forgotten at the prospect of being able to share something sensational, Mrs Chapman sat down. "Margaret Turner, you remember her," she said. "Dressmaker – on New Square." She looked from Chapman to me and back again. "Good heavens, does neither of you ever listen to me?" She shook her head. "No matter. Margaret is a good dressmaker – not the finest, but certainly the fastest I have ever known. When she's stitching, you can barely see her needle, it's moving that quick. And because of this, she's popular with the..." she dropped her voice into a whisper, "theatre folk."

"Theatre folk?" repeated Chapman, stirring the teapot vigorously. "What do you mean, theatre folk?"

"Performers," said his wife, rolling her eyes and raising her voice. "Actors – on the stage. They often need their costumes refitted, or mended, and so they call Margaret. Sometimes," the voice dropped again, "she even has to make the alterations while they're wearing their costume – the men!"

Her husband poured three cups of tea and pushed one across the table to me. "Well, if they get too amorous, she can always jab 'em with her needle," he suggested.

"I'll suggest that," said Mrs Chapman.

"Is that what the dressmaker told you," I asked, blowing on my tea, "that she had to fend off advances from an amorous actor?"

"Oh good heavens," she said, putting down her own cup with a clatter. "He's the one who suggested that." She nodded at her husband who was studiously trying not to laugh. "No: she said that one of them has died." She looked at us and seemed to think that we now looked serious enough. "One of the actors was found dead in his lodgings last night. Mr Rowley. He was supposed to be on the stage yesterday evening, and when he didn't turn up they went to find him – and there he was, dead." She shook her head. "And him only a young man too – no more than thirty, Margaret said."

"Did they send for the coroner?" I asked.

"Course they did," she replied. "Mr Chevell lives near the the-atre, so the constable went for him." She took another drink of tea and waited.

"And did the coroner say anything?" asked Chapman, curious despite himself.

"Well," said his wife with relish, "as Mr Hardiman will tell you, nothing is certain until the inquest," she looked at me and I nod-ded, "but Mr Chevell told the constable that there was no wound on Mr Rowley, so he wasn't attacked. I reckon he must have been ill already because when the landlady cleared out his room, she found boxes and boxes – all empty – of those pills I used to take. Morison's pills."

Chapter Four

HORSES

With William Bird's permission, I had readied the horses for the *Norfolk Regulator* and left careful instructions with Poor Jamie to help the driver put them into harness at midday. Jamie – simple-minded and often overlooked because of it – was pleased as Punch with his new responsibility, and as I did my final checks of the animals he was at my elbow.

"If you have any trouble at all, Jamie," I said, buttoning up my coat, "you're to go straight to Mr Bird. But you know the driver," Jamie nodded solemnly, "and the horses are all fit and fed," he nodded again, "and you've helped me dozens of times," another nod. "You're a good lad, Jamie, and there'll be extra wages for you."

Raising my hand in farewell, I left the yard just as the bells marked the quarter hour. I crossed Bridge Street and ducked into Dolphin Lane, walking round the south side of the church before turning into Trinity Street. The yard of the Blue Boar was full of activity as I arrived, with the *Ipswich* being prepared to leave at half-past nine. Leaning against the wall, taking a bite from an enormous roll stuffed with meat, was the driver Jack Colman. He spotted me and swallowed his mouthful before smiling at me. I walked over to him.

"Mr Hardiman," he said with mock formality. His heavy Suffolk accent always sounded friendly.

"Mr Colman," I said in turn. "I have a favour to ask of you. The horse fair is at Stourbridge today. You will pass it on your way to Bury..." I stopped as Jack held up his hand.

"You can sit up top with me, Gregory," he said. "There's no speed to be had along the road during the fair, so letting you down will be easy. And in return," he nodded towards the coach, "you can check my animals. You've the surest hand in Cambridge for horses."

Half an hour later I was walking along Garlic Row towards the horse fair. The other stalls were still there, but most were closed as the holders knew that today's visitors – like me – would have little interest in anything else until they had seen the horses. And doubtless the stallholders themselves would enjoy a day of rest after a busy week. As I approached the area set aside for the horse fair, I could hear the familiar sound of unsettled horses – whinnying, stamping, neighing. The horse fair served two main purposes: it was a marketplace, and it offered a chance for people to watch and wager on races. I did not wish to participate in either, but I did love to see the horses.

The horses were fenced in, crowded together, with one small enclosure left empty for the sale; each animal would be led in, walked around to show it to advantage, and then auctioned. The beasts for racing were given a little more space, but I knew from my visits to Newmarket that they were nervous animals and as I approached them they rolled their eyes and danced on the spot. I pitied the men who would be riding them.

I spent perhaps half an hour walking along the fences, enjoying as I always did the beauty of the animals, but their fear and confusion saddened me. I said some quiet words of reassurance to one or two of them standing near me, but most of them had withdrawn into themselves. It reminded me uncomfortably of the voyages I had taken with horses in the army, crammed together in the swaying holds of ships, trying to calm myself by calming them. I had had enough of the horse fair.

I decided to take a look at the river before heading back to town. As I left the horse fair and walked towards the leather fair, I saw a crowd gathered in front of a man who was standing on an upturned box. Alongside the stalls that were booked months in advance by businesses, the fair naturally attracted all manner of itinerant pedlars and hawkers, and this one seemed particularly popular. I stood at the back of the crowd, which was about three people deep, and listened.

"Imagine, if you will, suffering terrible pain for more than three decades," cried the hawker. "Pain here," he said, pointing to his chest, "and here," now to his head, "and here," now to his stomach. "Imagine going to doctor after doctor, and doing exactly what they tell you, and still," he dropped his voice, "the fearful pain." He shook his head sadly. "That, ladies and gentlemen, is what happened to Mr James Morison." I knew that name, and I started to edge my way forwards until I could see the man properly. He was about my own age, lean, soberly dressed. He had a mobile, expressive face and his accent told me he came from London. "More than three decades of agony." He chewed that word carefully. "Agony. After suffering terrible pain and discomfort for more than three decades, Mr Morison decided to find his own cure in the natural world. And he succeeded!" With that, he delved into the bag at his feet and stood up again, a box of Morison's pills in his hand – just like the box I had burned in Mrs Chapman's stove. "Ladies and gentlemen, these are Mr Morison's pills – a vegetable universal medicine made entirely of natural ingredients." He tucked the box into his coat pocket so that he could tick the ingredients off on his fingers. "Rhubarb," he intoned. "Cream of tartar. Myrrh – yes, as in the Bible, given to the Lord Jesus at his birth. And gamboge – a rare and valuable substance harvested at great expense from a tree in Indo-China." A few people in the crowd drew in their breath. "And within a few days, those thirty years of horrific pain – gone!" He threw up his hands like a conjurer on stage. "Never to return!" Another flourish of the hands. "And now, ladies and gentlemen, Mr Morison is sharing his universal remedy with you. No matter your ailment – dropsy, gout, inflammations, smallpox, fatigue, apoplexy, jaundice, whatever you care to name – these pills will rid you of it. And remember, ladies and gentlemen, they are completely natural. No need to trouble the doctor with his leeches or the surgeon with his knife: simply take Morison's pills as often as you need and all will be well." He looked around at his audience, smiling encouragingly. "And, for today only, Mr Morison has given me permission to offer a special gift. But for today only." He paused for effect and the crowd leaned forward slightly. "Buy two boxes of Morison's pills for a shilling each, and I will give you a third box of thirty-six pills for nothing! That's three boxes of Morison's universal remedy – universal, remember, and a total of more than a hundred pills – for only two shillings. For today only, ladies and gentlemen."

A woman next to me barged forward, clutching coins in her hand. She paid for her two boxes and the hawker made a great show of adding a third to her hand. This seemed to encourage the others, and within a matter of minutes almost everyone in the crowd had walked off with three boxes of Mr Morison's miracle cure. The hawker jumped down off his box and turned his back to me, and I guessed he was putting his bulging purse of coins into a secret inside pocket. He turned round and smiled uneasily.

"Can I help you?" he asked, his eyes catching on and then sliding off my scar – a constant reminder of my soldiering days. "You look like a strapping fellow, but a soldier like you must have all sorts of hidden pains. Night sweats, I shouldn't wonder." He was sharp, I'll give him that. He smiled conspiratorially. "I'll tell you what. As I've had a good day," his hand slipped towards his hidden pocket before he remembered himself and halted it, "I am sure Mr Morison would approve of me honouring the great service you have done for your country. One shilling, and you can have three boxes." He tilted his head, assessing my response. "I can't say fairer than that, can I?"

"It's a very generous offer, Mr...?" I said.

"Longman," he said, holding out his hand for me to shake. "Jeremiah Longman."

"Gregory Hardiman," I said in turn. "You're from London, I think, Mr Longman?"

He smiled broadly. "You've a good ear, Mr Hardiman. Whitechapel, me – born and bred."

"Whitechapel," I repeated. "I spent a few weeks there back in, oh, it must have been '15, before I left for Ireland. I had lodgings just off the high street." You'll know, of course, that I have never spent a minute in Whitechapel, but I was fairly certain it would have a high street. And it never hurts to know exactly where someone can be found.

"I'm at the other end of Whitechapel Road," replied Longman. "Norfolk Street."

"There's a coincidence," I said. "I'm a Norfolk boy myself. You're in town for the fair, then?"

"Too good an opportunity to miss," he said, squatting down to do up the buckles on his leather bag and then lifting it onto his shoulder. "All these folk, gathered in one place – a good number of them suffering terribly from who knows what ailment or disease.

And if I can offer them some relief from their pain, some hope," he put a hand to his heart, "I am grateful to do it." His success had made him chatty – and careless. "Shall we?" He indicated in the direction of the road and we started strolling towards it together.

"Oh, there's plenty of people in Cambridge," I agreed. "The University men, the merchants, and then everyone passing through. This week we even have a company of actors in town." Although they would be a man short when they returned to London, I thought to myself, remembering my conversation with Mrs Chapman.

"Yes, at the Barnwell Theatre," said Longman. "I was there myself Friday last."

"Have you been to a performance?" I asked. "Do you recommend it?"

"Oh, I was not there for my own entertainment," said the hawker seriously. "I was fulfilling an order for Morison's pills for a long-standing customer. An actor. William Rowley. Perhaps you have heard of him?"

"I have indeed," I said. "Mr Rowley was found dead in his lodgings yesterday evening."

Longman stopped walking and his smile disappeared. "I am truly sorry to hear it," he said sadly.

"He was your long-standing customer," I observed. "How long had he been taking Morison's pills? Had they not cured him?"

A watchful look came over Longman's face. "I don't believe you told me why you are here, Mr Hardiman," he said.

"I'm an ostler," I said easily. "Here to see the horses." I waved an arm towards the horse fair.

"Then perhaps it's best if you stick to what you know," said Longman, a menacing tone creeping into his voice. "And I shall do the same."

"I am also a constable, Mr Longman," I said calmly. "Just to be clear, did you go to the Barnwell Theatre..." But I had no chance to finish my question. Longman's right fist came from nowhere and caught me squarely on the chin. I stumbled backwards, tripped over a rope holding up a tent, and fell onto my backside. By the time I scrambled to my feet, Longman had disappeared into the crowd.

CHAPTER FIVE

BANKS

"Good heavens, no," said George Fisher, laughing. "Henry Adeane, squire of Babraham Hall, is far too grand a personage to bank with us."

We were sitting in the parlour of the Black Bull, having a drink before the meeting of our book club.

"He's not with Mortlock's, surely," I said.

George made a mock horrified face. "A Whig sympathiser banking with the Mortlocks? I should say not." He reached for his tankard and looked into it with disappointment. "He's with Foster's on Bridge Street." He tipped his head back to drain the final drops of his drink. "Why do you ask?"

"I need to report a matter to a magistrate," I said. "Something that happened a couple of days ago. And it occurred to me that Mr Adeane might come into town to call on his banker or his lawyer."

George glanced at the clock on the wall and stood up. "Ten to," he observed. "We had better go up and sign in. And I can introduce you to Adeane's banker."

George Fisher was as good as his word. Once the business of the evening was completed, he made his way quickly across the room, dragging me in his wake, and introduced me to Ebenezer Foster. He was a serious-looking man, perhaps ten years my senior, with a high forehead and neat white hair. But his smile, as he shook my hand, was surprisingly childlike. George bade us both goodnight and left us to our conversation.

"A university constable, eh?" said Foster. "I've lived in Cambridge all my life, and you're the first one I've met close up." He leaned forward to stress the point.

"Ah well, we have not been in existence for that long," I said. "In fact, my term of office comes to an end this month, although I hope to be reappointed."

"Bound to be," said George stoutly. I smiled my thanks at him.

"I know the Senior Proctor, of course," continued Foster. "Mr Tomkyns, of King's."

"The undergraduates call him 'Ten O'Clock Tomkyns'," I said. "Thanks to his habit of reminding them about the curfew."

Foster smiled delightedly. "I shall call him that myself, next time we meet," he said. "Now tell me: how can a simple banker be of assistance to a university constable?"

"There is a matter I wish to bring to the attention of Mr Adeane," I said, "in his capacity as a magistrate." I looked around to make sure that we were not being overheard, but I dropped my voice just in case. "I could report it to the town constables, but…"

I had no need to finish my sentence. The banker shook his head. "I know, I know," he said. "The town constables are not best pleased to have university constables interfering in their work."

"Precisely," I agreed. "I am concerned that they will not take the matter seriously enough, and anyway, I know more about it than they do." Foster raised an eyebrow. "Not that I am a better constable," I added hastily, "but simply that I have more information."

"I am dining with Mr Adeane on Tuesday next," said the banker. "If you are still a university constable by then, come to the bank at six o'clock and you can meet him before we leave."

CHAPTER SIX

MAGISTRATE

The bells of St Sepulchre's were tolling the hour when I arrived at the door of Foster's bank as arranged. Just as I raised my hand to knock, the door was pulled open by a young man in a dark coat and trousers that were too short for him. He jumped a little when he saw me and then laughed.

"Sorry," he said cheerfully. "We're closed now. Open tomorrow morning at nine o'clock." He paused, cocked his head as though he had heard something, and went back into the bank. He reappeared a moment later. "If you're Mr Hardiman," he said, "you're to come in. Mr Foster is expecting you."

"I am indeed Mr Hardiman," I said. The young man stepped smartly to one side, holding the door open for me, and then left as I entered.

The banking hall was set out in the familiar way: a high counter along the back wall, with a closed door leading to – I assumed – the partners' parlour.

"Hello?" I said.

Ebenezer Foster's head appeared above the counter. "Good evening, Mr Hardiman," he said. "We are a shilling short, and I am just checking the floor. Otherwise it will have to come out of my pocket. One moment, if you please." And he ducked down again.

"Aha! Here it is." He stood up again, holding a coin triumphantly in his hand. He opened a drawer behind the counter, dropped the coin into it and closed it again. "All present and correct."

There was a knock at the door. "Shall I?" I asked.

"If you would, Mr Hardiman," said the banker.

I returned to the door and opened it. Standing there was Henry Adeane. He was about my own age, tall and lean, with thinning hair swept back from his forehead. His nose was long and straight, and the set of his eyes and mouth suggested that life amused him.

"Mr Adeane," I said, holding out my hand for him to shake, "I am Gregory Hardiman. It is very kind of you to agree to meet me." I held the door open and the magistrate came into the banking hall. He stopped and looked more keenly at me.

"I know your face," he said. "Ah yes. You work at the Hoop."

"I do, sir, yes," I said. "I am the ostler there, and I serve as a university constable."

"Mr Hardiman was reappointed only yesterday, Henry," said Mr Foster, coming forward and shaking his friend's hand. "The proctors change, but the constables are constant."

"The good ones, at any rate," said Mr Adeane. "Delighted to see Sedgwick is to be Senior Proctor. Good man."

"Mr Sedgwick does not take up his duties until the start of Michaelmas term next week," I said. "I have not met him."

"Shall we sit in comfort?" said Mr Foster. He opened the door at the back of the hall and, as I had guessed, it led to the parlour. It was larger than the one in George's bank, with four armchairs and two low tables. On a sideboard was a tray with two decanters and some glasses. The banker poured three drinks and handed one to each of us, and we sat down.

"Geologist – rocks and the like," said Mr Adeane. I must have looked puzzled. "Sedgwick," he explained. "Founded that place, you know, Ebenezer – in Sidney Street. With the library, and lectures." He waved his free hand about. "The Philosophical Society, that's it. Good brain in his head." He took a sip of his drink. "Foul stuff, Ebenezer," he said, smiling. He turned to me, suddenly serious. "Now then, Mr Hardiman, I believe you have something you need to tell me."

The banker rose to his feet. "If this is a confidential matter, gentlemen," he started.

I shook my head. "Not at all, Mr Foster," I said. He sat down again, and both men looked at me expectantly. "I live on Jesus Lane," I began, "and my landlady, Mrs Chapman, was taken ill during that warm spell at the beginning of September." I told them of Mrs Chapman's recourse to Morison's pills, and the death of William Rowley at the Barnwell Theatre, and my unpleasant encounter with Jeremiah Longman at the horse fair. Mr Foster listened silently; Mr Adeane interrupted now and again with a question.

"And so you think that this Mr Longman," the magistrate looked at me and I nodded, "should be held accountable?" I nodded again. "But these people – however unfortunate the outcome may have been – took the pills of their own volition. They were not tied up and the pills pushed down their throats," reasoned Mr Adeane.

"No," I agreed, "but there has recently been a similar case in London. At the Old Bailey. There was a report of it in a London newspaper – the coach drivers often bring them for me." I reached into my coat pocket and pulled out the folded piece of paper. I flattened it on my knee. "An agent in London sold his customer," I looked again at the paper, "thirty Morison's pills for a pain in his knee. When the pain did not go, the agent – Francis Little – sold him forty-five more pills, advising taking five in the morning and five at night. The customer – a sea-captain called Wilson – complained to his wife of irritation in his stomach. His bowels were very loose and he started to vomit up any food or drink he was given." I looked up at the two men. "The agent returned, and said that Wilson was not taking enough pills. Mrs Wilson objected, but, as she explained to the coroner, 'Mr Little told me I was alarming myself without the least occasion because my husband was doing well, and of course everything must come to a height before it would take the turn'. Mrs Wilson wanted to call a doctor, but Little said that if he saw any medical gentleman at the bedside, he would turn him out. He then," I consulted the paper again, "gave Mr Wilson twenty pills mashed up in jelly. Ten minutes later, Mr Wilson vomited the jelly, the pills and some blood. It went on like this for two more days – Little bringing more pills, Wilson vomiting and growing weaker. Eventually Mrs Wilson disobeyed Little and called in a doctor, but it was too late: her husband could not hold down any food or drink, he worsened and died a day later, leaving his wife a widow with five children under the age of seven."

"Poor mites," said Mr Foster, shaking his head sadly.

"And what of the agent Little?" asked Mr Adeane, more business-like.

"Several people spoke in his defence," I said, "saying that he had been kindness itself, offering his medical advice for no fee, and that the Morison's pills had cured them. Mr Little himself said that what he was facing was the unfair damnation of the medical profession, who were frightened of losing their income. In the end, Mr Little was found guilty of manslaughter, but recommended to mercy," I looked again at the paper, "in consequence of his not being the compounder of the deleterious pills in question. He was fined two hundred pounds."

Mr Foster made a low whistle. "A significant sum," he said.

"But of little comfort to the widow and her children," I said before I thought. "Forgive me, sir."

"No, no, quite right," said the banker.

"May I take that report?" asked Mr Adeane, holding out his hand. "Want to read it myself. Make notes. Consider the matter. You'll get it back." I gave him the paper and he folded it up. He reached into his pocket and took out a notebook, rather like my own. He tucked the folded report into it. "And you say you have an address for this agent – this Longman?"

"He told me his name, and the street where he lives," I said.

The magistrate handed me his notebook. "Write it down, would you. Enquiries can be made." I did as he asked and handed the notebook back to him. He glanced at what I had written and then put the notebook away. He drained his glass and shook his head. "Abominable wine, Ebenezer."

CHAPTER SEVEN

BROTHERS

"I am a good-natured man, Will," I said through gritted teeth, "but the combination of a new term and your wife can test even my limits."

"I know, Gregory, I know," said the innkeeper, looking impatiently through the piles of paper on his desk. He sat back in his chair with a sigh. "It seemed such a good idea, moving here from the Sun, adding the new meeting rooms, offering hot lunches as well as cold plates..." He shook his head. "But when we have every room filled and Hannah in full sail, I wonder whether I have made a rod for my own back."

At that exact moment the office door flew open and there stood Hannah Bird. I have grown no fonder of her in the years I have known her, and I daresay the feeling is mutual. She thinks herself better than me – better than almost everyone, truth be told – and it brings out the mischief in me. She glared at me and I smiled back.

"I am surprised you have time to loll about in here, Mr Hardiman, considering how busy we are today," she said crossly.

"I came in to confirm the number of horses with your husband," I said mildly. "With the *Star* on its way and the *Norfolk Regulator* passing through at midday, I needed to know how many stalls will be occupied tonight by private animals."

"I would expect you to prepare all the stalls, just in case," she said, folding her arms.

"And so I have," I replied. "It is simply that if there are to be empty stalls, I will spread the animals out to allow them better rest. And if we are to have a full house, I will pay particular attention to the temperament of the animals so that I can create good neighbours."

Hannah Bird sniffed. "Well, be quick about it," she said. "And William, I expect you to put on a clean shirt before you show yourself in the public rooms. This is a family hotel, not an alehouse."

"I know, my dear," he said. "That is why I had it painted on the front of the building." He stood and went over to his wife, taking her hands in his. "Hannah, you are like this at the start of every term. We are busy, we are making money, and all is well." He kissed her cheek. "Now go and see to the kitchen so that Mr Hardiman and I can finish our discussion." He opened the door for his wife and she left.

William returned to his chair. "It all comes from uncertainty," he said, jerking his chin towards the door. "Her father was a drunkard and a gambler – living high on the hog one day and scrabbling in the gutter the next. She's frightened of ending up back there." He looked at me sharply. "You must never let on that I have told you that – she likes people to think she's from respectable stock."

"I take little notice of where a person has come from," I said. "It's what they make of themselves that matters. Now, the stables."

William reached for a ledger. "Four from the *Regulator*," he said, "three singles booked in, and a message from Mr Bendall about his curricle and pair."

"Mr Bendall?" I repeated. "Gerard Bendall?"

William looked at his ledger again. "That's the one," he said. "Do you know him?"

"I met him at Stourbridge," I said. "A young man recently come into a fortune, and setting his brother up as a fellow commoner at St Clement's. Five pounds a quarter."

"I shall make sure to tell Hannah," he said, winking. "No-one could mistake us for an alehouse when we have a curricle on the premises."

I was checking the mouse traps in the stables when I heard the sound of hooves and wheels in the yard. I straightened up and walked outside. In the doorway of the kitchen was Poor Jamie, standing slack-jawed as he stared at the new arrival. Sitting high on the seat of his curricle, the hood raised against the drizzle, were Gerard Bendall and another man I guessed to be his brother. Edward? No, Edwin. The vehicle itself was richly painted in glossy midnight blue with sunshine yellow outlines to the panels. And in the traces stood two perfectly-matched grey horses, sweating and stamping. Bendall slotted his long whip into its holder and stepped down to the wheel and then to the ground. He grinned when he saw me and held out his hand to shake mine.

"The constable," he said happily.

"Gregory Hardiman, sir," I replied.

Bendall beckoned to his companion. "Come down, Edwin – this is the constable I told you about."

Edwin Bendall had the same dark colouring as his brother but was taller – a fact he tried to hide by stooping. He seemed as shy as his brother was sociable, and barely met my eye as we shook hands.

"And this," I turned to Poor Jamie, "is our expert kitchen-hand Jamie."

"Delighted to meet you, sir," said Bendall, bowing his head and clicking his heels. Poor Jamie gaped anew. Bendall turned back to me. "When Mr Vaughan let slip that you are also an ostler, I knew that there would be no-one better to take care of Apollo and Hercules." He turned to indicate the horses.

"They are very handsome animals," I observed. "Jamie, if you could show the gentlemen into the parlour and tell Mrs Bird that they are there, I can settle Apollo and Hercules in their stalls."

"Edwin, the bag," said Bendall to his brother, pointing. Despite being the younger brother, he was clearly in charge – money will do that to a man, I have observed. Edwin climbed back into the curricle and retrieved a leather bag from under the seat. "Our overnight requirements," explained Bendall to me. "Edwin's trunk has been sent ahead to the college." I moved towards the horses. "When you have seen to them," continued Bendall, "perhaps you would join us for some refreshment in the parlour. I am pleased to see a familiar face, and I am sure it will do Edwin no harm at all to claim friendship with a constable."

"I wouldn't be sure about that," I replied, smiling. "Most undergraduates turn on their heel when they see me coming. But I will happily join you once I have groomed and watered your Greek gods."

Half an hour later I checked the doors on the seven occupied stalls in the stables, told the horses quietly that I would be back at half-past five to give them supper, and went into the Hoop. It was busy, as it always is at the beginning and end of term, and the pot boy passed me almost at a run as he hurried to clear tables and provide fresh drinks. The Bendall brothers were sitting at a corner table in the parlour, a glass in front of each of them. Gerard saw me and beckoned me over.

"A glass of Madeira?" he asked.

I shook my head. "I am on duty tonight and need a clear head. If the Senior Proctor smells drink on me, I will be in trouble."

"But term does not start until tomorrow," said Edwin. It was the first time I had heard him speak.

"It does not, no," I agreed. "But as we constables have been off duty since the end of the Easter term in early July, the proctors think we should practise our patrols this evening. I doubt we will stay out until ten, but we are to gather as usual at six o'clock – all eight of us – and walk the town in pairs. Nearly all the undergraduates are, like you Mr Bendall, arriving today, and I think the proctors like to remind them that we will be keeping an eye on them."

"You have nothing to fear from Edwin, Mr Hardiman," said Bendall, nodding at his brother. "He knows what an opportunity this is for him – he will not squander it on high jinks."

Edwin Bendall blushed.

"St Clement's is not known for its high jinks," I assured Bendall. I signalled to the pot boy and asked for a glass of cordial. "Mr Vaughan is an excellent Master, and has a good reputation for encouraging young men who are serious about their studies. Are you looking forward to your lectures, Mr Bendall?" I asked.

"I... I don't... that is, sir, I don't know what to expect," said Edwin in a rush. He leaned towards me and spoke quietly. "I was only a middling scholar at school. I was quite content working with our father, taking care of the accounts and order book, but then Gerry came home with this idea I should go to Cambridge and take a degree and go into the church. I had never thought about it really..." He tailed off and sat back.

"The fact is, Mr Hardiman," said Bendall as my cordial arrived, "there is no point my taking a degree – I have an estate to manage and investments to oversee and I cannot hide myself away in Cambridge for three years. We have four sisters, but Edwin is the only other boy in the family. If a Bendall is to be educated, then it falls to Edwin. He must learn to live in this modern world of ours. You'll soon make friends, Ed, and work out the lie of the land." He reached over and patted his brother's leg.

I paused but then pressed ahead. "I hope you don't think me impertinent, sir," I said, "but when I met you at Stourbridge you spoke of an unexpected inheritance, and now you mention an estate and investments. Yet your background is not dissimilar to my own." I paused again.

"You want to know my story?" asked Bendall, but he smiled.

"I did tell you I was curious," I said.

Edwin got to his feet. "If you are going to talk about all this again," he said to his brother, "do you mind if I go for a walk? Find my bearings."

"That's a good idea," said Bendall. "Just make sure you are back here in time for supper. You'll need to be rested for tomorrow."

Once Edwin had left the parlour, Bendall settled back into his chair. "I can date my good fortune very precisely," he began. "It began just over a year ago, on the last day of August. A Thursday. I was nearly seventeen years old."

I raised my eyebrows. "That is precise."

"I can remember it precisely because it was the day I was travelling back to school," he said. "I had been a bright pupil from a young age, and my parents made sacrifices to send me to Shrewsbury School, under the tuition of Dr Butler. The plan was to prepare me for the church – as it is now for Edwin." He took a sip of his drink. "It was my usual habit to travel from Bedford to Birmingham, and then to meet a schoolfellow there and travel on with him to Shrewsbury. But when I arrived in Birmingham on, as I say, the last day of August last year, there was a message waiting for me at the inn, telling me that my friend had mistaken the date and had already travelled on ahead of me, the day before. I was shown into the inn parlour – one quite like this – to wait the two hours on my own. And sitting by the fireplace, a newspaper in his lap, was an elderly gentleman." Bendall gestured at the empty fireplace and smiled to himself. "We nodded at each other and I sat down. And then he picked up the newspaper, waved it at me, and said, 'Tell me, young man, what do you think of Mr Telford's suspension bridges? Would you dare walk across one?'"

"Suspension bridges?" I repeated.

Bendall grinned. "Two of them," he confirmed. "Conwy and Menai – both in Wales. I remember it clearly, as it was my first conversation with Mr Robert Gilmartin. We talked while we waited in the parlour and then, as luck would have it, he too was travelling on to Shrewsbury and we talked in the coach. Not just about bridges, of course, but all manner of things. I did venture the opinion that suspension bridges were all very well in certain conditions but might prove unstable in high winds and that I would choose whether or not to cross accordingly. We parted in Shrewsbury and he wished me well in my studies. Three days later a message arrived at the school asking me to call on Mr Gilmartin at his home; I did so, and that is when my fortune changed."

Despite myself, I leaned forward in my chair. Young Bendall certainly knew how to tell a story.

"Mr Gilmartin lived in a substantial but not flashy house near the guildhall. His man served us tea in Mr Gilmartin's study, and I could tell from the globe and books and ledgers and cases of papers that he was a man of wide business interests. We spoke for about an hour, and at the end of it Mr Gilmartin said that he had enjoyed meeting me. He said that he was impressed by my intelligence and my ability to make a reasoned argument about the bridges. And he said that henceforward we would be friends. And so it proved."

"Mr Hardiman," said a stern voice from the doorway and I jumped. It was Mrs Bird. "I am sure that Mr Bendall would rather not be kept from his reading by our ostler."

"On the contrary, madam," said Bendall. "Mr Hardiman is here at my request. I apologise if I am keeping him from his duties – has a horse arrived in need of his attention?"

Mrs Bird gave a tight smile. "No," she admitted. "As long as you are quite sure..."

"I am, madam, yes," said Bendall. "The Hoop has delivered everything your advertisement promised, and more."

"Our advertisement?" repeated Mrs Bird.

"Indeed," said Bendall, reaching into the leather bag leaning against the leg of his chair. He took out a large notebook and leafed through it until he found a folded page torn from a newspaper. "From your local paper, I believe – an excellent idea."

He handed the paper to me and I read aloud. "William Bird of the Hoop Inn and Hotel, Cambridge, begs to return his grateful acknowledgement, and so on... ah, here we go: he has made considerable additions to his house by entirely re-furnishing it and making other extensive improvements." My eyes scanned ahead. "Good horses and careful drivers, well-aired beds and wines of the first quality."

"Every word of it true," said Bendall, lifting his glass in salute to Mrs Bird. "Thank you, madam – I have everything I need."

We both waited in silence, and after a few moments Mrs Bird left the room.

"You have earned yourself the gratitude of William Bird," I observed. "His wife was most upset at the money he spent on placing that advertisement."

"A businessman has to spend money to make money," said Bendall. "I admire him for it. Now, where was I?"

"You became friends with Mr Gilmartin," I prompted.

"Ah yes," said Bendall. "From then on, I called on him at least once a fortnight, and he seemed to enjoy the company and the conversation. He told me that he had never married and I think he was lonely. On my third visit he asked about my plans for the future, and promised to help me find a good living in the church. But in early November, he caught a chill that went to his chest, and his health started to fail. Our discussions took on a more urgent nature, and one day he admitted that he sensed death approaching. I was sorry to hear it, as I had grown fond of him. And on my very next visit he said the most astonishing thing. He said that he wanted to give me everything. All of it, then and there." Bendall threw his arms wide. "His house, his business interests, his investments – everything. I protested, saying that it could wait, but he was adamant. He said that should the Lord spare him, he knew that I would take care of him, and that it was more important for my position in the world to be secured. What kindness, Mr Hardiman. What kindness." He sat quietly for a moment. "From then on, our meetings were almost all about business. He told me his financial secrets, instructed me in how to conduct transactions, entrusted me with the names he had used to conceal his property in foreign countries..." Bendall looked at me. "I hope I have not shocked you, sir."

"I am no innocent, Mr Bendall," I said.

"I guessed as much," said Bendall. "I knew I was right to tell you my story. In short, Mr Gilmartin told me everything about his extraordinary – and sometimes criminal – life. He made me a deed of gift of his entire fortune – a generous but not outrageous amount. And within the month he had died. On the fourteenth day of December." He took a handkerchief from his pocket and dabbed at his eye. "I miss him still, Mr Hardiman."

"It is quite a responsibility for someone of your age," I said.

Bendall nodded. "It is, yes. But when I waver – and I do waver from time to time, you know – I remind myself that Mr Gilmartin was a man of great experience and wisdom, and he obviously thought me capable." The bell of St Clement's sounded the hour. "And on that, Mr Hardiman, I must return to my papers." He gestured at the leather bag by the side of his chair. "Once I have seen Edwin settled in college tomorrow I am travelling to London to meet some men of business and my banker. And my lawyer, dull fellow that he is. Taking a leaf from Mr Gilmartin's book, I will settle my estate on Edwin – our father is a good man, but knows nothing of business."

I stood and shook his hand, taking care that he did not see me smile. Hearing such a slight young man talking in that way, it reminded me of how as a boy I would follow my father through the fields, stretching my legs to put my own boots in the prints he had left in the mud – trying to be grown before I was.

CHAPTER EIGHT

BALLOON

"Can you see anything from your window?" asked Mrs Chapman as soon as I walked into the kitchen.

"Of course he can't, Mary," said her husband, looking at me and rolling his eyes. "His window looks towards Butts Green, not the manor."

"George is right," I said, sitting down at the table. "I can hear them, right enough, but I can't see anything." My landlady put my plate down in front of me. "You could still get a ticket," I suggested.

"Pay to watch someone do their work?" she sniffed, folding her arms.

"I'll tell you what, Mrs Chapman," I said. "From what I hear, it will take them several hours to get the balloon ready, and I know you're far too busy to spend all that time watching them." I glanced across at George and he carefully avoided my eye, applying himself to his own breakfast. "But if I can get a ticket for you from Mr Bird, perhaps you could go over later and watch as they take to the sky."

For days, seemingly everyone in Cambridge – from the greenest of the new undergraduates to the most grizzled of the Masters – had been talking about Mr Green and his balloon. In what was going to be his sixty-eighth aerial voyage, according to the gaudy advertisement he had placed in the local newspaper, Mr Green was planning to launch his splendid balloon from the paddock at the back of the manor house, which itself was just behind our very own Radegund Buildings. As to where it would go, well, you know as well as I do that it would depend on the winds.

"Oh, Mr Hardiman," said Mrs Chapman, looking girlishly excited at the prospect. "Could you do that, d'you think? The tickets had all sold out when I..." She stopped suddenly, realising that she had given herself away, and put her hand over her mouth.

"I'll ask Mr Bird if he can spare any tickets," I said, reaching for another piece of bread. "And if George can take a few hours off and call me for at, say, half-past one, we'll come back here and then the three of us can go over to the paddock and see what's what."

In the end, we were a party of four. Poor Jamie had heard about the balloon and that morning he had overcome his natural shyness to ask everyone he met whether they had seen it and was it really bigger than a building and did they think it would fall from the sky and a dozen more questions. When I asked whether he had any tickets to spare and reached into my pocket for the money, William Bird had stayed my hand.

"Gregory," he had said through gritted teeth, "if you take Jamie with you, I'll give you the tickets – all four of them. He's driving us all to distraction with his questions. And anyway," his face had softened, "there's not much colour in that poor lad's life. He'll remember this balloon until the day he dies."

And when I had gone into the kitchen and told Jamie that he was coming with me, I knew that William Bird had spent his money wisely. After splashing his face with water and scrubbing his hands and making me inspect his clothes for any stains or rips, Jamie had all but skipped along Jesus Lane at my side. As we rounded the bend and saw the top of the balloon peeping – no, looming – over St Radegund's manor house, he stopped in his tracks and pointed, silent for the first time that day. Eventually I persuaded him to move and at just gone two o'clock the Chapmans, Jamie and I made our way to the side of the manor house, where a temporary gate had been built to control the flow of people into the paddock behind. I showed our tickets and the man at the gate made a little tear in each of them and handed them back. Jamie had, without asking, taken Mrs Chapman's hand, and she seemed to like it.

"You hold on tight to me, Jamie," she said as we walked around the side of the building. "There will be lots of people, and we don't want you getting lost and being carried up into the sky with the…"

And then we all stopped in our tracks. It was magnificent. There is no other word for it. I had read the description in the advertisement – 110 feet in circumference, 60 feet high with the car attached, made of 1,200 yards of silk – but seeing it in front of me, well!

"Look at that, Jamie!" breathed Mrs Chapman.

The balloon was almost fully inflated, and the alternate stripes of crimson and gold made it look like a huge piece of jewellery.

"How did they blow it up?" asked Jamie, his eyes wide. "Did they all blow into it?"

"No," I said. "It is filled with coal gas, from the works at Barnwell. Look." I pointed. "You can see the pipes coming into the field. When they judge that it is full enough and they are ready to launch it, they will disconnect the pipes and tie the bottom of the balloon closed. Then they will untie the ropes," I pointed again, "and up they will go."

"But how can it lift so much weight?" asked Mrs Chapman. "The basket thing, and two men?"

"Well," I said, "I was wondering that myself, so I asked Mr Vaughan at the college and he explained that the coal gas is lighter than the air around us. So it wants to rise upwards."

"And how will they ever come down again?" asked my landlady, concern on her face. "They surely won't just go up and up forever?"

"Mr Green has done this many times before," I said. "More than sixty times, I am told. I understand that that is the real skill of the thing: when he is in flight, he has to gradually let the gas out of the balloon so that he descends slowly and gently. Too quickly and well, you can imagine."

The paddock was crowded with people trying to get a good look at the spectacle. Standing near the basket – and yes, it was simply a large woven basket, nothing more substantial than that – were three men, two in the neat dark clothes of gentlemen and one in the rougher wear of a workman. This man would periodically climb into the basket and gaze upwards at the mouth of the balloon, where the gas pipes snaked into it. He would then go to one of the other men and say something to him, presumably reporting on the progress of the inflation. We watched this for perhaps a quarter hour and then Jamie asked if we could walk around a little to see the balloon from the other side. I rather suspect he had spotted the stalls set up around the edge of the paddock. George and I said that as we had a good view we would stay put to reserve our spot.

"In that case," said Mrs Chapman, "Jamie can escort me." She took firm hold of his arm and they set off.

The bells had just tolled three o'clock when they returned. Jamie was beaming.

"Mrs Chapman bought me a balloon," he said with delight, and pulled from his pocket a rough little wooden model of a balloon and basket, hastily painted to match the one we could see.

"It was only a few pennies," she said under her breath to her husband, "and he was so desperate to have one." She spoke to Jamie. "And what else did we find, Jamie?"

"Balloon biscuits," he said, grinning broadly.

Mrs Chapman reached into her bag and took out a small package of brown paper tied with string. She untied it, and there were four biscuits in the shape of a balloon. Jamie reached out his hand and then quickly put it behind his back. "Sorry," he said. "Ma says I'm too greedy."

"Good lad," said Mrs Chapman. "And as a reward for being polite and thinking of others, you can choose first."

Jamie took quite a few moments to inspect the four biscuits before selecting the largest. We three each took one and then touched them together, Jamie quickly doing the same. "To Mr Green and his balloon," I said, and Jamie laughed.

A short while later, someone came forward with a wooden crate and positioned it in front of the balloon's basket, facing us. One of the two gentlemen climbed onto it, a speaking trumpet in his hand. He raised it to his mouth and started to speak.

"Ladies and gentlemen," he said, "my name is Charles Green. And I am delighted to be here in Cambridge today to show you my gas balloon. Isn't she magnificent?" There was a cheer from the crowd. "This very balloon is the one in which I performed my nocturnal ascents from the Royal Gardens at Vauxhall in London last year. Today I shall have a passenger with me – Mr Scott of Trinity College." He indicated the other gentleman and there was some applause. "My men and I have been observing the weather conditions today, and we are almost ready to launch." Jamie cheered loudly and Mr Green smiled before stepping down from the crate.

A few minutes later, the crate was moved much closer to the basket and Mr Green and the man in working clothes climbed into the basket. Together, they carefully disconnected the gas pipes and other unseen men pulled them away across the field. The two men then pulled on cords at the mouth of the balloon, sealing it closed, and winding the cords around several times with elaborate knots. They then spent several minutes checking those cords, and the ropes holding the basket to the balloon. Finally, they shook hands and the workman climbed out of the basket. He walked over to Mr Scott of Trinity College, who squared his shoulders, paused for a moment and then climbed onto the crate and into the basket.

The workman beckoned and three other workmen joined him. They positioned themselves at the end of the ropes tethering the balloon to the ground, and one by one they untied them. As each rope was released, the basket shuddered and shifted, the gas balloon straining to rise into the sky. As the final rope was untied, the basket left the ground and rose, not quickly, but – let me think of the right word – yes, majestically into the sky. The two aeronauts waved Union Flags and bowed to the crowd. Up and up it went, and we tipped our heads back and watched as it floated above us. It drifted slowly southwards.

"Can we follow it, Mr Hardiman?" asked Jamie without taking his eyes off it.

"You can walk me home, Jamie," said Mrs Chapman, "and then Mr Chapman will take you onto Butts Green and you can watch it from there. I wonder where it will land."

"Well, that depends on the wind and on Mr Green's skill," I said, looking down at the ground and massaging my neck with my hand. Staring up for a long time had given me an ache. "Now, I'm on patrol this evening, so I need to be heading home myself." I held out my arms to usher our little party towards the gate, and then something caught my eye. A young couple was walking ahead of us arm-in-arm, and someone jostled them from behind. The man of the couple turned with a frown, and I was almost certain it was

Gerard Bendall. I was about to call out to him when Jamie tripped on a stone and fell to his knees. By the time we had righted him and dusted him down, the young couple had gone. It must have been a mistake, I realised later: Bendall had told me that he was returning to London to attend to business, and if he was in Cambridge he would surely have come back to the Hoop.

CHAPTER NINE

MARKETS

"Chatteris!" said George Swanney, checking his reflection in the looking glass in the Proctors' Court. "All that way."

"Were you at the manor house watching the launch yesterday?" I asked. It had been so crowded that the King himself could have been there and I doubt I would have noticed.

George shook his head. "No. Kate and I walked to Parker's Piece and watched from there. The balloon went right over our heads and we waved at it. Then it went higher and changed direction – the wind must be different up there."

"Jamie said the same this morning," I said. "He was watching from Butts Green and it came right back over him, heading north. Going fast, apparently."

"Well, it must have been," said George, his voice muffled as he struggled with his cloak. "I saw a lad from the *Chronicle* on my way here, and he said that they landed in a field three miles west of Chatteris at about quarter to six. So that's, what, 27 miles in just an hour. Imagine."

"I'll have to tell Jamie," I replied. "And how did they get the contraption back again?"

"Apparently," said George, "they packed it up when they landed – folded up the balloon, I suppose – and then went for supper with a local bigwig, who gave them plenty of champagne and provided them with a chaise and four to drive back to Cambridge. The balloon will be collected on a cart today."

The door opened and in came our new proctors, Mr Sedgwick and Mr Turnbull. The former looked around, counting under his breath. "Seven, eight," he finished. "Good morning, gentlemen."

"Good morning, sir," we chorused back at him.

"Line up, if you would," he said, "and Mr Turnbull will check your appearance."

We did as instructed and the Junior Proctor moved along the line, smiling at each of us in turn.

"All the most senior officers of the University will be there," continued the Senior Proctor, "as well as the Mayor. So we must look our very smartest and uphold the dignity of the University at all times. One small glass of wine each, gentlemen – please remember that. No more. Mr Turnbull, will you please check that my hood is correctly squared, and I shall do the same for you."

He turned his back to the Junior Proctor, who lifted Mr Sedgwick's hood, flattened it and draped it across the Senior Proctor's shoulders like a cape. Both men then turned around, and Mr Sedgwick did the same for Mr Turnbull. We heard bells marking a quarter to the hour and, forming ourselves into a neat procession, we walked round the corner to the Senate House. As promised, the senior officers were all on show, and at eleven o'clock the Vice-Chancellor arrived. Wine and cakes were served to everyone; the Senior Proctor need not have issued his warning, as the tiny glasses they used contained barely a mouthful of wine. After about twenty minutes the Registrary rang a bell and organised us into a larger procession.

"That wine was foul," said George Swanney quietly as we stood side by side. "I needed the cake to take away the taste."

"Silence, if you please," said the Registrary, and we set off at a funereal pace. Townsfolk who had gathered to buy provisions at the market stood to the side and gawped at us. When we reached Peas Hill the Mayor and aldermen were waiting for us, and Mr Purchas and Mr Wordsworth bowed stiffly to each other. As doubtless you know, there is little love lost between the Mayor of the town and the Vice-Chancellor of the University, regardless of who is holding those posts.

Mr Hustler – the Registrary – then unfurled a roll of parchment and started to read the Proclamation in his soft Suffolk accent. "Prince William Frederick, Duke of Gloucester and Edinburgh, Chancellor of the University of Cambridge doth in the time of our sovereign lord King George the Fourth strictly charge and command that all millers have their measures well sized and sealed after the standards of the University..." On he went, dealing next with bakers, butchers, grain merchants, sellers of ale and beer, vintners, and anyone selling victuals of any kind, warning them to sell good produce in fair weights and measures or face the penalty of the law. He finished with the usual plea to God to save the King, before handing the parchment to Mr Jiggins, the Yeoman Bedell, who read it aloud all over again. I turned to look questioningly at George Swanney and he just shrugged.

Over George's shoulder, in the watching crowd, I saw a sudden movement as someone ducked from view. I raised myself a little on my toes to get a better look, but Mr Sedgwick cleared his throat noisily and widened his eyes at me. I sighed and turned my attention back to the Proclamation. Again, I could have sworn I had seen Gerard Bendall.

CHAPTER TEN

CAP

A few days later, all talk of fairs and balloons was finished and Cambridge was quiet once more. The lamplighter was walking away up Trinity Street as we constables started our patrol. I had been paired with Tom Blake, who worked at Bacon's tobacconist on Market Hill. He was tall and good-looking, but quiet and shy with it. We were patrolling with the new Junior Proctor, Mr Turnbull, who did not care at all for this part of his proctorial responsibilities; from the way he pulled his coat close about him and shot dark looks at anyone we passed, I guessed he was happiest sitting by his fireside reading books.

"Mr Sedgwick has instructed me to look particularly at Silver Street," said Turnbull gloomily. "The boatmen's alehouses are proving a temptation to the young gentlemen of the University."

"The alehouses, sir?" I asked. "But the Three Crowns, the Black Lion – these are rough and ready places."

"Indeed," agreed Blake. "I shouldn't like to go in to them in these fine clothes."

Turnbull looked uneasy. "I don't imagine there's any need for me to actually go into the premises," he said. "In fact," he continued with more certainty, "I think it would be unseemly for me to do so. I shall stay outside and you constables can go in and warn any University men that they must leave. Yes, that is what we shall do." He walked on, and Blake and I exchanged glances.

We passed a few small groups of undergraduates on Trumpington Street and reminded them that they should be back in their colleges by ten o'clock at the latest. We paused at the Black Bull Inn and Blake and I waited outside while Turnbull went in; apparently it was not unseemly for him to be seen in this venerable establishment, and he obviously preferred the warmth indoors as we constables were left waiting outside for upwards of quarter of an hour. I peered through the window of the parlour and could see him talking to a group of young men. Eventually he glanced at the clock on the wall and took his leave of them; I saw them burst into laughter as soon as he had left the room.

"Come along, gentlemen," he said irritably when he rejoined us, as though we had kept him waiting.

We walked southwards and turned into Silver Street. At the town end of the street were some perfectly respectable premises – including the milliner's shop above which lived our fellow constable George Swanney – but as the lane led down to the river, its character changed. Working on that river were scores of boatmen, sweating and toiling as they steered their loads to and from Newnham Pool, and every one of them liked to slake his thirst in an alehouse, be it the Cock or the Wheatsheaf or the Anchor. The landlords kept their premises simple and their prices low – and undergraduates liked to dare each other to step into this unknown world.

We were just approaching the first of the alehouses when we heard someone running up behind us and shouting, "Constable! Constable!"

We stopped and turned, and saw a young lad of about sixteen in dark trousers, a pale shirt and a sturdy apron. He looked horrified.

"What is it, boy?" asked Turnbull. "We are engaged on University business."

"Please, sir, I'm from the Cap – the Cardinal's Cap Inn," he said, half turning back. "You must come, constables. Please!" He beckoned urgently.

"We must attend, sir," I said to the Junior Proctor.

"But surely the town constables..." he began.

"Are nowhere to be seen," I finished, and Blake and I followed the lad who was heading back to the corner while looking over his shoulder to check that we were coming.

The Cardinal's Cap is certainly not an alehouse, but an inn. Indeed, only a few weeks ago William Bird had shown me an advertisement placed in the newspaper by the innkeeper of the Cap, boasting of his neat and convenient coffee room, where gentlemen of the University would find the latest newspapers alongside coffees, teas, jellies and other refined refreshments. Mrs Bird had decided that the Hoop should offer something similar and was pestering the cook to devise some sweet pastries and biscuits to tempt hungry undergraduates.

"In here, sirs," said the lad, standing to one side so that we could go in through the main door of the inn. "I have them, Mr Jeffers."

Mr Jeffers, it turned out, was the innkeeper. He was a plump man, in clean but not fine clothes, and I saw the same shock on his face as on his lad's.

"Thank you for coming, constables, and sir," he said, wringing his hands. "I saw you passing and sent my pot boy after you."

"What is it, Mr Jeffers?" asked Turnbull.

"In one of our rooms," he said. "Upstairs." He pointed. "There is a body. And we think he might be one of yours."

"One of ours?" repeated Turnbull. "You mean a gentleman of the University?"

The innkeeper nodded. "I thought you might like to know before we call the town constables," he said.

"I see," said Turnbull. "But why would you need the constables? If someone has died in his sleep then the coroner..." He stopped as the innkeeper shook his head emphatically.

"Do you mean to tell us, Mr Jeffers, that the person in the room upstairs has been killed?" I asked.

"Yes," said Jeffers. "There is a great deal of blood. And the young gentleman was not alone. There is another body – a woman. They were obviously... together when they were set upon."

I turned to look at the Junior Proctor, who had gone pale. I took pity on him. "Mr Blake and I will go upstairs," I said. "The pot boy can show us the room. Perhaps you should stay here, Mr Turnbull, and find out what you can about the dead man from Mr Jeffers. There will be a ledger showing who is staying in which room."

"There is, yes," said Jeffers. "If you wait in the parlour, sir, I will bring it to you." He indicated a door and Turnbull walked off without a word.

"Up there," said the pot boy, pointing down the corridor. "Up the stairs, then turn left and it's room 3. The number is painted on the door."

"Who found the bodies?" I asked.

"Joanna," replied the pot boy. "The maid. She screamed and I was at the bottom of the stairs and went up to see what was wrong. She's in the kitchen with Mrs Jeffers."

"We'll see them afterwards," I said to Blake. "Upstairs first." Halfway up the stairs I stopped and looked at him. "Have you seen a dead body before?" I asked him.

"Only my grandfather," he said. "In bed. Quiet. Not something like this."

"Let me go in first," I said. "You stay outside the door. I'll call you if I need you."

Blake swallowed hard and nodded.

We reached room 3 and I looked again at Blake. "Make sure no-one comes in – including you, unless I call for you," I repeated. I opened the door just enough to squeeze into the room and quickly pushed it closed behind me. What I saw made me thankful that I had done so.

As you know, I served many years with the 48th Northampton-shire. It was never the intention that I should see battle, but at Albuera I was taking my officer's second horse to him and found myself trapped in the thick of things. My face is a daily reminder of that day, but there is little chance I will ever forget the screams of men and horses, the choking, sulphuric stink of gunpowder, the smoke clearing only to reveal bright blood and slippery entrails. The images crowd my dreams to this day. And if I could protect someone else from the same torment, I was glad.

There were two bodies in the room; a woman face down on the bed and a man on his back on the floor. As Jeffers had said, it seemed the pair had been disturbed while they were lying with each other as both were in their underclothes. They had rags tied across their faces, which I assumed were to stop them crying out – or at least, to stop their cries being heard. The woman's hands were bound behind her back and there were several spreading blood marks on her garments. I crouched by the man and could see the handle of a knife sticking out of the left side of his chest. I reached up to his face and pushed aside the rag. What I saw made me cry out. It was Gerard Bendall.

"Hardiman?" I heard Blake outside the door. "Shall I come in?"

"No, no," I called hurriedly. I gently replaced the rag on Bendall's face and got slowly to my feet. I opened the door a sliver and spoke to Blake. "Go and fetch Mr Ingle," I said.

"The coroner?" asked Blake. "But he will be at home."

"He will," I agreed. "But tell him that he must come. He is used to being called out. I will stay here to make sure that no-one comes in until he arrives."

"What shall I say to Mr Turnbull?" asked Blake.

"Tell him that it is not a University man, but that I do know him and so I cannot leave," I said.

I saw Blake's eyes widen. "You know him?" he repeated.

"An acquaintance," I said. "Now, go and fetch Mr Ingle, and then you and Mr Turnbull will complete the patrol."

I closed the door again and turned back to the horrible scene. Just then, the woman groaned. I hauled open the door and yelled after Blake. "A surgeon! Fetch a surgeon first – the coroner can wait!" I saw Blake lift his hand in acknowledgement as he disappeared down the stairs.

I bent over the bed and carefully took hold of the woman, turning her onto her back. I unwound the rag from her face and her eyes fluttered open. She looked terrified.

"My name is Gregory," I said softly, speaking to her as I spoke to nervous horses. "I shall not hurt you. A surgeon is coming to help you."

She licked her lips and tried to speak. "Three," she said, before fainting away.

Chapter Eleven

CORONER

Hannah Bird was in two minds about holding inquests in the upstairs assembly room at the Hoop. On one hand, it brought important people to the inn – people who might take some refreshment, or return another day for an entertainment. But on the other hand, it meant that a dead body had to be carried through the building and up the stairs and laid on the grand table (requiring careful scrubbing before and after), and then brought back down again. She actually had no choice in the matter, as William Bird had agreed when taking on the Hoop that the assembly room (large and central as it was) would still be made available for inquests. But still, she was not happy and she made sure that we all knew it.

"Mr Hardiman," she barked at me as I came in from the yard at ten minutes to the hour. "I hope you are not neglecting your duties to attend this performance."

"An inquest is an essential part of the work of the coroner," I said mildly, "and must be conducted in public. I have cleaned and prepared the stables, and will be in the yard from noon onwards, to ensure that the *Norfolk Regulator* gets away on time."

"You make sure you are," she said. "And don't sit down in the assembly room; the chairs are for important people, not gawpers."

"I have been requested to attend as a witness, given what I found two days ago," I replied, "but I will certainly make sure to stand throughout."

"Ah yes," she said, catching hold of a passing maid. "I had forgotten that you are mixed up in this distasteful situation." She looked into the basket of linen that the girl was carrying. "This should have been brought down hours ago," she said crossly, and I smiled apologetically at the maid and took my chance to escape upstairs.

This would be my second inquest at the Hoop. Despite what Mrs Bird might think, I can assure you that I have no interest in attending such gatherings unless I have to. The first I went to was at the start of 1825, after the drowning of a man I had known and liked, and I attended so that his wife – his widow, I should say – would not have to face it alone.

The assembly room this day was set out in the way I remembered: the body laid on the table with a cloth over it, the windows wide open to keep the room cool, a chair at the head of the table for the coroner, and more either side of the table for the jury – I counted fourteen of them. There were about a dozen other chairs provided for more important or infirm visitors, but I stood, as I had promised. The room filled quickly, the jury members taking their seats after confirming their names with the clerk. Two chairs near the door had been left vacant, and when Francis Vaughan and Edwin Bendall came in, they were directed to them by the clerk. Edwin sat looking down at his lap and the Master put a comforting hand on his shoulder. As the nearby church bells marked ten o'clock, the coroner walked into the room and everyone stood. He made his way to his seat, bowed to the covered body on the table and sat down. Those who had chairs did likewise.

John Ingle is an important man in Cambridge. He has been one of our coroners for over thirty years, and the University's solicitor for over twenty. But unlike many important men, who take all of the credit and do little of the work, he is diligent in meeting his responsibilities. And unlike many important men in Cambridge, he treats everyone with respect and patience. He smiled at the jury and said, "Please stand, gentlemen." They did so. "Hearken to the foreman's oath," he advised them, "for the oath he is to take on his part is the oath you are severally to observe and keep on your part." He looked along the table at Mr Seaton, the clerk. "You may begin."

Seaton squeezed his way around the table until he was standing in front of the foreman of the jury, who raised his hand to take the oath. The clerk read from a paper in his hand. "You shall diligently inquire, and true presentment make, of all such matters and things as shall be here given you in charge, on the behalf of our sovereign lord the King, touching the death of Gerard Bendall, now lying dead, of whose body you shall have the view; you shall present no man for hatred, malice or ill-will, nor spare any through fear, favour or affection; but a true verdict give according to the evidence, and the best of your skill and knowledge, so help you God."

"So help me God," repeated the foreman.

The clerk then looked at the other jurors, first on one side of the table then turning to look at those on the other side. "The same oath your foreman has taken on his part," he said, "you and each of you are, severally, well and truly to observe and keep on your parts. So help you God."

"So help me God," repeated each man.

"Thank you, Mr Seaton," said the coroner. The clerk returned to his position at the foot of the table. "Gentlemen," continued Ingle, "you are sworn to inquire, on behalf of the King, how and by what means Gerard Bendall came to his death. Your first duty is to take a view of the body of the deceased, wherein you will be careful to observe, if there be any marks of violence thereon, from which, and on the examination of the witnesses intended to be produced before you, you will endeavour to discover the cause of his death, so as to be able to return me a true verdict upon this occasion." He had spoken these formal words so many times he had no need to read them from the paper in front of him. He looked solemnly at the jurymen, several of whom I recognised as tradesmen from the town. "The jury having been sworn in, I shall now open this inquest into the death of Mr Gerard Bendall, whose body was found in a room at the Cardinal's Cap Inn on Tuesday last. Gentlemen of the jury, please draw near to view the body."

People who attend inquests fall neatly into two camps: those who are hugely curious about the body, and those who cannot bear to look at it. I watched as the first group leaned forward, hoping to glimpse something as the jurymen gathered around the table and lifted the sheet, while the second group turned away and, in some cases, closed their eyes. The coroner spoke quietly, pointing out injuries and marks to the jury, although I doubt any of them would be uncertain as to the cause of death. After a couple of minutes, the sheet was pulled back over the body and the jurymen and coroner returned to their seats. Three of the jurymen looked pale; I guessed this was their first inquest.

The coroner put on his spectacles and looked down at the papers in front of him. "I call the surgeon Mr Abbott," he said.

Alexander Scott Abbott is another important man in Cambridge. He has been a surgeon at the hospital for a decade and I understand he also served a year as mayor, but that was before I came to the town. To my eye he looks like an innkeeper, with his jolly face and ruddy cheeks. He stood and approached the table.

"Good morning, Mr Abbott," said Ingle.

"Good morning, Mr Ingle," replied the surgeon.

"The oath, if you would, Mr Seaton," said the coroner.

The surgeon turned to face the clerk and raised his hand. "The evidence you shall give to this inquest," said the clerk, "on behalf of our sovereign lord the King, touching the death of Gerard Bendall, shall be the truth, the whole truth and nothing but the truth, so help you God."

"So help me God," said Abbot. "I have my notes, which I made on the day." He showed a sheaf of papers to the jury. "I was summoned to the Cap – the Cardinal's Cap Inn – at about half-past six on the evening of Tuesday last. I was shown upstairs and in room 3 I found a man and a woman. The man was deceased. The woman was severely injured but alive. I sent for the hospital porters and she was conveyed to the hospital. She is recovering under our care. Her injuries were brutal." He paused. "Do you wish to hear more about the woman?" he asked the coroner.

Ingle shook his head. "We shall confine our deliberations today to the deceased."

"Indeed," said Abbott. He turned back to his notes. "The deceased was a young man. I estimated him to be twenty years of age."

Several of us looked at Ingle as the surgeon said this. It was common knowledge that the coroner's own son had died at the same age some twelve years earlier, and as a consequence the coroner was always more than usually affected when presiding over the inquest of a young man. And indeed, he looked down for a moment before turning his attention back to Abbott.

The surgeon continued. "From speaking to the victim's brother, we know that the victim was in good health prior to the attack. My own examination revealed him to be sound of limb and well-fed." He glanced at Edwin Bendall, who was pale but dry-eyed – I could imagine the effort of will this took. Abbott went on. "The victim was in a state of undress, wearing only his undergarments, lying on his back on the floor. He had a rag tied around his face. I confirmed that he was deceased and that nothing could be done to save him. I then examined the body. There was a knife which had penetrated between the fourth and fifth ribs on the left side. You will have seen the wound yourself."

"The knife was still in the body when you examined it?" asked the coroner, making a note.

"Yes," confirmed Abbott.

"Can you describe the knife, please?" asked Ingle.

"I have it here," said the surgeon. "It has been cleaned." He reached into his satchel and took out a flat cloth package. He passed it to the clerk, who in turn handed it to the coroner. Ingle unwrapped the cloth and took out a knife, which he held up for everyone to see. It was about eight inches long, with four inches of that making the blade. It was not a pointed kitchen knife, nor a dagger, but had a wide, flat blade with a blunt end. Ingle passed the knife to the jury foreman. This man looked at it and handed it to his neighbour, who stared at it for a moment and then turned to the coroner.

"Mr Ingle, sir," he said. "I recognise this type of knife. It's a skiving knife – used by boot makers to thin the edges of leather pieces."

"Mr John Hunter," said the clerk, checking his papers.

"Thank you, Mr Hunter," said the coroner. "You are a boot maker yourself?"

"I sell boots," clarified the juryman. "But I use the services of boot makers and have seen skiving knives in their workshops."

The coroner made some more notes, then turned again to the surgeon. "Did you remove the knife from the body?" he asked.

"I did," replied Abbott, "but not until the body was at the hospital, so that I could examine the wounds more closely. You have seen that the body has four wounds: three in the chest and one on the right hand. I assume this happened when the victim raised his hand," the surgeon put up his own right hand to demonstrate, "to try to fend off his attacker or attackers. The wound on the hand

and two of the chest wounds were nasty but not serious. It was the fourth wound – the one with the knife left in it – that killed him. From the position of this wound, I think it highly likely that the knife penetrated the heart. I will be able to confirm this if you require me to open the body."

The coroner held up a hand to stop the surgeon. "In your opinion, Mr Abbott," he asked, "were all four wounds caused by the same knife – the skiving knife?"

"I believe so, yes," confirmed Abbott. "The wounds all have the same shape and width."

"Thank you, Mr Abbott," said Ingle. "Is there anything else you think the jury should know?"

"Two things, if I may," said the surgeon. "Firstly, for the fatal wound, the knife had penetrated the body for the full length of its blade – four inches or so. Given that it is a round-ended knife rather than pointed, this would have taken a great deal of force. It was a very deliberate wounding, done with determination. And secondly, the wounds on the woman were not caused by the same knife. She was attacked with a pointed blade."

Ingle looked searchingly at him. "In other words, Mr Abbott," he said, "there was an attacker with two knives, or more than one attacker."

"Precisely so," agreed the surgeon. "It is not for either of us to pursue those enquiries, Mr Ingle – that is the job of the town constables – but I thought it important to make it a matter of public record."

"Thank you, Mr Abbott," said the coroner. The surgeon returned to his seat. "I call Gregory Hardiman, university constable."

I carefully pushed my way to the front and stood at the foot of the table.

"You are Gregory Hardiman?" asked Ingle.

"I am, sir," I said.

As the surgeon had done, I turned to look at the clerk, raised my right hand and took the oath.

"I understand that you found the victim," said the coroner, once I had finished.

"Not exactly, sir, no," I replied. "The first person to see the victim and the injured woman was a maid at the Cap. She told her employer, Mr Jeffers, and he sent his pot boy to fetch me and my fellow university constable, as he had seen us go past on patrol. But I was the one who looked most closely at the victim before the arrival of the surgeon."

"Is this right, Mr Abbott?" asked Ingle.

The surgeon rose to his feet again. "A university constable called Blake called for me at my home," he confirmed, "and we went together to the Cap. When we arrived, we found Mr Jeffers downstairs, and Mr Hardiman in the room with Mr Bendall's body and the woman. At his suggestion I dealt first with the woman, sending for the hospital porters as I said, and then with the man, who was beyond helping."

"Thank you, Mr Abbott," said the coroner, and the surgeon sat down again. "I have one or two questions for you, Mr Hardiman," said Ingle, looking down at his notes and then up at me. "Was the victim dead when you first went into the room?"

"I thought they were both dead," I said. "I looked at the man and could be certain that he was dead."

Ingle cocked his head at me. "You have seen many dead bodies, Mr Hardiman?" he asked.

"I was at Albuera," I said starkly.

"Then I am sorry for it," said the coroner kindly. "Please continue."

"I thought the woman was also dead," I said, "but then I heard her make a noise – a groaning sound – and that is when I told Mr Blake to fetch a surgeon."

"When the surgeon – Mr Abbott – arrived," said Ingle, looking back through his notes, "he said that the knife was still in the body. Why did you not try to remove the knife, Mr Hardiman?"

"As the victim was dead," I said, "removing the knife would not have helped him. Although there was a lot of blood on the woman and on the bed, there was not much on the victim or on the floor around him. Sometimes, if there is a weapon left in a wound, it stops the blood from flowing out. It plugs the wound, I suppose. I thought that if I pulled out the knife, it would make more mess, to no purpose."

"Thank you, Mr Hardiman," said Ingle as he wrote. He looked up at me. "Is there anything more you think the jury should know about the cause and manner of death of Mr Bendall?"

"No, sir," I said.

The coroner nodded at me, and I returned to my place at the back of the room. Ingle gathered his papers and glanced at the clerk, who shook his head. "Does any member of the jury wish to call a witness?" the coroner asked, looking first to one side of the table and then to the other. No-one replied. "In that case," said the coroner, "the body has been examined and all the evidence has been heard. The jury will now consider its verdict."

The fourteen jurymen stood and edged their way towards the window in order to have some privacy, while the coroner remained where he was. He was permitted to assist them with advice about the evidence they had heard, should they need it, but was not allowed to influence the decision they would reach. It took them only a few minutes and then they returned to their seats, with their foreman stopping to whisper their verdict into the coroner's ear. He nodded and made a note on his papers.

Once the foreman was back at his seat and at a signal from the clerk, he stood and addressed the room. "Having heard evidence concerning the death of Mr Gerard Bendall," he said, "we the jury return an open verdict. By this, we mean that we acknowledge a crime without being able to name the criminal." He bowed to the coroner and sat down.

"Thank you, gentlemen of the jury," said Ingle. "An open verdict is recorded. Should further evidence come to light, this inquest can be re-opened in the future. The verdict will be recorded on the inquisition. All members of the jury must sign the inquisition. And then," he glanced down at his papers again and read aloud, "you good men of this county who have been impanelled and sworn of the jury, to inquire for our sovereign lord the King, touching the death of Gerard Bendall, and who have returned your verdict, may depart and take your ease. God save the King."

Chapter Twelve

BOLIVIA

As I had promised Mrs Bird, I was back in the yard in plenty of time to meet the *Norfolk Regulator* as it arrived from London at half-past noon. It had had an early start from the White Horse Inn in Fetter Lane and the driver and his passengers were all exhausted. The passengers clambered down from the coach – smoothing their clothes, stretching their backs, gathering their belongings – and were shown into the parlour. The driver had scampered to the privy as soon as he arrived, and now returned to check the coach and the horses for any damage or injuries that he would have to report. A great deal of autumn mud was clinging to the wheels of the coach, and sprayed up its back and sides, but the structure itself was sound. The horses had come from the Crown House in Great Chesterford; the ostler there was a good man and they had been well-fed and well prepared, but they too were in need of their rest. I released them from their traces one by one, looping their reins through the rings on the walls of the yard while I ran my hands across their shoulders and back, which took the weight of the shaft, and then – more carefully – down each leg, finally lifting the hoof to look at the shoe. The waiting horses stamped and snorted impatiently, but they knew as well as I did that they would not see their stalls or their supper until the driver and I had agreed on their condition.

"All well, Mr Hardiman?" asked the driver, who had crouched on the ground and was looking frantically through his satchel. He stood up again and patted his pockets, finally smiling in relief as he found his tobacco pouch.

"All well, Mr Pym," I confirmed. "You are not staying with us tonight?"

He shook his head. "I'm to board in Newmarket," he said. He cocked his head and counted the church bells as they sounded. "Quarter to," he said. "I'll head in for my belly timber – leave you to the beasts. Are they well?" He glanced at the stables, where the fresh horses were waiting.

"On good form, Mr Pym," I said. "They will be ready at half past. Enjoy your meal."

I had a busy afternoon, seeing Mr Pym off to Newmarket, then the *Dart* to Peterborough and the *Hero* on a quick changeover from Fakenham to London. I was grateful for Poor Jamie's help; the lad might not be quite right in the head, but he had a calm way around animals, and horses were always content to stand and listen to his nonsense, flicking their ears while he held their reins and I swilled out the stalls and laid fresh straw. But at last I had finished, and I had two hours until I was to report to the Proctors' Court for my evening patrol. I took Poor Jamie back to the kitchen, to thank the cook for lending him to me, and sat on a stool in the corner trying not to wolf down too quickly the generous pork roll that had been put aside for me.

"This is really good, Seth," I mumbled through a mouthful.

Seth Young smiled. William Bird was ambitious for the Hoop, and he knew that people choose an inn for three reasons: clean stables for their horses, fresh bedding for themselves, and quality food for both man and beast. With the horses in mind, William paid a little more for top quality hay, and personally left out a saucer of milk each morning for the beefy mouser that kept the stables free of vermin. And for his human guests, William paid a little more for Seth Young, an energetic and exacting cook. All the staff at the Hoop were grateful for this, as Seth insisted on using only the freshest ingredients and had quickly worked out which shops and stalls in town were worth using and which were to be avoided.

"I'm trying a new butcher," he said. "The Willimott brothers on Market Hill. I like how they hang their meat." He wiped his hands on his apron. "She's not keen on the extra cost," he jerked his head towards the rest of the inn, suggesting Mrs Bird, "but when is she keen on anything, except complaining?"

Poor Jamie looked from the cook to me with wide eyes, and when we both laughed he joined in.

Ten minutes later I was stepping in through the gate of St Clement's. I raised a hand in greeting to George Chapman and he opened the little window of his lodge.

"Is the Master in his rooms?" I asked.

"He is," replied the porter. "Bendall's brother – poor lad – was with him for a while, but he's on his own now." He leaned towards me and dropped his voice. "He's cagged today, Gregory. He snapped at Mr Wells, and that's not like him."

He was right: the Master rarely let his temper get the better of him, and if he was barking at his poor footman, something was obviously bothering him.

"Noted," I said, and set off around the court to the Master's rooms. Wells was nowhere to be seen, presumably keeping out of the way, and so I knocked on the door myself.

"Come in, come in," called Francis Vaughan, and I could hear for myself the irritation in his voice. I squared my shoulders and went in. The Master was standing at his desk leafing through some papers and glanced over his shoulder at me.

"An open verdict, Mr Hardiman," he said without greeting me. "What use is that to anyone?"

"I'm not sure what you mean, sir," I said. "The jury had no other option. Mr Bendall was clearly attacked but no-one knows who the attacker was."

The Master turned to face me. "You could ask questions," he said.

"I could," I said slowly, "but it is more properly the duty of the town constables. The victim was not a University man, and the attack took place at the Cap, not on University premises."

I found myself wondering again about Bendall's actions: why he had made such a show of leaving Cambridge and why, when he returned, he had gone to the Cap rather than back to the Hoop.

"But Bendall's brother is a University man," said the Master. "Or at least he was." He paused for a moment, biting the corner of his mouth. "And the University is perhaps more... concerned than you realise. Well, not the University so much as St Clement's." He indicated the two armchairs. "Take a seat, Mr Hardiman."

I did so. "Concerned, sir?" I asked. "Involved, you mean?"

"What was the woman like?" he asked in turn. "The one you found injured with Bendall."

I remembered the terrified creature, lying on the bed, her hand reaching out to me for help.

"She was badly hurt, sir," I said.

"I mean, was she a lady? His wife, perhaps?" asked the Master, looking uncomfortable. "He may have married in secret, without his family knowing."

"I think it... unlikely," I said carefully. It had been obvious to me that the woman in Bendall's room had been paid to be there. Her appearance, her words, the clothes strewn about the place – none of them suggested a wife. "In my view, she was what you might call an unfortunate woman."

The Master sighed deeply.

"But surely the moral choices of Mr Bendall do not concern St Clement's," I said, confused. "It is his brother who is in your care."

"Indeed, indeed," said Vaughan, looking away distractedly.

I waited a few moments. "Is there something else, sir?" I asked gently.

I was shocked when the Master looked back at me, as there was such anguish on his face.

"Mr Hardiman," he said. "I have been a fool. And not just on my own account. I have endangered St Clement's with my actions." His hands in his lap gripped each other so tightly that the knuckles were white. "I shall be discovered, Mr Hardiman, and I shall be dismissed. I shall deserve it, but what am I to do? I know nothing but my life here." He looked around him miserably. "Where am I to go, Mr Hardiman?" I stood up and the Master's hand shot out and took hold of my arm. "Please do not leave me, Mr Hardiman," he said.

"I am not leaving, sir," I said. "I am fetching you something to calm you." I walked over to the sideboard and uncorked the decanter of dark liquid that he had so often offered to me. I poured him a glass, gave it to him and sat down again.

"Port," I said. "You always say it's good for shock."

He took a sip. "You must have one yourself, Mr Hardiman," he said. "You might well need it."

I shook my head. "I am on patrol this evening. If the Proctor smells drink on me, I will be in the suds." The Master smiled wanly at me. "So I will have to bear whatever you tell me without the benefit of strong drink."

Vaughan took another sip of port, then put the glass down on the small table beside him. "Do you know where Bolivia is?" he asked.

"In the Americas," I said. "Neighbour to Brazil, I believe."

"Ah yes, a soldier would know his globe," said Vaughan. "Until recently, under Spanish colonial control, but now its own country."

"I think the book club library has something about it," I said. "*Wanderings in South America?*"

"Mr Waterton's book," said the Master. "But he did not venture as far as Bolivia." He took a deep breath. "I was told about the country by Gerard Bendall. When we met you at Stourbridge, do you remember that he mentioned coming into an unexpected fortune?"

I nodded, and thought back to my conversation with Bendall in the parlour of the Hoop.

"One of the business interests that he inherited was a silver mine in Bolivia," explained Vaughan. "And silver is very valuable. And the demand for it is growing."

"For jewellery?" I asked.

"No," the Master shook his head. "I made a note of what Mr Bendall said." He walked over to his desk and took a small journal from one of the compartments. He sat down again next to me and opened it, turning over a few pages covered in writing until he reached the one he wanted. "Here. It's all to do with trade across the world. 'European countries want goods from China – silk, tea, porcelain, opium.'" He looked up at me and I nodded. He continued. "'China does not want European goods in exchange but wants to be paid in silver, which is used as their main currency. European traders need more silver to buy more goods from China.'" He closed the journal. "And that's as much as I know, Mr Hardiman."

"But why…" I started.

"Mr Bendall invited me to invest in his silver mine," said Vaughan quickly. "He said that I would double my money, perhaps more." He stopped. "Not my money. The college's money." He sighed deeply. "As you know, we have been without a bursar since Mr Galpin left us last year." I nodded. "And none of the other Fellows could be persuaded to take it on, so I – as Master – have been doing my best. But I am a mathematician, Mr Hardiman – not a banker. You know that I enjoy the occasional wager," he smiled sheepishly, "but this," he tapped the journal in his lap, "this is beyond me. I should not have been so foolish. I fear that I have been taken in by a whipster."

"Might I ask how much money you invested, sir?" I asked.

He closed his eyes. "It is a fearful sum, Mr Hardiman," he said quietly. He looked at me. "Friday last after entertaining Bendall in the dining hall, I promised to invest four hundred pounds in his silver venture. And I sent a letter to Fisher's Bank instructing them to make payment to him as soon as possible."

It was only as I crossed the court that I realised that the Master had spoken of Edwin Bendall in the past tense. I rapped lightly on the window of the porters' lodge. George Chapman opened the door.

"George," I said, "what has happened to Edwin Bendall?"

"Gone," he said.

"Gone out?" I asked.

"Gone home," he replied. "Half an hour since. His father came with a cart, Edwin loaded his trunk, and off they went."

"But surely his brother left enough money to pay his fees," I said. "I can't believe the Master would have thrown him out before..." I stopped – the porter was shaking his head.

"Nothing to do with the Master," he said. "Mr Bendall – Mr Edwin Bendall – he was never happy here. The studying and the church, well, that was all his brother's idea. Mr Edwin, he's a farmer to his bones – you only had to look at him. Spent every moment he could out of doors." He looked keenly at me. "Shutting him in a library would be like taking you away from horses. Cruel."

Chapter Thirteen

LETTER

Thankfully there are no early arrivals or departures at the Hoop on a Friday, and as soon as I had fed and saddled up the two horses that had stayed overnight and left them in the yard with Poor Jamie, I made my way quickly down Sidney Street. By the time the church bells were sounding quarter to the hour I was waiting outside Fisher's Bank, and five minutes later George Fisher appeared round the corner.

"Gregory," he said warmly, holding out his hand.

"I did not expect to see you outside," I said. George Fisher lived above the bank with his older brother and his sister-in-law, and I knew that there was a narrow staircase leading between the family's private rooms upstairs and the bank below.

"My brother and his wife are altogether too Godly for me at the breakfast table," he said with an impish smile. "Too much Bible and not enough butter. As a consequence, I rise early, dine alone with a newspaper, and then go out for a walk before shackling myself to the bank for another day." Unlike his brother Thomas, George did not have a natural inclination towards the family business. "Shall we go in?" Without waiting for an answer, he knocked smartly on the door of the bank. We could hear a bolt being drawn back and then the door opened and a young man put his head around it. The stern expression on his face disappeared when he saw George and he smiled.

"Good morrow to you, Mr Fisher," he said. "I thought you were the general public. Arriving too early."

"Good morning to you, Stevens," said George. "And instead of the bothersome public you have me, arriving just in time. With Constable Hardiman."

Stevens opened the door fully and we went inside. He closed the door behind us and bolted it again. "Mr Thomas is in his office," he said. "Do you want to see him?"

George shook his head emphatically. "I do not, no. We shall go to the parlour," he said.

"As you wish, sir," said the clerk, and with great ceremony he pulled a watch from his pocket and consulted it. "Six minutes to nine," he announced, before carefully putting the watch away and returning to his stool at the counter.

I followed George to the small banking parlour and we sat in the two armchairs either side of the little fireplace. "Stevens is terrifically proud of his watch," he observed. "He saw it in the window of Mr Wilson's shop a few doors up, and put money aside every week towards it. Not a new one, of course, but a fine piece nonetheless."

"I have known young men spend their money on far more foolish things," I said.

"Are you planning to buy something foolish, Gregory?" asked George with a smile. "Is that why you are here – to take out a loan to squander on high living?"

I laughed. "You know me better than that," I said.

"I do," he admitted. "And it would be hard to find a less profligate man in the whole of Cambridge."

My hand went to my pocket and I pulled out my vocabulary book. "What was that again?" I asked.

"Profligate," said the banker slowly, watching as I wrote. "That's it: I, then gate as in fence. Reckless, wasteful. It can also apply to morals as well as things – a profligate is a person without good principles. A useful word for a constable, I should think."

"Thank you," I said, putting my notebook and pencil away. "And no, I am not here on my own business. I understand that St Clement's College has its account with you – with Fisher's."

George nodded. "You were right the first time – I am banker to the college." I must have looked surprised. "I know: you are wondering why my brother would allow such a thing. But he thinks that giving me more responsibility will enhance my love for banking, and – between you and me – the St Clement's account is the smallest and least important of the four college accounts that we have. And even then, I do not have free rein. For large and unusual transactions, I must seek approval from Thomas."

"Well, it is a large and unusual transaction that I have come about," I said.

"Ah," said George. "Much as I like and respect you, Gregory, I cannot discuss the business of St Clement's College with you."

I held up my hands. "I understand that, of course," I said. "And I am sure Mr Vaughan would be here himself had he had the same idea as I have had. But having had the idea, I did not want to mention it to him and give him hope in case it came to nought. My suggestion is this." I leaned forward, and George did likewise. "I will tell you everything I know about the transaction. And I will ask you questions that require simply yes or no as an answer."

"So I will merely be confirming or denying information that you already have, rather than telling you anything new," said George slowly.

"Precisely," I agreed.

"I think that would be permitted," said George with satisfaction. "Let us commence!" And he sat back, an expectant look on his face.

"I know that Mr Vaughan is currently acting as bursar for St Clement's College," I said. "He is therefore permitted to spend money on behalf of the college. Is this right?"

"Yes," said the banker.

"I know that there are several ways he can do this," I continued. I held up a hand and counted on my fingers. "He can come into the bank and ask for cash to spend. He can write a cheque and give it in payment. And he can send a letter to the bank asking you to make a payment on behalf of the college. Is this right?"

"Yes," agreed George. "Standard banking practice."

"I know that on Friday last – a week ago today – Mr Vaughan agreed to invest four hundred pounds of the college's money in a silver mine owned by Mr Gerard Bendall." George lifted an eyebrow but said nothing. I continued. "That evening or the next morning, Mr Vaughan wrote a letter to you, instructing you to pay four hundred pounds from the college account to Mr Bendall. Is this right?"

"I cannot know when Mr Vaughan wrote his letter, Gregory," said George, smiling, "and so I cannot truthfully answer yes or no."

"Quite so," I conceded. I thought for a moment and then tried again. "I know that Mr Vaughan wrote and posted a letter to you concerning a four hundred pound payment to be made to Mr Bendall. You would have received this letter on Monday. Is this right?"

The banker paused a moment, considering whether he could answer. "Yes," he said eventually.

"And did you make that payment?" I asked.

"That I cannot answer," said George. "But perhaps you can ask something more general, less specific to one customer..."

"I see," I said slowly, thinking. "Did you receive correspondence from customers in the post on Monday last?"

"Yes," confirmed the banker.

"And were you able to fulfil all the instructions in that corre-spondence?" I asked carefully.

"No," he replied.

"Why not?" I asked.

He shook his head. "Yes or no," he reminded me.

I tried to remember what he had told me. "Did some of the correspondence make reference to a large or unusual transaction?" I asked eventually.

"Yes," he said, smiling.

"And as such, would require the permission of your brother?" I asked.

"Yes," he said.

"And did your brother give his permission?" I asked.

"No," he said. "It is a matter of public record that my brother devotes Mondays to visiting his most important customers at their homes and business premises, to discuss any concerns they may have."

"Which means that any transaction that requires his approval must wait until Tuesday?" I asked.

"Yes," said George.

"Did you ask your brother for his approval on Tuesday?" The banker looked a little uncomfortable. "Did you ask him?" I repeat-ed.

"I intended to," he said in a rush. "But having thought about it for a day myself I was uneasy about the transaction, and I thought that if I went to see Mr Vaughan first thing on Tuesday and then could present Thomas with a more complete picture of the situa-tion, he would see that I am capable of running my own accounts. I am tired of being held on a string, always having to answer to Thomas. Banking is dull at the best of times, but banking like this – having no freedom to make my own decisions – well, it's deathly."

"Mr Vaughan did not mention that he had seen you," I said, puzzled.

"Because he did not see me," said the banker. "I went to St Clement's but he was out, and your porter friend…"

"Chapman," I supplied.

"That's the one – said that the Master had gone from town and would not be back until after dark," continued George. "I fully intended to visit him on Wednesday morning but by then…"

"Mr Bendall had been killed," I finished for him.

"When Stevens opened up on Wednesday, he was full of the news," said George miserably. "A visitor to our town, killed in such a gruesome way."

"Indeed," I said. "And you will forgive me for seeming heartless, but what happened to the letter?"

"I have it still," said the banker.

"You have it?" I repeated. "Here?"

George reached into the pocket of his coat and pulled out his leather wallet. He opened it, dipped into its largest compartment, and pulled out a letter. He handed it to me. I knew Mr Vaughan's hand straight away – I had seen it often enough on college documents and in his own notebooks. I did not open the letter – there was no need.

"Has your brother seen this letter?" I asked. "Have you mentioned it to him?"

"No," said George.

"Thank you, George," I said. "You have been most helpful. I will now be as honest with you. I am uneasy about Mr Bendall and his business dealings. I do not believe that his death was a robbery that went too far. And I know that St Clement's cannot afford to lose its money or its reputation investing in a silver venture that may well prove to be a racket. If I am wrong about any of this, then Mr Vaughan can invest later, once the dust has settled and Edwin

Bendall has picked up the reins of his late brother's business ventures. But for now, can we agree that Mr Vaughan's letter should be returned to him?"

"Yes," said the banker.

It was just after ten o'clock when I knocked on the door of the Master's rooms at St Clement's. Wells the footman opened it.

"How is he today?" I asked in a low voice.

"He did not sleep well," said Wells. "The toast is too cold, the coffee is too hot."

I smiled. "You go to the kitchen," I suggested. "I have some news for him that may put him to rights."

"That would be exceeding welcome, sir," said the footman, and scampered down the stairs before I could change my mind.

"Who is it, man?" called Vaughan from inside his rooms. "Close the door – there's a draught."

"Good morning, Mr Vaughan," I said, walking in.

The Master was standing at his desk, sorting irritably through some papers and tutting as he did so. He looked up at me, and I could see the shadows of sleeplessness under his eyes.

"Constable Hardiman," he said flatly.

"There seems to be a great deal of correspondence when you are Master of a college," I observed, walking over to him.

"Hmmm," he said.

I took the letter from my pocket and placed it on the desk in front of him. "More vexatious still when a letter is returned to you."

Vaughan glanced over at the letter, then snatched it up and looked at it. "My letter to Fisher's," he said wonderingly.

"Mr Fisher asks me to convey his apologies to you, for not having attended to the matter in a timely fashion," I said.

The Master sat heavily on his chair. "Not attended to?" he repeated. I shook my head. "So the four hundred pounds..." he continued.

"Not paid out," I confirmed.

"Not paid out," he echoed.

"Might I suggest..." I said, nodding towards the fireplace.

"An excellent thought," said Vaughan, jumping to his feet. He walked over to the small blaze and carefully tore the letter into tiny pieces, feeding them into the flames. When the last of them had crackled into ash, he turned to me.

"Mr Hardiman, St Clement's is once again in your debt," he said.

I shook my head. "The proper order of things has been restored, that is all," I said.

"If you say so," said Vaughan, "but I know better. If there is anything I – we – can do for you to express our gratitude, you have only to ask. Now, I must summon Wells and apologise to him – I have been rather beastly to him."

CHAPTER FOURTEEN

SCARS

"Mrs Booth?" I said, "Mrs Sarah Booth?"

The young woman who had just walked out of the gates of the hospital turned towards me. She was dressed in a blue skirt with white petticoat, a green bodice and a faded red shawl pulled tightly about her shoulders. But what was most noticeable was the way she had arranged the shawl to cover the lower half of her face, with the ends tucked under her straw bonnet. Above the mask this created, her eyes looked at me fearfully.

I tipped my hat and smiled at her. "My name is Hardiman, Mrs Booth – Gregory Hardiman."

She looked again and then walked a little closer.

"You," she said quietly. "You were there."

"Ah yes," I said, indicating my face. "Once seen, never forgotten."

She shook her head. "No, not that," she said. "I remember your voice. That's what you said to me. My name is Gregory. I heard that." She leaned towards me and put her hand on my arm. "Thank you, sir. It was kind of you."

I thought back to that gruesome room, Gerard Bendall lying dead on the floor and this poor woman on the bed, gravely wounded and so very frightened. After I had sent Blake for the surgeon, I had pulled up a chair so that I could take hold of her hand and talk to her, keeping her awake until Mr Abbott arrived.

"Did you hear that Mr Bendall – the gentleman you were with – died?" I asked.

She nodded, touching a hand to her throat. "And I was sorry for it," she said. "He was a kind sort – like you. Younger, of course…" She stopped and blushed.

"Much younger," I agreed, to put her at her ease. "And a deal more handsome." Her eyes suggested that she was smiling, but I could not see her mouth. "I knew him, a little," I said. "Mr Bendall. I met him a few times. He has a brother, Edwin, who would like – deserves – to know why his brother was killed so brutally. And I was hoping I could talk to you about it." She stepped back again and I put out a hand – she flinched. I withdrew my hand and stepped back myself. "Forgive me, Mrs Booth. You have suffered a terrible attack, and you have every reason to be wary of men." She looked at me appraisingly. I lowered my voice. "Mrs Booth, I know that you were lying with a man who was not your husband, and I make no judgement of you for it. You need hide nothing from me." I saw tears come to her eyes and she reached up and wiped them away with the heel of her hand. "But I need your help, Mrs Booth. You are the only person who saw whoever attacked Mr Bendall. All I want is to talk to you." I looked at her. "Please."

"Very well," she said eventually. "Where?"

Hoping that she might agree, I had made arrangements on my way to the hospital. "Do you know Nicholson's – the bookseller?" I asked.

"Near Market Hill?" she said. "On the corner?"

"That's right," I said. "The bookseller there, Mr Giles, is a good and kind man, and he has said that we can sit in the parlour behind the shop. It will be warm and quiet, and no-one will disturb us.

There may be tea and cake." I gave her a half-smile. "I need only a half-hour of your time, Mrs Booth."

A cold wind whipped down Trumpington Street and she shivered. "Very well, Mr Hardiman," she said. "I am partial to tea and cake."

We walked in silence back through town. When we reached Nicholson's, I pushed open the door and ushered her inside. Geoffrey Giles was standing at the foot of a stepladder, a pile of books in his hand, but he quickly put them onto the counter and came to greet us.

"Mr Hardiman," he said, shaking my hand. "And I see you have found Mrs Booth. Welcome." And he made a small bow to her. "I have cleared the chairs in the parlour, but mind your step – I have cleared them onto the floor. The kettle is waiting on the stove, the tea is in the pot, and – at Mr Hardiman's special request – there are some sweet buns from Mr Mustill's shop on Sidney Street. And now I must return to my books. Monday is a busy day for deliveries." With a sweep of his arm he indicated the heavy curtain that concealed the door to the parlour. I walked ahead of my guest and pulled back the curtain and opened the door so that she could walk through. I closed both behind us, so that no-one coming into the shop would know that we were there. As I had promised, the small room was warm, and I heard Mrs Booth sigh with relief as she sank into one of the little old armchairs.

I put the back of my hand to the battered old kettle on the stove and quickly pulled it away again. "Well, that's ready," I said, and used the pot-holder to lift the kettle and pour the water into the waiting teapot. I swirled it a few times, and then sat down to serve two generous cups. I lifted the cloth covering the little plate on the low table between our armchairs and offered my guest first the cloth and then one of the plump buns studded with dried fruit. She balanced them on her lap and paused. Then she put her hands to her face and slowly pulled the ends of her shawl free while looking down. She let her hands fall into her lap and looked up at me, her eyes wide and tearful. On her right cheek, about two inches long, was a cut, its angry edges held together by small knots of thread.

"Oh my dear," I said quietly.

"We are twins, then, sir," she whispered.

"May I look more closely?" I asked.

She nodded, and I got on to my knees in front of her and slowly put my hand to her chin, turning her face so that I could look at the wound.

"That is very fine work," I said. She looked sideways at me. "Such neat sutures. Done by a skilled hand." I got to my feet and sat back in the armchair. "Not twins at all, Mrs Booth," I said in as jolly a tone as I could muster. She looked at me, frowning. I continued. "My mark," I indicated my own face, "was given to me on the battlefield. A sabre, I am told. It took two days for the surgeon to attend to me, and he was a rough fellow – did his best, I daresay, but from his stitching I think he must have been apprenticed to a cobbler." She rewarded my feeble joke with a smile. "But you, well, there's all the difference in the world. You were injured by a small knife – a dagger, perhaps. And within two hours you were in the capable and skilled hands of a surgeon at our modern hospital."

"He was very kind," she said.

"And very good at his work," I observed. "It looks angry now, but the cut is fine and the skin will heal."

"But I will always have a mark," she said sadly.

I nodded; it would serve no purpose to lie to her. "You will, yes. But it will be nothing like mine, I promise you." I leaned forward and turned my face so that she could see my scar more clearly. She put up a hand and then drew it away again. "Touch it," I said. "I don't mind." In truth, I was nervous: she was the first woman I had ever allowed to do so. She reached out and with the very tip of her finger she followed the dark line across my face. I shivered.

"Does it pain?" she asked quietly.

"At first it did," I said, "and the itching as it healed – I felt like scratching my own face off!"

She gave a sudden laugh. "That's how mine feels," she said. "Sometimes I have to sit on my hands to stop myself touching it."

"But not now, no," I said. "No pain at all. From inside, it feels the same as the rest of me – you don't know your skin is there, do you?" She shook her head. "The only time I remember it is when someone stares at me and looks shocked."

She sat back in her chair, looking sad again. "That's what will happen to me, isn't it?"

"Maybe," I admitted. "And I know it will be harder for a woman. I was hardly handsome to begin with, so the loss of my looks was not so great." Now I was lying to her; as a young man, I had felt it badly, and can still remember the sting of seeing a woman look away from me in disgust.

"But my work..." she started. "I work for Mrs Ind – the milliner, on Sidney Street. She will not want her customers to see this."

"Mrs Booth," I said, "I may have some thoughts on that. But first: tea, and eat that bun. You need to keep your strength up while your body is healing."

We sat in a comfortable silence for a few minutes, eating and drinking. Mrs Booth gazed around her at the books and papers that spilled from every shelf and covered most of the floor in the parlour.

I swallowed my mouthful. "Can you read?" I asked.

"I can," she said proudly. "Well, mostly. I went to school. The Old Charity School on King Street. For two years, until my father died – and then my mother needed me to go out and earn a wage."

I held out the plate again. "Here: have another bun," I said.

"Really?" she said.

"Mr Giles will be offended if we leave any," I replied.

"I only saw one of them," she said suddenly, holding the bun in one hand and picking at the currants in it with the other.

"One of your attackers?" I asked. She nodded. "How many of them were there?"

"Three," she said. "And maybe one outside the door. But three came in." She put the bun onto the cloth on her lap. "Do you think Mr Giles will mind if I take it home with me? Hattie – my little one – would love it."

"You have a daughter?" I asked. "So do I. But mine is far too old for currant buns – she's all grown and married now."

"Hattie is nearly four," said Mrs Booth, her face softening. "She lives with my ma, out in Fen Ditton. We used to live together in town, when my husband was alive. But now I lodge above the shop and go to my ma's on Sundays. She's a bright one, my Hattie – learning her letters already." She looked sad again. "This will frighten her." She put her hand to her face.

"Only the first time she sees it," I said. "My advice is to tell her that you had a little accident. Let her look at it and touch it, and she'll soon get used to it. And that bun will make up for a lot." She wrapped it carefully in the cloth and then slipped it into her pocket. "Tell me about the man you saw. It was a man, not a woman?"

"A man, yes," she said. "Mr Bendall and me, we were, well, you know." She looked at me and I nodded. "I know it was wrong, Mr Hardiman, but he was so nice to me. I met him when he came into the shop to ask for directions, and when we closed up that day he was waiting for me. He asked me to walk with him and I saw no harm in it – I've been a widow for two years now, and when I told him about Hattie he said he was very fond of children. I know I should have waited until..." She hung her head, but after a moment seemed to gather herself and sat up straighter. "But I did not, and here we are."

"Mrs Booth, you do not have to explain anything to me," I said. "Loneliness is a terrible weight to bear."

"It is, sir." She sighed. "But you wanted to know about that day. We were both on the bed when the door opened and they came in. Three of them. One of them said, 'You keep watch,' so I think there was someone else outside the room. I couldn't see them very well because Mr Bendall was on top of me," she blushed as she said this, "but then they came over and pulled him away from me. I was scared so I hid my face under the cover. Daft, isn't it – thinking they might not notice me." I smiled and she continued. "But of course they saw me. One of them pulled me out; I had my back to him and he tied something over my face then pushed me back onto the bed. I could hear them talking roughly to each other – sort of loud whispering – but I couldn't hear what they said. Then I heard Mr Bendall – 'Please no, please no,' and then he screamed. I jumped up – maybe thinking I could stop them. But someone came over to me and grabbed my arms. We struggled and he must have had a knife and I can't remember anything after that. Until you telling me your name."

"We thought you were dead too," I said. "Then you made a noise – good job you did, otherwise we might not have sent for the surgeon."

We were both silent for a while as we thought about how things might have turned out.

"I should be thankful, I suppose," said Mrs Booth, looking at me with a brave smile. "I may have this," she gestured to her face, "but I am better off than poor Mr Bendall." She sighed. "But as for my work..."

"Ah, now," I said, putting down my cup, "as I said, I have had a thought about that. I can't promise anything, mind, but I can try.

You know the Hoop Inn?" She nodded. "Come to the yard there tomorrow morning at nine o'clock, and I'll see what I can do."

Chapter Fifteen

JOB

William Bird shook his head. "It's not for me to say, Gregory," he said. "The hiring of female staff is up to my wife. You'll have to convince her."

"Convince me of what?" said a voice at the door, and William and I both jumped.

The innkeeper's wife came into his office. Hannah Bird was usually a fearsome presence at the inn but today she looked tired. Her husband noticed it too, and stood to steer her to a chair. She smiled at him as she sat down, and with that smile I could see the pretty woman that he had chosen to marry. He patted her arm and returned to his own chair.

"George's teeth are coming in," he said to me. "The big ones at the back. And the poor fellow can't settle with them. Keeping us awake at night, isn't he?" His wife put her hands to her eyes and sighed. "And when he wakes, he disturbs his sister, and here we are – all of us dead on our feet." He frowned. "And why should that make you smile, Gregory?" he asked.

"I think I may have a solution," I said.

Sarah Booth sat down abruptly on the upturned crate. "A job?" she repeated. "Here?"

I pulled over another crate and sat down alongside her. "Well, several jobs really," I said. "It won't be much like the elegant surroundings of Mrs Ind's shop, I am afraid. You are to help the maids tidy the rooms in the mornings – sweep the floors, empty the pots, change the linen when necessary, all of that." She nodded. "If Mrs Bird needs fetching and carrying, that's you. And she can be stern, Mrs Bird. Frightens me sometimes." I smiled at her and she smiled shyly back. "And you're not to go into the public rooms unless you're given permission."

"Is that because of my face?" she asked.

"Maybe," I said, considering it. "The same rule applies to me." I winked at her. "And there's more, if you decide to take on the position," I continued. "The Birds have two children: Emma is four, like your Hattie, and George is just coming up on two. Three nights a week, you're to stay over in the nursery – their house is just up there, on Jesus Lane."

"They want me to look after the children?" she said softly, her eyes bright.

I nodded. "Just overnight to begin with," I said, "to give their worn-out parents a rest, but if you do well..." I left the idea unfinished. "For the other four nights, you will stay here."

Mrs Booth blinked at me. "Here?" she repeated, looking around her. "Here at the inn?"

"The maids share one of the attic rooms," I said. "There used to be three of them, but Agnes left a while ago – she's Mrs Grantham now – and you can have her cot." I stopped. "Goodness, Mrs Booth – whatever is the matter?" I felt in my pocket for a handkerchief and handed it over.

She took it and wiped her eyes. "It's just that I've been so worried about it all," she said, sniffing. "I've been staying in my old room but Mrs Ind was starting to get vexed with me and needs to take on someone else who can work in the shop. And I thought I would have to go back to Fen Ditton and it's all farm work there." She stopped and shook her head. "And now this. Wait 'til I tell my ma and Hattie!" She smiled and handed back my handkerchief.

I glanced over her shoulder. "And here's someone else you need to know," I said. "This is Jamie – he washes the pots in the kitchen, and there's no-one better at holding a horse steady."

Mrs Booth turned to look at Poor Jamie. He stared at her. "You're like Mr Hardiman," he said, pointing to her face. "Does that mean you're kind like him? Can you read with me?"

"I think that's a very good idea," I said quickly. "We can all three practise our reading together, so that we all improve."

Mrs Booth stood and held out her hand. Jamie looked down at it – he was at least a foot taller than she was – and then carefully took it and shook it gently, as though she was made of glass.

"I am very pleased to meet you, Jamie," she said. "My name is Mrs Booth, but I think you should call me Sarah."

Jamie blushed bright red and dropped her hand. "Sarah," he repeated wonderingly. "Sarah. I think that is the prettiest name in the whole wide world."

You can imagine my thoughts – but let us leave that problem for another day.

Chapter Sixteen

ATTORNEY

The area outside the entrance to the Black Bull Inn was crowded as I walked up.

"Mr Hardiman," said a voice at my elbow. I turned to see Geoffrey Giles. "Our speaker this evening has attracted a crowd," he observed. "Why, even Mr Hodson is here." James Hodson was the proprietor of the *Cambridge Chronicle and Journal*, our town's most popular weekly newspaper. "Mr Hodson, have you met Mr Hardiman, one of the University's constables?"

I found myself shaking hands with a man of about my own age, perhaps a few years older, in a dark but dusty outfit. When he retrieved his hand, I saw that it was stained with ink. His face broke into a ready smile as he waggled his fingers at me. "The time-honoured mark of a printer," he said. "My father was the same before me. And no amount of energetic scrubbing makes a scrap of difference, to the despair of my good wife. Ah, here we go."

The door leading to the upper floors of the inn had been opened, and gradually we made our way to the room on the top floor where our book club held its meetings every Wednesday. Taking our leave of Mr Hodson, Giles and I went first to the library to return our volumes. I decided not to take out another as I still had one unread in my room, but Giles pounced with delight on something that had just been handed in by another member. I angled my head to read the spine.

"*The Atrocities of the Pirates*," I read aloud. "By Smith."

"Aaron Smith," said Giles as he signed the borrowing ledger. "Quite the character – acquitted of piracy himself." He handed the book to me. "Read the frontispiece."

I did so; it promised that the book would describe the unparalleled sufferings endured by the author while in the hands of pirates in Cuba.

"Thrilling, isn't it?" asked Giles, a schoolboy grin on his face. "I shall read it aloud to Father, and we shall imagine ourselves adventuring on the high seas." I laughed at the image of these two gentlest of men and the fate they would undoubtedly suffer on those high seas. "Now, Mr Hardiman, let us find ourselves a good perch to hear Mr Holman's adventures."

Some months earlier, Mr James Holman – the celebrated blind traveller – had spoken at a University gathering, and a member of our book club had heard him and persuaded him to return to Cambridge to speak to us. Unusually, the club had issued an invitation to the town at large, and the room was filled to bursting, with every chair occupied and men standing two deep along the side and back walls. Sitting on a chair on a raised platform that had been created at the front of the room was our speaker, a well-built man with a generous beard and bright, although unseeing, blue eyes. In his right hand was a stick that he used to emphasise certain words by thumping it on the floor. He enthralled us for an hour with stories of his travels in Russia and Siberia, including how the then-Emperor Alexander was so alarmed by Mr Holman's ability to recall everything he was told that he suspected him of being a spy and had him "conveyed by force beyond the boundaries of his dominions" – a phrase so stirring that I quickly scribbled it in my vocabulary book to share later with Jamie. Mr Holman is soon to leave England for the coast of Africa, and there cannot have been many in that room who did not dream of accompanying him. He would not have seen us rising to our feet in acclaim at the end of his talk, but he would have heard the thunderous applause. When we had finally stopped and taken our seats again, Mr Holman placed his hand on the shoulder of our club president and the two men squeezed their way through the throng and headed downstairs for, I guessed, a well-earned drink.

Just as Giles and I were about to rise from our seats, I felt a hand on my own shoulder and turned to see a man I did not know leaning towards me.

"Mr Hardiman?" he asked.

"Indeed," I said, standing.

"My name is Nicholas Trew," he said, and we shook hands. "Attorney."

"Ah, yes – I know the name," I said. "I have seen it on a plaque outside an office on St Andrew's Street."

"That's the one," he said. Nicholas Trew had pale skin and what looked to me to be prematurely greying hair. He had a long, straight nose and his eyes seemed to miss nothing. "Might we have a word, Mr Hardiman?"

Giles tapped me on the arm. "I must be off, Mr Hardiman," he said. "Father said he will not sleep tonight until I tell him something of Mr Holman's adventures." He nodded at our companion. "You will forgive me, Mr Trew."

Once the bookseller had left, Mr Trew looked around him. There were still some men standing around in small groups talking, but no-one was taking any notice of us. "Shall we?" said the attorney, gesturing to the chairs. We sat down.

"How can I help you, Mr Trew?" I asked.

"It is more a matter of how I can help you, Mr Hardiman," he replied. He turned to face me, dropping his voice. "I understand that you were involved in the discovery of the poor young man who was killed at the Cap. Mr Bendall.”

“I was, sir, yes,” I said. “I gave evidence to that effect to the inquest.”

“And the verdict of that inquest was an open one,” said Trew. “May I enquire as to whether any progress has been made in discovering the poor man’s attackers?”

“As you know my name,” I said carefully, “you must know that I am a university constable. And the murder of Mr Bendall is a matter for the town constables.” I looked at the attorney, whose face gave away nothing of his thoughts. “But you said attackers, not attacker, which tells me that perhaps you know something more.”

The attorney smiled suddenly. “And you said murder, Mr Hardi-man, which likewise gives you away.” He looked searchingly at me, as though weighing me up. “But you are right: I do know something more. I could go to the town constables, as you say, but should I do so and what I tell them is… inaccurate, I might be accused of using my position as an attorney to settle scores. On the other hand, I am reluctant to say nothing and simply swallow my suspicions.”

“I see,” I said. “And you think that if you pass on those suspicions to me, you will have done your duty without putting your reputa-tion at risk.”

“And perhaps helped to bring a man’s murderers to justice,” added the attorney.

I considered. In truth, having met Sarah Booth I was even more keen to do just that: make sure that someone answered for the death of Gerard Bendall and the wounding of Mrs Booth. “Tell me what you know, Mr Trew,” I said.

He held up a finger. “I can tell you what I suspect,” he corrected me. “If I had known anything, I would of course have told Mr

Ingle." I inclined my head to show that I had understood. "Well, then." He sat back in his seat and I did likewise. By now, there were very few people left in the room with us. "You will be aware of Pemberton, Fiske and Hayward of Trumpington Street?"

"Another firm of attorneys," I said.

"Indeed," he agreed, "but we have very different clients, Mr Pemberton and I. As Clerk of the Peace, Receiver General and attorney to the University, he moves in our town's most rarefied circles. I, on the other hand..." He smiled again. "Let us just say that my clients are not quite as elevated. And as I draw up their deeds and draft their contracts and help them to decide who to put into their wills and who to leave out," he flashed me another smile, "they talk to me. They tell me of their worries and their disagreements. Their assets – those they have and those they want and those they have lost. Their friends – and their enemies." I raised an eyebrow. "And here, at last, I will get to the point, Mr Hardiman. As I understand it, Mr Bendall was found in his room with a young woman to whom he was not married. A Mrs Sarah Booth." He looked at me and I took care not to react. "I have a client who owns a shoemaking business on Peas Hill. And one of his workers is a young man called Charles Booth. Mrs Booth's husband."

"I see," I said, still keeping all expression from my face.

The attorney continued. "Two years ago, Mr Booth appeared before the magistrates on a charge of affray and spent some time cooling his heels in gaol." He looked over first one shoulder and then the other. "I merely suggest that were I a young man with a hot temper and ready access to, what did the juryman call it, a skiving knife, and I discovered that someone was taking liberties with my wife..."

Chapter Seventeen

ERNESTO

It had been several months since I had visited the Howards, and so on the first Sunday in November I walked briskly to their comfortable and airy villa in Lensfield Road. The maid smiled as she opened the door to me, which pleased me enormously. Margaret was fiercely protective of her invalid mistress, and her approval meant a great deal.

"Mr Hardiman," she said, taking my hat. "They are in the parlour, but the missus is having a bad day."

"I'll not stay long," I promised.

I knocked quietly on the door and went in. George Howard was sitting in an armchair, reading aloud from a book in the circle of light thrown by the lamp at his elbow, and his wife was lying on the sofa, a blanket tucked around her. They both looked up at me, and Mr Howard put down the book and came to greet me.

"Look, Henny," he said. "It's Mr Hardiman come to visit us."

"I can see that, George," she said. "My legs might not be much use these days, but my eyes are perfectly serviceable, thank you." But she smiled as she said it. She held out her hands and I went over to the sofa and took hold of them. "How well you look, Mr Hardiman," she said. She kept hold of my hands and studied my face. "Happier," she declared. "But your hands are cold. Go on: warm them by the fire."

"Leave the poor chap in peace, Henny," said her husband. The maid appeared at the door. "Coffee and biscuits, please, Margaret," said Mr Howard.

I did as Mrs Howard suggested and stood by the fire, rubbing my hands to warm them. "There's a strong wind still," I observed, "but nothing like the other day."

"A hurricane, if you please," said Mrs Howard. "George read about it in the paper. Two sails torn off the windmill in Chesterton, and that poor farmer's thatch blown away." She shivered. "We are lucky to live in such a sturdy house."

Once the refreshments had arrived and the Howards had pressed me to take three biscuits while sharing just one between themselves, we settled into our seats.

"Tell us all about it, Mr Hardiman," said Mrs Howard. "The admission of the new Vice-Chancellor. Did you all look splendid?"

"We did, Mrs Howard, yes," I said. "Thankfully I was not on duty for the election – only two constables are required for that – but we had to turn out as a full complement for the procession to bring Mr Davy to the Senate House for his admission. Everyone in their best bib and tucker. Although I don't mind wearing my heavy cloak on a day like today, with that northerly wind slicing down Trinity Street."

"And did Mr Davy speak his lines well?" she asked.

"Very clearly," I replied.

"Of course, it is not his first time," said Mr Howard. "When was it, my love?"

"His first term as Vice-Chancellor?" replied his wife. "Oh, twenty years ago, perhaps more." She smiled impishly. "Tell me, Mr Hardiman: is Mr Davy still as handsome, with his thick curly hair?"

I looked at her husband and he rolled his eyes at me.

"Mr Davy holds himself well," I reported, "and speaks his Latin with a Norfolk accent, of which I approve, but the curly hair, alas, is no more."

"Ah well, my dear," said Mr Howard, "you will have to put up with your ancient husband a little longer." He smiled at his wife. "But this second term for Mr Davy will be an interesting one. I understand that he has lost some of the certainties of youth, and now espouses more Whiggish principles. There is even talk of his supporting the admission of non-Conformists to the University."

Mrs Howard held out her cup and I leaned forward to take it from her and put it on the table. "An excellent idea," she said decisively. "A university should concentrate on attracting men of brains, regardless of their religious beliefs. But enough of dreary University talk for now." She settled back and looked at me. "Have you had a letter from Father Carrasco? With news of your daughter?"

My Spanish daughter Lucia Maria had married her sweetheart the previous year, and I had enlisted the help of the Howards – specifically, Mrs Howard's dull brother-in-law who lives in Lisbon – to send Lucia Maria some money to form part of her dowry. And to do this I had had to take them into my confidence about my past, about my beloved Lucia – and about my own religion. I can tell you it gave me some sleepless nights beforehand, but they could not have been more caring and considerate. And the story of Lucia Maria's courtship had enthralled the romantic Mrs Howard; with three sons and no daughters, she was starved of breathless discussion of weddings and babies. So I knew that the letter I carried today would give her great pleasure.

I reached into my coat pocket and pulled out the folded letter. "I have indeed, Mrs Howard," I said. "Shall I read it all to you, or just summarise the main points?"

Her husband laughed.

"The deliciousness is in the detail, as well you know, Mr Hardiman," she said. "Every last word, if you please." She folded her hands over the blanket and looked at me expectantly.

"Very well," I said. "As much as I can manage, at any rate." Father Carrasco, the priest in my daughter's village, very kindly sent me a couple of letters a year with news of my daughter and her neighbours. He wrote in Spanish, naturally, and my own mastery of that language had always been limited. Indeed, my very first purchase from Geoffrey Giles had been a dictionary to aid with translation of those letters. When I had bought the dictionary Giles was not such a friend as he is now, and so I did not confide to him my reason for buying it. One day I shall. In readiness for this visit, I had written a translation of Father Carrasco's letter in my notebook and so I handed the original to Mrs Howard.

"What a fine hand he has," she observed. "I daresay they are taught that in the seminary. Is that the word, George? Where priests learn to be priests?"

"I believe so," he replied.

"You may start, Mr Hardiman," she commanded.

"Father Carrasco opens with the usual pleasantries, enquiring after my health and so on," I said. "He says that the summer has been hot in the village, with some difficulty finding enough water for the crops, but that despite this my daughter's husband's family's wheat harvest was good. The pigs and goats are thriving. And," I looked up at Mrs Howard and smiled, "and something else is thriving too."

She clapped her hands. "A baby!"

"I have a grandson," I said. "Born on the 20th of May. They have called him Ernesto after his father, as is proper. And then Gregorio." I smiled broadly – it felt so good to share my happy news.

"Gregorio after his mother's father, just as it should be," said Mrs Howard. "We shall have to look in the trunks in the attic, George, and see what little toy we can find to send to young Master Ernesto Gregorio. Perhaps something of William's." She smiled a bit too brightly. I knew how keenly they still felt the loss of their beloved youngest son, whom I had brought home from Australia to die three years earlier.

Mr Howard jumped to his feet and came over to shake my hand. "Congratulations, Mr Hardiman," he said. "A grandson – that is something to be proud of." He walked to the door and called to the maid. "Margaret, bring a bottle of Madeira, if you would." He turned back to me. "We must toast the health of your grandson, Mr Hardiman."

An hour or so later, as Mr Howard and I were discussing a fine pair of horses I had seen in town, I glanced across and noticed that his wife had drifted off to sleep. I looked back at my host and put my finger to my lips. He nodded and we both rose quietly to our feet and tiptoed from the room. He slowly pulled the door closed behind us. Margaret was coming down the stairs with a jug in her hand.

"Mrs Howard is taking a little rest," Mr Howard said quietly.

Margaret nodded. "I've made some chicken broth for her supper," she said. "I'll give her an hour and then take it in to her." She put the jug down and retrieved my hat and cloak from the hook, and handed them to me.

"Before you go, Mr Hardiman," said Mr Howard, "might we have a quiet word in my study."

He led me into that room and indicated that I should close the door. "Just in case she wakes," he said. "Nothing to worry her really, but she has had such a happy afternoon. Poor Margaret will doubtless spend all day tomorrow going up and down to that attic, bringing toys to be inspected." He smiled. "Thank you for entrusting us with your happy news."

"It was my great pleasure," I said, and I meant it. I waited.

"Now, this other matter," said Mr Howard. He scratched his cheek as he considered. "It's something and nothing, I daresay." He walked over to the fireplace and stared at the small pile of smouldering coal. "Do you know a Mr Trew?" he asked eventually, turning to look at me.

"Nicholas Trew?" I said. "The attorney?"

"That's the one," he replied. "Ah. I see I touch a nerve."

"Not exactly," I said. "More that it's a coincidence. Mr Trew is a member of my book club."

"The one at the Bull Inn," said Mr Howard. "Come: take a seat, Mr Hardiman."

We both sat. "I had never been introduced to Mr Trew," I said, "but at the meeting of our club on the Wednesday just gone he approached me with some information about a man who was killed in town about a fortnight ago. I am sure you heard of it: Gerard Bendall. His brother was a fellow commoner at St Clement's."

"I did hear something of it, yes," said my host sadly. "Another young life cut short. And Mr Trew – he knew the poor man?"

"No," I said. "Or at least, not that he admitted to. He gave me the name of someone who might be responsible for the killing – someone who works for a client of his. He said he was uneasy about going to the town constables with just a suspicion, but thought that I could ask questions in the right places."

"And have you?" asked my host.

"Not yet," I admitted, "but I will." I looked at him. "But why do you mention Mr Trew to me?"

"I was in town myself on Friday," said Mr Howard, "visiting my bank and calling on an old friend who is unwell. I have met Mr Trew on a few occasions, although he is not my own solicitor. Cambridge is really only a large village, you know, and eventually we all meet each other." He smiled. "I passed Mr Trew's premises on St Andrew's Street and a few moments later heard someone coming up behind me. I turned and there he was."

"Chasing you?" I asked.

"Not exactly," said Mr Howard, "but I had the oddest feeling that he had been looking out for me. We enquired politely after each other's health, made a few observations about the weather and the poor condition of the streets, and then he asked about you."

"Me?" I said, surprised.

"Oh, he was subtle about it," replied Mr Howard. "He mentioned that he had had the pleasure of speaking to you at the book club and that he was impressed with your good sense during the discussions there. He asked how long we had known you, and what we thought of you – not in those words, but that was the gist of it."

"And what did you say?" I asked.

"No more than I would tell anyone," said Mr Howard stoutly. "That you served with our son, and that both he and I regarded you as a good friend."

"And was Mr Trew content with that?" I asked.

"I think he was hoping for a little more," said Mr Howard, "but I said that I had an appointment elsewhere and needed to be on my way. I did not warm to him, Mr Hardiman – he nettled me, as Margaret would put it. And I thought you should know that such a man is taking an interest in you."

As I walked home I turned it over in my mind. Nicholas Trew had seemed friendly enough at the book club. Indeed, he had given me what might turn out to be very valuable information. So why was he now digging into my past?

CHAPTER EIGHTEEN

SHOEMAKER

Once I had seen the *Star* off to London the following Thursday morning and readied the stables for the arrival of the *Norfolk Regulator* that afternoon, I stuck my head around the door of the kitchen to let Jamie know that I was going into town on an errand. Now that his writing was coming along so well, he took great pride in drying his hands, taking his notebook from the pocket of his apron, touching the end of his pencil to his tongue, and carefully noting where I was going and when I would be back. And then if anyone called into the yard and couldn't find me, someone would tell them to ask Jamie.

You will have noticed that I have stopped calling him Poor Jamie. Now that I know him a little better, I can see that he does not consider himself unfortunate – and no more should I.

James Day made everyday shoes and boots for the townspeople and gownsmen of Cambridge, leaving the fancier slippers and dancing shoes to other shoemakers. As I pushed open the door of the small workshop and quickly closed it behind me to keep out the chill November mists, I could see that everything was kept admirably tidy. Wooden lasts were stored on shelves along one wall and tools were hanging from hooks along the opposite wall. In the middle of the floor was a sturdy workbench with two high stools pushed underneath it, and near the front of the shop was a wooden chair with a low stool in front of it – I assumed this was where the shoemaker would measure his customers' feet. Standing at the workbench, cutting shapes from a piece of brown leather, was a striking-looking man. Clean-shaven but with rich red side whiskers and thick curly hair to match, he wore dark trousers and waistcoat, a white shirt and a heavy brown apron to protect them. On his feet was a pair of black leather slippers. He looked up at me.

"Take a seat, sir," he said, glancing quickly at my boots. "I'll be with you presently."

"I'm not here to..." I began, but he had bent again to his cutting. I sat in the wooden chair and waited. The shoemaker walked to the shelves of lasts and ran his fingers across them, selecting the one he needed. He took it to the workbench and draped a piece of leather over it before picking up a pair of pliers and using them to stretch the leather smoothly. He then exchanged the pliers for a small hammer and quickly tacked the leather into place on the last. He put down the last and the hammer, wiped his hands on his apron, and walked over to me.

"Forgive me for making you wait, sir," he said, "but once the leather is damp I must work quickly before it dries out."

Just then a boy of about twelve came into the workshop from the back, wearing an almost identical outfit to his master, down to the black leather slippers on his feet. He glanced at me before retrieving a tall boot from the corner where it stood with its mate, sticking his arm into it and starting to buff it energetically with a brush that he had taken from his apron pocket.

"Good lad," said the shoemaker. "Now then, sir, what can I do for you?" He sat on the low stool.

"Are you Mr Day?" I asked.

He cocked his head. "I am, yes," he replied. "Another pair like this, is it, sir?" he asked, pointing at my foot. "Usually we could get them to you within a fortnight, but just at the moment we're short-handed and you'd have to wait another week. But they'd be fine boots – see you through several winters. You need good boots for your evening patrols." Ah, so he recognised me, even if he didn't know my name.

"Mr Day," I said, leaning forward and tucking my feet under the chair so that he would stop concentrating on them. "Mr Day, I am not here to order a pair of boots. I wanted to speak to Charles Booth, and I am told he works for you."

The boy stopped his brushing and Day stood up. "Ah, well, if it's Charlie you're after," he said after a moment, "I am afraid you're too late."

I rose to my feet as well. "Too late?" I repeated. "Surely he's not..."

"No, no," said the shoemaker quickly, shaking his head. "Tom," he looked over his shoulder at the lad, "we're running out of thread. Take a shilling from the drawer and go to Mrs Rickett's for me." The boy hesitated for a moment and then put down the boot and did as he was told, throwing a curious look my way as he went out of the door shrugging on his coat.

"They took him away yesterday morning," said Day once the door had closed. "Two of them – two town constables."

"Did they say what they wanted with him?" I asked.

The shoemaker shook his head. "No. They asked his name, then told him to put on his coat and go with them. I asked whether he would be back by the end of the day as I needed him to make some deliveries for me, and they just laughed." He looked downcast. "I fear for him, sir. I know he's had his troubles, but the work here – it has settled him. It's quiet work: a man can lose himself in it – leave the rest of the world outside." He sighed mightily. "I suppose he was caught up in that trouble the other night."

"Trouble?" I said. It seemed a strange word to choose to describe a murderous attack on two people.

"The riot," he said. "All around here, it was." He waved both his arms to indicate the market and surrounding streets. "Just gownsmen to start with – asking for trouble, mind you, after the magistrates put out that notice banning squibs and fireworks. They think because they're gownsmen the law doesn't apply." He gave me a rueful smile. "As I am sure you know only too well, sir."

"Some of them do run wild," I agreed.

"Aye, and then the local lads started joining in," he continued. "We were lucky they didn't cause more damage – putting in the windows and the like. But from what I have heard, their main sport was aiming squibs at the town constables and high-ups from the University." He paused. "I'm surprised you weren't called out, sir."

"I was," I said. "Not my regular patrol, but when it was clear that there was real unrest, the proctors sent messages to call in all the university constables."

"Well, then, you'll have seen it for yourself," said Day. "I daresay Charlie – Mr Booth – was caught up in the excitement of it. You know how young men can be."

"Does his wife know that he has been arrested?" I asked.

The shoemaker frowned. "Wife? Charlie never mentioned that he was married."

Jamie's eyes grew as round as plates, and nearly as large. "Gaol?" he repeated, his pencil pausing over the page. "You're going to gaol?"

I laughed. "Not exactly," I said. "I am going to the gaol to find out about someone who has been taken there. The town gaol on Downing Place – not the one up the hill." I pointed in the general direction of Castle Hill and the county gaol and shook my head. "Do you have that?"

Jamie's tongue poked out of the corner of his mouth as he concentrated on his writing. He nodded slowly. I glanced down at his notebook and could see that he had written 'town goal', but it was near enough. "What time will you be back?" he asked.

The bells had just tolled two o'clock and as I was not due on patrol this evening and I had already prepared the stables for any late arrivals I knew I would not need to rush. "By six o'clock," I said. "To check the horses before I go home."

I picked my way carefully along Birdbolt Lane; the rain earlier in the day had done little to clear the slurry of blood, guts and waste that was swilled out of the beast market further along the street. Turning left, I walked to the end of Downing Place and the entrance to the town gaol. The rough wooden door was of course closed tight, and I banged on it with my fist.

After a moment a face appeared at the small grille. "Yes?" growled the turnkey.

"My name is Hardiman," I said. "Constable. I would like to speak with Mr Payne."

"Wait there." The face disappeared again.

I pulled my coat tighter about me as I stood on the chilled cobblestones; the wind was whistling down the lane and I turned my back to it. Eventually the door scraped open and the turnkey looked around it.

"Yer to come in," he said. I could now see that he was very old, stooped and grey-haired, his hands gnarled. I helped him push the door closed again and he grunted at me. "Thanking ye," he said.

I looked about me; it was some time since I had come to this miserable place. I was standing in a small courtyard, thankfully protected from the wind but open to the grey sky above. In it was a pump and a channel to take away the waste; the smell coming from it was none too pleasant, and I could imagine that in the warmer months it would be suffocating. I looked up at the gallery.

"Debtors," said the turnkey. He pointed, with some effort. "Men in that room," he pointed again, "and women in that one." He turned a bit further and pointed to a room on the opposite side. "Day room." He looked at me and then spat on the ground. "Spoilt, they are." I must have looked unbelieving. "They have beds," he continued. "Two shillings a week they pay. And every Friday the colleges send them broken bread. Live better than old Jones, they do." He spat again.

Just then I heard boots coming up some stone steps in the corner of the courtyard and turned to see John Payne the gaoler.

"Thank you, Mr Jones," he said. "I can attend to the constable now." The turnkey muttered something to himself before shuffling off to a small cubbyhole near the entrance. "He was working here when I arrived," said Payne, "and I have not the heart to turn him out." He looked at me more closely. "Ah, but you are a university constable, not a town man. We have none of yours here, you can assure Mr Davy."

I shook my head. "I am not here on behalf of the Vice-Chancellor."

"Then how can I help you, Mr Hardiman, was it?"

"Gregory Hardiman," I confirmed. "It is irregular, I know, sir, but I was hoping to speak to Charles Booth."

The gaoler folded his arms. "Were you, indeed?" he said. "And might I ask what interest a university constable might have in Mr Booth?"

"I knew the man who was killed," I said. "His brother was an undergraduate at St Clement's. And I have since become acquainted with the young woman who was badly hurt in the attack. I gave her my word that I will find out why they were targeted by Mr Booth and the others. It may give her some peace of mind."

The gaoler sniffed. I could see him turning it over in his mind. "Very well," he said. "Booth was brought in with another man. We are not full so I have put them in separate cells, but they did not seem keen to chat anyway. A falling out, I suspect."

"Only two?" I asked. "I understood that there were at least three, maybe four of them involved."

"I thought as much," said the gaoler.

"What do you mean, sir?" I asked.

"We have five cells down there," he said, pointing at the stone steps. "They are dark and cold and very small. When you leave a man in one, he starts to think. Some decide to tell you everything. Some decide that they will never tell you anything. And some, well, they want to tell you but they're scared. Something scares them more than the rats and the dripping and the stench and even the judge. And your man, Booth – he's one of those." He sighed. "Maybe he'll talk to you, but he's said nothing to me." He walked over to the stone steps. "Mind your head," he said. "And watch where you put your feet. You don't want to slip over, I can assure you."

I followed him down the steps, turning almost sideways as the steps were narrow and the walls seemed to close in on us. The basement of the prison felt colder than the street and I shivered even in my heavy coat. As my eyes adjusted to the gloom, I saw six dark wooden doors, each with an iron grating above it. One of the doors had another iron gate across it. Payne saw me glance at it. "The solitary cell," he said. "For our more troublesome guests."

He stopped outside one of the ordinary wooden doors. "I have to shut you in with him," he said, glancing at me. "But he's not been rowdy, and if you shout we'll hear you." He pointed to the iron grating above the door. "Shout loudly, mind." He pulled the bolt across, opened the door and stood aside. "Visitor," he said curtly.

I edged past him into the cell. The smell was almost over-powering. I heard the door being pushed closed again and the cell grew darker. The bolt scraped home, the gaoler went back up the steps, and I felt my fear rising. I wanted to take a deep breath to calm myself, but the stench made that almost impossible.

"You can sit down," said a man's voice. "There's a stool – here." I felt a hand on my elbow and I was guided to a low stool. I sank onto it and waited a few moments for the pounding of my heart to quieten. It was very dim in the cell but gradually I could make out some details. On the floor was a pile of sacking that would serve as a bed, and I was sitting on the only furniture in the place. In one corner was a pot with a cloth over it. And standing in the opposite corner, leaning against the wall and looking at me, was a young man of about twenty.

"Feeling better?" he asked. "It's the stink. You do get used to it, but it's bad at first." He held up a hand as I tried to get to my feet. "No, you stay there. There's not much room if we're both standing anyway." He was right about that. The cell was smaller than the stables at the Hoop – perhaps only nine feet by six, and about seven feet high from floor to ceiling. "I would shake your hand," he continued, "but mine are a bit grubby." He wiped them on his trousers as he said it.

I finally felt able to speak. "My name is Gregory Hardiman," I said, trying not to breathe too deeply. "I am a university constable and on the 23rd of October I was walking past the Cap and was called to help a man and a woman who had been attacked in their room. When I went to them, the man was dead and the woman was very badly hurt. And I believe that you have been accused of being one of their attackers." I stopped. "Is that right, Mr Booth?"

Charles Booth said nothing. He was a compact man, slight and lean – well-suited to shoemaking, which could be uncomfortable for a tall or heavy man, with hours spent bending over a workbench or crouched over a last. His fair hair showed signs of once having been trimmed to shape, but he now looked untidy with several days' growth on his chin.

"I have already been before the magistrates," he said eventually, a surly edge to his voice. "I am committed for trial at the next assizes. I do not see what business this is of yours."

"I knew the man who died," I said. "Gerard Bendall. He was just eighteen years old. He has parents and a brother and four sisters, all of whom will mourn him."

"Eighteen?" repeated Booth. "I had no idea."

"The woman who was injured," I continued. "She was your wife." The prisoner looked sharply at me but said nothing. "Mr Booth, did you know your wife would be there?"

"Of course not," he burst out. "I would never have..." He stopped.

"Mr Booth," I said quietly. "I know that you did not attack your wife. Her injuries were from a sharp, pointed knife but you were armed with a skiving knife. Which you used to murder your wife's lover."

Booth pushed himself away from the wall and took a step towards me. "Mr Hardiman," he said pleadingly, all bluster gone. "I did not intend to kill him. If I meant to kill someone, I wouldn't do it with a skiving knife." He spoke quietly now, defeated. "It was meant to be a warning, but he struggled and the knife went in deeper."

"A warning about what?" I asked. "To stay away from your wife?"

Booth shook his head. "It was nothing to do with Sarah," he said. "I was delivering a message. To Bendall."

"A message?" I repeated. "Who sent you?" The prisoner was silent. "Who sent the message, Mr Booth?" I asked again.

"I think you'd better leave," he said, folding his arms. "I've said all I'm going to say."

I put my hands on my knees and pushed myself up from the stool. "As you wish, Mr Booth." I walked to the door of the cell and hammered on it with the side of my fist. After a moment I could hear footsteps. "Turnkey," I called. "I am ready to leave." We heard the bolt being pulled across and then the door opened. As I walked towards it, Booth suddenly put his hand on my arm.

"Tell Sarah I am sorry," he said. "For all of it."

CHAPTER NINETEEN

UNNATURAL

One of the horses that had come in with the *Norfolk Regulator* had a small wound on its fetlock – likely caused by using its own hoof to scratch at some irritation – and I decided to apply a bread and milk poultice. Jamie stood by the horse's head and talked nonsense to the animal while I tended to it.

"What is wrong with the horse?" said a woman's voice, and I looked up from where I was crouched to see Sarah Booth peering over the door of the stall.

"He has kicked himself," said Jamie, "and Mr Hardiman is mending it with bread."

I bent again to my work; the horse would stay patient only so long. "A bread and milk poultice," I explained. "To draw out any infection and encourage the skin to mend." I patted the last bit of the poultice into place and stood up slowly so as not to startle the horse. I wiped my hands on my apron.

"Thank you, Jamie," I said. "That was a great help. We'll let the horse sleep now, and in the morning we can look at the leg again."

I opened the door and Jamie walked out of the stall ahead of me. I closed the door behind us, bolted it and checked it by pulling on it. When I turned around, Jamie was standing staring at Sarah Booth.

"Jamie," I said gently. "You must not stare at Mrs Booth like that."

She put a hand to her damaged face.

"Sorry," said Jamie, looking down. "But her face is prettier than anyone I else I know." He leaned towards me and spoke in a loud whisper. "She has eyes the same blue as a kingfisher."

I forced myself not to laugh. "That she does," I agreed. I put a hand into my coat pocket and picked out two pennies. "These are for you," I said, putting them into Jamie's hand. "They are your wages for being my assistant ostler this afternoon. Take one home to your ma, and spend the other one on yourself."

Jamie looked at me with shining eyes, then smiled broadly and walked out into the yard.

"I'd like a word with you, Mrs Booth," I said, "but it's too cold to stand out here for long." I had seen her pull her shawl tighter around her shoulders. "I am sure Mr Young will not mind if we sit quietly in the corner of his kitchen."

We walked across the yard and I pulled open the door of the kitchen to let Mrs Booth walk in ahead of me. A cloud of steam and warmth came out to meet us.

"Close that door quickly!" shouted the cook. "I have meat resting."

"It's just me, Seth," I called into the haze. "Mrs Booth and I need a warm spot to talk for a while."

The cook emerged. He was a handsome man of about thirty, his hair close-cropped to his head and his clothes covered by a long apron that he changed twice a day. He was drying his hands on a cloth draped over his shoulder.

"Gregory, Mrs Booth," he said, nodding at us. He looked around. "Jamie's counter is clear. Pull over another stool, Gregory, and you can sit there. I have some coffee warming, and a fruit loaf, if Mrs Booth would care for some."

"If you are sure you can spare it, Mr Young," said Mrs Booth.

"Three slices it is," he said, smiling. "And how is young Hattie, Mrs Booth?"

"Full of chatter, always asking questions," said Mrs Booth with a laugh. "From dawn to dusk. My poor ma." She shook her head.

Once Seth had brought our refreshments and Mrs Booth had served us both, I looked at her. "Mrs Booth," I said.

"I would feel more comfortable if you called me Sarah," she said. "I have never really taken to the name Booth. It's my husband's name, but it never really suited me, I felt."

"Thank you, Sarah," I said. "And it is your husband I wanted to ask about." Sarah looked a little uneasy but said nothing. "You told me that you are a widow," I continued. "But this morning I went to the town gaol. They have found two of the men who attacked you and Mr Bendall. And one of them is called Charles Booth."

Sarah put down her cup so quickly that the coffee splashed out onto the counter. "Charlie?" she said. "Charlie attacked me? Charlie did this?" She covered the scar on her face with her fingers.

I put out a hand to calm her. "Charles Booth attacked Mr Bendall, not you. We're sure of that. He didn't know you were in the room, and he was very upset when I told him. He said to tell you he was sorry for all of it." I waited a moment. "But Charles Booth is your husband, isn't he?"

Sarah picked at her fruit loaf, then nodded slowly.

"Why do you tell people that he is dead?" I asked gently.

A tear dropped from her face onto the counter. I reached into my pocket and passed her my handkerchief. She took it and wiped savagely at her face, wincing as she touched her scar. "Charlie Booth is not fit to be a husband," she said quietly but fiercely. "He's not fit to be a father."

"Because he is violent?" I asked.

"Because he is... unnatural," she replied. She looked at me, her eyes now full of tears. "He prefers to... spend his time with men."

"Ah," I said. "And you did not know this before you married him?"

"I did not know such a thing was possible before I married him," she said. "He was very careful with me. Said he didn't want to rush me, to force me." She looked at me, blushing, and I nodded. "We managed to – well, you know – just twice, and then he lost interest. I thought it was me, doing something wrong. But then I found that I was going to have a baby and it didn't seem to matter so much. But one day." She stopped. She put her hand across her mouth, closed her eyes and shook her head. I waited. "One day I came home and I found him. With another man, against the wall. I couldn't make sense of it, but there was no mistaking what I saw. I ran and went to my ma and told her. And she knew – I could tell from her eyes. She was not surprised. He came to my ma's later, and we decided that the best thing was for him to leave Fen Ditton and go to Cambridge for work. And if anyone asks, I tell them I'm a widow."

"And Hattie?" I asked.

Sarah jabbed at the counter with her finger. "I am not having him make her filthy. I told him I would keep his disgusting secret as long as he stayed away from us. He has never seen Hattie and he's never going to. I made myself that promise."

Chapter Twenty

GAOL

It was not all that difficult for Sarah Booth to keep her promise. Two days later I was in one of the stalls, replacing the hook that held the water bucket after a horse had kicked out and bent it. There was an urgent knocking on the doorpost and Joe Lassiter appeared. He's by no means the only messenger boy in town but I would wager he's the hardest-working. With a little sister to care for, Joe spends every waking moment doing everything he can to keep them from falling onto the parish. Although he is only eleven years old, he carries a man's responsibilities on his shoulders – but you would never know it from his cheery manner and dancing feet.

"Morning, Mr Hardiman," he said.

I looked up from my work. "Joe," I said. "And how is Mistress Sally?"

He smiled, as he always did at any mention of his beloved sister. "She is getting prettier by the day," he said stoutly. Poor little Sally had a hare lip, but she was beautiful in the eyes of her doting brother.

"I don't doubt it," I said. I pulled on the hook to make sure that it was secure and then hung the bucket back on it. I swept the straw back over the bare floor where I had been working and came out of the stall to meet Joe. "You have a message for me?" I asked.

"From Mr Payne at the gaol," he said importantly, holding out a folded piece of paper.

I took the message, opened it and read it.

"Bad news, Mr Hardiman?" asked Joe, suddenly serious.

"It is, yes," I replied, folding the paper again. "But it's nothing for you to worry about, Joe." I felt in my pocket and found a tanner, then a second one. I put them into Joe's outstretched hand and he carefully picked up one of them and held it out to me.

"Only sixpence to deliver to you, sir," he said gruffly.

"Sixpence for the delivery," I said, "and sixpence for Sally."

His face broke into a wide grin. He curled his fingers over the coins, touched his other hand to his forehead in salute, and skipped from the yard.

This time the door to the gaol was opened as soon as the turnkey saw my face. Again I helped him push the door closed, and again he growled, "Thanking ye." He pointed to the far corner of the courtyard. "Mr Payne is waiting fer ye in his office."

I walked the very few yards and knocked on the door that had "Keeper" written on it in uneven, faded letters.

"Come in," came the reply.

I opened the door and went into a tiny room. It was about the size of one of the stalls in my stables, and all but filled by a desk with a chair on either side of it. A window looked out of the back of the gaol, into another yard, and through its grimy panes some milky light fell onto the desk. In the corner of the room was a little stove, giving out enough heat to warm the office to an almost uncomfortable level.

John Payne was behind the desk and had stood to greet me. We shook hands. "Thank you for coming so promptly, Mr Hardiman," he said. He indicated the second chair and we both sat down.

"When did you find him?" I asked.

"When Mr Jones took him his breakfast this morning," he replied.

"Mr Jones lives in?" I asked.

The gaoler nodded. "He has a cot in the gatehouse. It would have been at about seven o'clock."

"And Mr Booth had hanged himself?" I asked.

"Tied his belt to the grille above the door," said Payne. "During the night. He was cold by the time Jones could get into the cell. He had to let out two other men to help him push open the door, with the body against it."

"I'm curious, Mr Payne," I said. "Why did you send for me? Self-murder is surely a matter for the town constables."

"Indeed it is, and I shall be sending word to them presently," said the gaoler. "But given your interest in the prisoner, I thought you might like to see the body before the coroner takes it. In case there is anything that might cause further distress to his family." He looked at me. "Given Mr Booth's interests." I raised an eyebrow. "If you ever want to know the local gossip," explained the gaoler, "you could do worse than take Mr Jones for a tankard of ale. He's quiet and slow, granted, but there's nothing wrong with his hearing or his eyesight. He told me that a young man visited Mr Booth several times, and their... affection for each other did not go unnoticed."

"I see," I said. "Is the body still in the cell?"

Payne nodded. "It's cool down there – cool enough for me to give you a few minutes before I inform the town constables."

It was more than cool in Booth's cell; the dank chill made me shiver.

"I'll not close the door this time," said Jones. He jerked his head towards the bedding sacks. "He's going nowhere. And I'll leave you my candle," he added, putting it on the stool. He turned away and I could hear him clumping up the steps.

I lifted the rough blanket that had been pulled over the body. I have seen several hanged men, and every time I vow never to take that particular escape myself. Like the others, it was clear that Booth had struggled. Above the angry red stripe made by his belt, there were claw marks on his neck. There was thick foam around his mouth and his tongue was hanging out, with dried blood where he had bitten it. And as I lifted the blanket a little further, I could see his clenched fists, and the stains on his trousers where he had soiled himself. I was thankful that someone had closed his eyes, as I did not want to see the terror I knew would be in them. I paused for a moment and said what I suppose would be called a prayer, hoping that God would be merciful and grant this poor man some peace.

Over his grubby shirt and trousers Booth was wearing a thick woollen coat which likewise was none too clean after more than a fortnight in gaol. I felt inside one of the large pockets and found a heel of bread wrapped in a cloth. The colleges sent their broken bread to the gaol each Friday, so I guessed this had been Booth's share. I wrapped it up again and replaced it. In the other pocket was what I had hoped to find: a letter. It was made of a poor piece of paper – I guessed that perhaps Booth's affectionate friend had brought it for him – and on the front, in neat letters, was the name Mrs Charles Booth. I slipped it into my own pocket. The town constables would have no interest in it; there was no doubt that Booth had taken his own life, and if the letter offered any information that might help the coroner, I would pass it on myself.

"I couldn't think where else to take her," I said in a low voice to Mrs Chapman as we stood at the stove. Behind us, Sarah Booth sat at the table, her husband's letter unopened in front of her. She held a handkerchief to her face, but her crying had quietened.

"You did right," said my landlady. "She won't want the other maids at the inn knowing her business." She poured hot water into the teapot and gave it a swirl before turning and setting it on the table. "There we are." She reached for a cup and poured hot tea into it before pushing it towards my guest. "I have bought a new blend from Mr Twiss on Market Hill, but I fear it's too bitter."

Sarah reached for the cup, blew on the tea and took a sip. "'Tis kind of you," she said quietly. "And not bitter, no."

Mrs Chapman smiled. "Mr Hardiman tells me you have a little girl," she said.

Sarah nodded. "Hattie. Well, Harriet – but she prefers Hattie. She's four." She gave a sudden sob. "I told her that her pa was dead – and now he is." She put down her cup with shaking hands. "Do you think he..." But she could not finish the question.

My landlady pulled out another chair from the table and sat opposite Sarah. She reached across to the younger woman and took both her hands in hers. "Now you listen to me," she said gently but with certainty. "This is a terrible thing that has happened. A young man has died by his own hand, and God alone knows the unhappiness he must have felt to do such a thing. But you," and here I could see her squeezing Sarah's hands, "you are not to blame. Your husband was caught in a trap of his own making. And you did what you had to do to protect your child. You could not have managed it any other way. Could you?" Sarah shook her head. "There, now," continued Mrs Chapman. "I was a widow myself, and I can tell you that there will be dark days. But you are young and you are strong and you have a child, and all of these will keep you going." With each of the last three words, there was another squeeze of the hands before she let them go.

Sarah smiled weakly. "Thank you, Mrs Chapman," she said quietly.

My landlady stood and pushed the chair back under the table. "Now, I've errands to run. You sit there as long as you like. But you will have to read it, you know." She pointed at the letter. "It was what he wanted."

Once we were alone, I sat down next to Mrs Booth. With the tip of one finger, she pushed the letter towards me.

"You read it first," she said.

"Are you sure, Sarah?" I asked. "It is meant for you."

She clasped her hands in her lap, under the table, and shook her head. I picked up the letter and carefully unfolded it. "Shall I read it out to you?"

She shook her head again. "You read it first," she repeated, "and then tell me the good bits. I don't want to know anything bad." She quickly wiped away a tear.

I started to read. "He starts with another apology," I said. "'My dear Sarah, I am very sorry for the pain I have caused you.'" I read a little more. "He says that he cannot live any longer with what he has done. He sends his best kisses to Hattie. And he says that if you go to his lodgings and lift up one of the floorboards – he has given directions – you will find his savings in a small wooden box." I looked up at Sarah. "You see: he was thinking of you and Hattie – thinking to take care of you."

"I do not need him to take care of me," she said fiercely.

"Perhaps not, but the money is rightfully yours," I pointed out. "Yours and Hattie's."

Sarah shrugged.

"Would you like me to go to Charlie's lodgings and fetch the box?" I asked. "Then you can decide whether it is worth having or not."

She looked at me and nodded. "Thank you," she said. "I don't think I could bear to – to see where he was."

I folded up the letter and handed it to her. "I shall go tomorrow," I said. "Before a new tenant moves in and discovers that loose floorboard."

Chapter Twenty-One

MATTHEW

It was a bitterly cold cobweb morning as I walked up the hill towards Charlie Booth's lodgings, and I quickened my pace to warm myself. There were not many people around; those who had not gone to church were staying indoors by their fireplaces.

I turned up St Peter's Street and on into Shallow Row, looking for the number that Sarah Booth had given me. It was a poor house, held up only by leaning on its neighbours. As I walked up to the door, it was pulled open and there stood a young woman, one child on her hip with his finger stuck up his nose, and a little girl of about four clinging to her skirt. They all stared at me.

"Good day," I said. "Does Mr Booth have a room here?"

"Charlie?" said the woman, pulling her son's finger from his nose with her free hand. He immediately put it back. I nodded. "Top floor," she said, jerking her head upwards. "Him and his brother. Stop that!" She slapped the boy's arm and he started to wail. I stood to one side and the three of them set off down the street.

I walked up the creaking stairs, past three closed doors on the first floor. The stairs narrowed as I climbed to the top of the house. Here there was only one door. I knocked on it. It was opened by a man of about twenty-five, small, with fine features and thick blond hair. He was wearing dark trousers and a clean white shirt, and he was putting on his coat as though to go out.

"Yes?" he said.

"I imagine you are on your way to see Charlie," I said. I glanced over my shoulder down the stairs. "Your brother." The man went to close the door in my face, but I put up my hand and stopped it. "It is no concern of mine what you tell your neighbours," I said, "but I am afraid I have some bad news for you and I think it best I tell you in private."

The young man looked at me for a long moment and then wordlessly held the door open for me. The room was in the roof of the house, with sloping sides and two windows, one looking into the street and one into the yard. There was a table with two chairs, a chest with an open lid – I could see clothes carefully folded inside it – and two narrow stump beds. They were pushed together. The young man watched me notice them, and his eyes stayed on my face.

"This," I said, pointing at the beds, "is also no concern of mine. I am here on behalf of Charlie's wife."

"Sarah?" said the man, surprised.

I nodded, and held out my hand. "My name is Gregory Hardiman."

He shook my hand. "Matthew Gibbs," he said. "Please, sit."

We sat at the table. He put his hands in his lap, then on the table, then back in his lap. He swallowed hard then looked at me. "He's dead, isn't he?" he said quietly.

"He is, yes," I replied. "I am very sorry for it."

"How?" asked Gibbs.

"He hanged himself at the gaol," I said. "The turnkey found him yesterday morning." I watched the man as he rubbed the knuckles of one hand with the thumb of the other, elbows tight into his sides. He nodded. "I think I know what he was to you," I said as gently as I could. "His wife told me of their arrangement."

"But she will go to the funeral," he burst out, "and everyone will comfort her."

"That is the way of things," I agreed.

"'Tis cruel," said Gibbs.

I nodded. It was. It occurred to me that there was something I could do. "Tell me about Charlie," I said. "Tell me why you loved him."

Gibbs's eyes widened at my use of the word. "I did, you know," he whispered. "He was so... certain. So hopeful that things would improve. Even this." He indicated the room and smiled. "He would look out of the window and point out the birds and the trees, and say how lucky we were to have our little nest up here. I've always been scared – timid. But Charlie had an appetite for life." His smile faded. "Until a few months ago, that is."

"What happened then?" I asked.

"He was more short-tempered," said Gibbs. "Nervous – looking behind him when we were out. As though someone was after him."

"But he didn't tell you who that was?" I asked.

He shook his head. "I kept asking him, but he denied it. He always wanted to protect me. I should have pressed him. Perhaps if I had..."

"We always have regrets, Mr Gibbs," I said. "They add an unkind sting to grief." I paused. "Charlie left a letter. But I am sorry: it was not for you."

"I expected nothing, Mr Hardiman," he said. "We have been so careful – he wouldn't give me away at the end. The letter was for Sarah, wasn't it?"

"More for Hattie," I replied. "He wanted to provide for her."

"The wooden box," said Gibbs flatly. "His savings." He picked up a knife from the table, then stood and walked over to a corner of the room. Kneeling, he used the tip of the knife to lever up a floorboard, then reached in and took out a wooden box. It was about nine inches long and five deep, with a domed lid. Gibbs got to his feet and brought the box to me, putting it on the table. "It is a tea caddy," he explained. "I work for Mr Beecheno on Sidney Street. When this was delivered it had been dropped and cracked – see, here." He turned the box so that I could see the break all the way down the back of it. "Mr Beecheno said it was worthless and he let me take it. Charlie is clever with his hands – was clever – and I thought he could fix it. In the end, he just used it for this." He opened the lid. "Every week he put aside two shillings for Hattie. Never missed."

"I did the same for my daughter," I said. "She's grown and married now, but every week for years I did that."

Gibbs tipped out the contents of the box; it was a mixture of notes and coins.

"Shall I help?" I asked.

Gibbs nodded, and together we sorted and counted the money, and then counted it again.

"Nineteen pounds and eight shillings," said Gibbs.

"Is that all there is?" I asked.

Gibbs frowned. "Two shillings a week for nearly four years – that works out right." He looked at me sharply. "Were you expecting something else?"

"No," I lied. "My arithmetic has never been much good – you're right, two shillings a week, making just under twenty pounds. Shall I take it to Sarah and Hattie for you?"

"I've no choice, really, have I?" asked Gibbs. "She knows about the box, and I can hardly turn up and introduce myself, can I?"

"No," I said, telling the truth this time. I carefully put the money back into the box and closed the lid. I stood and held out my hand again. "Mr Gibbs," I said, "I am genuinely sorry for what has happened. Losing someone we love – no matter how or why we love them – is dreadful. If you find yourself adrift, come and see me at the Hoop. I am the ostler there, and horses at rest are very calming beasts."

As I walked down Castle Hill with Charlie Booth's box tucked safely under my arm, I turned things over in my mind. Charlie had told me that he was delivering a message when he attacked Gerard Bendall. Messengers are usually paid for their work, and I had expected to find such payment in that wooden box. But it was as Mr Gibbs had said: two shillings a week for four years, and no more. Charlie's motive for attacking Bendall had not been personal (the two men had been strangers) and it had not been robbery (the constables had found money and a gold watch in Bendall's luggage). And now it seemed he had not been paid for it. What then could have been his reason for committing such a brutal act?

CHAPTER TWENTY-TWO

THREATS

Tempting though it was to stay tucked up in my warm ostry after I had seen off the coach to London, I knew I had to speak to Booth's fellow prisoner. I turned up the collar of my coat, pulled my hat low on my head, shoved my hands deep into my pockets and trudged off down Sidney Street. A cold northerly wind was whistling down the hill into town; on my return journey I would have it full in my face.

Jones the turnkey thanked me again as I helped him push the door of the gaol closed.

"Swells in winter, she does," he growled. He looked at me. "If it's Mr Payne you're for, he's not here. Gone to visit them up the hill." He indicated the direction with a frown.

"The county gaol?" I guessed.

"Aye," said Jones, spitting on the ground. "To see Mr Orridge's treadmill."

"You don't approve of the contraption?" I asked.

"Walking and walking to go nowhere?" said the turnkey bitterly. "What's the use of that? Better to get them doing something useful – learning a trade."

I looked at Jones with surprise.

"I've eyes in my head," he said defensively. "And many who come through here just need showing a better path. Not the debtors, mind you. Live better than Jones, they do." He spat again. "Now, what do you want, bothering me this morning?"

"I would like to speak to the man brought in with Charlie Booth," I said. "The other attacker from the Cap. I understand two were caught and two ran off."

"John Lodge," said Jones. "Warehouseman for John Swan the auctioneer. Not your usual thug."

"No more was Charlie Booth," I said.

The turnkey looked at me. "I've something of his that might interest you. I'll look it out while you talk to Mr Lodge. You know the way."

"You trust me to open the cell door and not let him escape?" I asked.

"D'ye want me to lock you in again?" he asked. I shook my head. "Thought not," he said, and winked at me.

The turnkey was right: John Lodge was no thug. He was sitting on a stool when I opened the door of his cell, and I have rarely seen a man look more defeated. He barely lifted his head to look at me.

"Mr Lodge," I said, "my name is Gregory Hardiman. I understand that you were one of the men who attacked Mr Bendall and Mrs Booth."

"I had nothing to do with the attack," he said wearily. "I was standing in the corridor outside the room."

"To what end, Mr Lodge?" I asked.

"I was to alert them if anyone came along while they were..." His voice trailed off.

"While they were attacking Mr Bendall and Mrs Booth," I finished for him.

Lodge stood up quickly, pointing an angry finger at me. "No," he said. "No. I did not know that they were going to attack them. They said they were going to speak to them, to make them see sense." He slumped down onto the stool again. "I keep saying this, but no-one believes me." He looked at me and opened his arms wide. "I ask you, Mr Hardiman: if you wanted a killer, would you pick me?"

"The more interesting question for me, Mr Lodge," I said, "is why you agreed to be involved at all. And before you say it was for money, let me save you the trouble. Charlie's savings have been given to his wife and daughter, and there's no sign of any payment." I looked down at Lodge, who had wrapped his arms around himself and was shivering. "John," I said quietly. "Here's what I think. I think you and Charlie were caught up in something that you didn't understand. I think the other two men escaped because they were more used to escaping than you two. And I think you were all acting on the instructions of someone else. What I don't know is why – and until I know that, I can't help you."

"Help me?" repeated Lodge bitterly. "Help me? I'll be up before the judge and swinging from a scaffold."

"Judge, yes," I agreed. "Scaffold, maybe not. If you can show that you had no idea there would be an attack, and that you took no part in it, you could be recommended to mercy."

The prisoner stared at me. "And you would speak for me?"

I shook my head. "I cannot promise that, but I would certainly make sure that the whole story was told to the judge and jury. If I knew the whole story."

Lodge fell silent. I waited. Eventually he spoke. "Blackmail," he said. "I was blackmailed." He closed his eyes for a moment and then looked up at me. "I had been taking pieces – small pieces only, pieces I thought no-one would miss – from the warehouse, and selling them. And somehow he found out. He said he would tell Mr Swan if I didn't do as he wanted. Just this one thing, he said: keeping watch so that his associates could have a private discussion with a man who owed him money." He shook his head. "I swear on the Bible, sir: I had no idea they were going to attack him. When I heard the screaming, I just ran. I nearly knocked over a maid on my way out – she must have described me to the constables." He stood and stared at the grille above the door. "To be honest, Mr Hardiman, it was a relief when they found me. The nightmares – I kept hearing the screaming." He shook his head as though to clear it.

"For that, you have my sympathy," I said, meaning it. "I have nightmares myself. But you said that *he* found out and *he* told you to keep watch – who?"

Lodge shook his head again, this time more forcefully. "No. No."

"But if you do not tell me who is blackmailing you, then why should I believe – why would the judge and jury believe – that you are being blackmailed?" I asked.

"Then my fate is sealed," said the prisoner. He shrugged. "It is the same, however it comes about. If the jury does not believe me, I will hang. And if I tell you his name, he will have me killed."

"Not if he is found and charged with blackmail," I reasoned.

Lodge gave a short bark of laughter. "Charged? Him? Never." He leaned towards me and dropped his voice. "He knows people. He makes sure to know them. He buys them, or blackmails them. Like Charlie, and like me." He turned away from me and dropped back onto the stool. "And not just scrubs like us – important men too. Magistrates. Judges." He looked at me with narrowed eyes. "Constables, for all I know. My advice to you, Mr Hardiman, is to stop asking questions and to watch your back. If you've secrets, he'll find them out."

"We all have secrets, Mr Lodge," I said. I opened the satchel that I had brought with me and handed the prisoner the stoneware bottle of ginger beer and the wrapped wedge of fruit loaf that I had begged from the inn kitchen for him.

"Thank you," he said, clutching them to him. "'Tis a great kindness."

"I could help you more if you would let me," I said.

He shook his head. "I dare not," he whispered.

"Did Lodge tell you that he is being blackmailed?" I asked Jones when I returned to his little room by the gate.

"I guessed as much," said the turnkey. "Those as do it for money will give up their paymaster to save their neck. But blackmail, that's different." He shook his head. "They'll go to the scaffold just to get the devil off their back." He wiped his dripping nose with the back of his hand. "Or see to themselves beforehand."

"Like Charlie Booth?" I asked. "You said you had something of his that might interest me."

The turnkey looked at me. I tried to look as trustworthy as I could. After a long moment he put his hand into his coat pocket and pulled out a folded piece of paper. "This was in his hand when I found him," he said. "I didn't want his missus to see it."

"That was kind of you, Mr Jones," I said. "If you let me have it, I can make sure it's seen only by those who need to see it."

Jones paused and then thrust the letter at me. "Glad to be rid of it, truth be told," he growled. "Blackmail is filthy stuff."

I was on duty that evening and so it was not until nearly eleven o'clock that I sat down in my room, a blanket around my shoulders as the small fire dwindled in the grate. I turned the letter in my hand towards the candle. The paper was heavy, of good quality, and the ink dark and clear. The message was also clear. *I trust you will not forget our arrangement*, it said. *Keep your mouth shut if you want me to do the same.* There was, of course, no signature.

CHAPTER TWENTY-THREE

LEDGER

After the two gentlemen who had stayed overnight at the Hoop had left, the stables were empty. I changed the straw in the stalls that had been used and took all the blankets out into the yard to shake and freshen them. I checked the troughs for rats and the water buckets for mould, and made sure that all the bolts on the stall doors were running smoothly. Nothing will unsettle a nervous horse like the screech of metal. When I had finished, I stood, hands on hips, and admired my work.

"Very tidy, Mr Hardiman," said a woman behind me, and I jumped. It was Sarah Booth, a pile of fresh bedlinen in her arms.

"Thank you, Sarah," I said. She smiled. "When you have finished what you are doing with those," I indicated the linen, "perhaps you could ask Mr Young for a pot of coffee and come back here. I have something for you. From Charlie."

Half an hour later, Sarah Booth returned. I had borrowed two chairs from the kitchen and put them in the narrow aisle between the stalls, along with a crate that could serve as a table. I could not risk Mrs Booth's reputation by inviting her into the ostry, and with fresh straw on the floor and hot coffee to drink, we would be snug enough. I took the pot from her and put it on the crate, wrapping the cloth tighter around it. I had brought down two mugs from the ostry and I poured our drinks as Sarah settled into her seat.

"And how is Miss Hattie?" I asked, handing a mug to Sarah.

Her face softened, as it always did at any mention of her daughter. "Miss Hattie," she echoed me with a smile, "is in good health, Mr Hardiman. She turns five next week."

"And your face?" I asked as I indicated the scar on my own.

Sarah's hand went to her damaged cheek. "It is as you said," she replied. "She was frightened when she first saw it, but now it is just part of me. Mama's thread, she calls it." She ran her finger along the mark.

"And it will grow finer and finer," I said. "It is already fading a little, I believe."

We drank our coffee in easy silence for a minute or two.

"Mr Hardiman," she said, putting down her mug, "if Mrs Bird catches me lolling about, my face will be the least of my worries." She smiled to take the sting out of what she had said, but she was right.

I reached under my chair and picked up the wooden box that Matthew Gibbs had given me. I pushed the coffee pot to one side and put the box on the crate. "Charlie left this," I put my hand on the box, "for you and Hattie."

"A tea caddy?" asked Sarah.

"Well, yes," I said, "but it's what is inside that he meant you to have." I opened the lid and we both leaned forward.

"Money?" asked Sarah.

"Nineteen pounds and eight shillings," I said. "He put something aside each week from his wages. He had lodgings with a friend," I was careful to put no weight on the word, "and the friend knew about the money and its purpose. He asked me to make sure it was given to you." I closed the lid, picked up the box and handed it to Sarah.

She took it and put it in her lap, and laid both hands on top of it, bowing her head. It was almost like a prayer. "This friend," she said without looking up. "He cared for Charlie?"

"He did, yes," I said quietly.

"I am glad of it," she said. She opened the box again and put her hand into it. Then she frowned slightly and peered more closely at it, closing the lid and opening it again. "There is something in here, Mr Hardiman," she said. "Look." She turned the open box towards me. "The lid is curved, but inside the lid it is flat. I think it's very thin wood. When you move the lid," she closed and opened it again, "you can feel something moving inside it."

"May I?" I said, holding out my hands. She gave the box back to me and I rested it on my knees, reaching into my pocket for my penknife. I carefully put the tip of the blade into the tiny gap between the edge of the lid lining and the side of the box and started to lever it. Slowly the lining lifted up, and then suddenly popped out. We both leaned forward. In the recess of the lid was a small notebook, about six inches by four. I tipped the lid and the notebook dropped into my hand. It had a dark blue leather cover and a strip of brown leather – perhaps an old bootlace – tied around it to hold it closed.

"Shall I open it?" I asked.

"Of course," said Sarah.

I untied the leather strip and opened the little notebook to somewhere in the middle. Someone had drawn lines down the pages, dividing them into columns. The first column contained dates, which were easy to read, and the fourth column had numbers in it, but the other information was harder to understand. I laid the notebook on the crate so that we could both see it.

"It's a ledger of some sort," I suggested. "Dates," I pointed, "and amounts – quantities, perhaps, or money?"

"But this is just letters, isn't it?" asked Sarah, pointing at another column. "That's not a word, is it?"

"No word that I know," I agreed. "Shall I take it away and try to work it out? Or do you want to try?"

"Not me, no," said Sarah, laughing. "Hattie is already better at her letters than I am."

Just then the door of the stables was pulled open and Jamie appeared. He looked at Sarah and blushed, putting a hand to his head to smooth down his hair. "Mrs.... Sarah," he said, stammering. "Mrs Bird is looking for you. I told her you were helping Mr Hardiman with the blankets."

Sarah jumped to her feet. "Thank you, Jamie," she said. "'Tis very kind of you to warn me."

I quickly closed the box and handed it to her. "Take this and put it somewhere safe," I said. "You could ask Mr Bird to keep it in his office, and then you can take what you need from it bit by bit."

"Thank you, Mr Hardiman," she said, taking the box from me.

"And I will let you know what I find out about this," I said, holding up the notebook. "I wonder what Charlie was up to."

Sarah looked at me, surprised. "Oh no, Mr Hardiman: that's not Charlie's writing. He was very proud of his hand, was Charlie. He would never have used a scrawl like that."

I was grateful not to be on patrol that evening – partly because the weather was filthy, with a sharp easterly wind carrying needles of rain on it, and partly because it would give me time to look more closely at the little ledger. George Chapman would be spending the night in his lodge at St Clement's and my landlady had retired early to bed, so after supper I had the kitchen to myself. I took the Argand lamp from the dresser and put it on the table and then opened the ledger in the pool of light that it cast. I also opened my own notebook so that I could write down anything I learned.

On each pair of pages there were six columns. The first, as we had spotted straight away, was a date. The first entry in the ledger was dated Monday 12th March of this year. I turned to the last entry, about two-thirds of the way through the book – it was dated Monday 22nd October. Between those two dates were perhaps fifty or sixty entries. The second and third columns contained a jumble of letters – a code, perhaps, or abbreviations. The fourth column, as we had guessed, was numbers. The fifth contained only either a cross, a check-mark or nothing. And the sixth was mainly blank, but occasionally had a scribbled note in it. I drew a picture in my notebook, showing the six columns, and labelled the ones I could understand: date, uncertain, uncertain, value, completed or not, uncertain. I was surer now that it was indeed a ledger of transactions or agreements.

I turned pages of the book backwards and forwards, looking at the columns of letters. The second column contained mostly pairs of letters – initials, I guessed, identifying people. The third column was harder to decipher, although I could see certain entries repeated. I wrote my findings in my own notebook, in case I should forget them, and decided to sleep on it.

CHAPTER TWENTY-FOUR

ADVENTURE

The driver of the *Star* threw his satchel up onto the seat and then turned to me. "I almost forgot," he said, patting his coat pockets. "Ah yes, here it is." He took out some folded paper and handed it to me. "It's one of those adventure stories. I know your simpleton in the kitchen likes reading them. Someone dropped it in the coach and I thought he would enjoy it."

I looked at the paper. It was one of a series of, as it said on the front, moral and religious tracts. "'The Black Prince,'" I read aloud. "'An account of the life and death of Naimbanna, an African king's son'. Thank you, Will – Jamie will be pleased, I know."

"Aye, well," said the driver gruffly, rubbing his nose. He climbed up onto the coach, took hold of the reins, called out to the horses and set off for London.

⁓⁓⁓

"For me?" asked Jamie, looking at me and then down at the paper that I was holding out to him. On the front was a stirring picture of a man about to strike a horse, and a black man – the prince, I supposed – holding up his arms in protest.

"Yes," I said. "Will Jones found it in his coach and thought you might like it. It's an adventure story."

Jamie carefully wiped his hands on a towel and then dragged them down his apron just for good measure. He took hold of the tract and read the title aloud very slowly. He stumbled on the name of the prince and I said it for him, but he managed the rest. "Will you read it with me, Mr Hardiman?" he asked. "During my break?"

"Only if you promise to do most of the reading," I said. "Bring your vocabulary book and pencil as well, and we can add some new words to your list. Come up to the ostry – it's too cold to be sitting in the yard."

The bells had barely tolled eleven when I heard a noise at the bottom of the ladder leading up to the ostry; it was Jamie kicking it because he had his hands full. I leaned down and he handed up a pot of coffee wrapped in a cloth and a small, stoppered flask. He then climbed up and we settled ourselves in the two chairs and laid out our refreshments on the crate that served as a table. Jamie reached into one of his coat pockets and added two slices of fruit loaf wrapped in another cloth. I poured a full mug of coffee for me and half a one for Jamie, which I topped up with water from the flask. When we had had a few sips of drink and some mouthfuls of cake, Jamie licked his fingers, wiped them on the cake cloth (which added crumbs back to his fingers but I said nothing) and with great dignity took the tract, his vocabulary book and his much-sharpened pencil from his other coat pocket. I sat back and steepled my hands.

Jamie read slowly and deliberately, tracking the words with his finger as I had shown him. After a few minutes he stumbled on the word 'navigation' and we talked about what it could mean. When he had understood, I reminded him to add it to his vocabulary list. He opened his little book and a piece of folded paper fell out. I reached for it and saw Jamie's own writing on it – he had been practising his letters. I unfolded it to check, turned it over, and there on the reverse was another hand that looked familiar. I frowned.

"What is it, Mr Hardiman?" asked Jamie. "Did I write it wrong?"

"No, Jamie," I said, smiling. "Your letters are very neat. But this piece of paper – can you remember where you found it?"

He nodded. "I was given it. By Mr Bendall. The one who died." He looked sad. "I liked him. He was nice to me. He wrote on it but only a bit, and was going to throw it away and I asked if I could have it to do my letters, and he said yes. It's nice paper, isn't it?"

"It is, Jamie, yes," I agreed. "Now, write down that new word – copy it carefully." I looked again at the handwriting on the sheet of paper and knew where I had seen it before. The little ledger: it was Gerard Bendall's.

Chapter Twenty-Five

DECIPHERING

"Well," said George Fisher, lifting his tankard and smiling, "that will certainly have shaken up the good burghers of Cambridge." He took a long drink.

I reached for my own tankard. "If it's good enough for His Majesty…" I added.

George and I had spent the evening at the Town Hall, with more than a hundred other people, listening to a concert of songs given by the Rainer family. The four brothers and their sister styled themselves the Tyrolese Minstrels, and appeared in the costume of their own country: soft leather knee-breeches and decorated breastplates for the men, a striped apron and pink waist bow for the woman, and high feathered hats for all of them. Their melodies were lively and mournful by turns, and after an astonishing run of eighty performances in London's Piccadilly they were note-perfect.

"I could have listened to them for an hour," said George.

"'Tis a shame, then, that they sang for two," I said.

"Aye," agreed George, and we both laughed. "Now," he continued, "show me this ledger of yours."

I reached into my coat pocket and took out the little notebook that Sarah Booth and I had found in the tea caddy. I handed it to

George, then retrieved my own notebook and pencil and turned to the page where I had made a start on working out what the contents of the ledger might mean.

"Goodness," said the banker, opening the ledger and turning it towards the light being cast by the oil lamp on the wall. "It certainly is small."

"But you can read it?" I asked.

George peered more closely. "I can make out letters and numbers, yes, but as to what they mean..." He turned over a page and then back again.

"Here," I said, putting my own notebook on the table and turning it towards him. "These are the columns in the ledger. A date, then two columns, then a value, then a check-mark or cross, and a final column. I think it is a record of transactions."

The banker put the ledger down next to my notebook and compared the two. "I agree," he said. "It would make most sense for this column here, next to the date," he pointed, "to identify the person involved in the transaction. But it seems to be initials only." He paged through the ledger. "Yes, no full names at all. But some of them have other initials in brackets after them. That might help."

I moved my chair a little closer to his and we both looked at the letters in the second column. He turned a page and we read that one, and then another. And then I saw something. "Wait," I said, putting my finger on the page. "There. 'FV(SC)'. Could that be Francis Vaughan, at St Clement's?"

The banker looked more closely, then leaned back and smiled broadly. "What else could it be?" he asked. "What is the date of that entry?" We both bent over the ledger again.

"'19 Oct 27'," I read aloud. I picked up my own notebook and looked through it. "Here," I said, pointing. "The notes I made after speaking to Mr Vaughan. Four hundred pounds to be invested in a silver mine in Bolivia. He agreed that with Mr Bendall on Friday 19 October."

"Then this column is the amount," said George, pointing at '400' in the third column, "and this one, the destination of the investment. See: 'Bol silv'."

I picked up my notebook and returned to the page when I had drawn the columns and quickly added what we had learned. "The fifth column," I asked. "What is in it for that entry?"

"Nothing," replied the banker. "It's blank."

"Because..." I started but could not finish.

"Because he had not received the money," said George. "Vaughan sent the letter to his bank – to us – but it was all cancelled because, well, because Bendall was killed. But as far as his records were concerned," he tapped the ledger with his finger, "it was simply that he had not yet received the money."

"So if we can work out the rest of the initials," I said, "we will know who Mr Bendall was doing business with."

George looked at me sharply. "And you think that he might have been killed because of that," he said quietly.

"It is a possibility," I agreed.

"Well, then," said the banker, pulling his chair closer to the table, "we had better start reading. When did Bendall arrive in Cambridge?"

An hour later we sat back, rubbing our eyes. We had gone through every page of the ledger. I had decided that entries made when Bendall was not in Cambridge would not be worth pursuing – partly because it seemed unlikely that an unhappy investor from elsewhere would know who to hire in Cambridge to do their dirty work, but mainly because we had next to no chance of being able to guess the identities of the investors. In my notebook now were five sets of initials which had been added to the ledger while Gerard Bendall had been in Cambridge, either in September or in October.

Interestingly, only one of those sets had a check-mark next to it in the fifth column. Even more interestingly, this entry also had a comment in the final column, which was uncommon in the ledger. It was the single word 'cave'.

"Cave?" I said, puzzled. "Is it something to do with the investment, do you think?"

"Unlikely," said George. "It looks like this person invested in the same Bolivian silver mine as was offered to Francis Vaughan, albeit a month earlier. Three hundred pounds, by the look of it. I suppose a mine is a sort of cave." He bit his lip as he thought. "Unless..." he said, his face clearing. "When I was at school, if a master was in a bad mood and might turn on you, the boys would warn each other about him by saying the word 'cave' – a pun on the Latin for beware. Bendall was away at school, wasn't he?" I nodded. "Well then, I'd put money on it being the same." He jabbed at my notebook. "Whoever this NT is, Bendall was reminding himself that he was dangerous."

CHAPTER TWENTY-SIX

BALL

"Holding a ball on a Sunday," sniffed Mrs Chapman. "I'm not sure that it's entirely seemly." She eyed me. "Turn around." I did so, and she pulled at the shoulders of my coat before picking a piece of dust from it and indicating that I should face her again.

"Good heavens, woman," growled her husband. "He's not going as a guest – he's on duty."

"I am well aware of that," replied my landlady. "But I hear from my friend Mrs Turner – you remember her…"

"The dressmaker on New Square," chorused her husband and I.

Mrs Chapman gave us both a look. "That's her," she conceded. "Anyway, Mrs Turner tells me that the steward for the ball has engaged two seamstresses for the evening, to help any ladies with repairs to their costumes. And," she paused and waited until I raised a questioning eyebrow, "one of those seamstresses is a young woman called Miss Swanney."

I forced myself to make no reaction at all, and I must have succeeded because Mrs Chapman looked disappointed and her husband tutted. "And just why would a university constable be interested in who repairs the outfits of the silly ladies of the county?" he asked, shaking his head at me in masculine sympathy.

"Indeed," I said gruffly, but you will have guessed that I was suddenly looking forward to the evening much more than I had been.

Normally my patrol ended at ten o'clock, but with dancing at the county ball not starting until half past nine and most guests not expected to leave for two or three hours after that, the Senior Proctor had asked if any of us would be willing to stay on duty until midnight. And as there is no early coach on Mondays, I was happy to earn the extra money that was promised. Not that any trouble was expected, Mr Sedgwick had said with a laugh: it was simply that the Mayor, Mr Purchas, had hinted that the town constables would be on duty in their smart uniforms and so Mr Davy, the new Vice-Chancellor, had decided that the University should parade its constables as well. In fact, the county ball is a notably staid affair, at which the fine families of Cambridgeshire display their unmarried daughters in the hope that they will catch the eye of a wealthy undergraduate. The young men, for their part, try to escape with a dance with a pretty girl and a few glasses of good wine.

At a few minutes before six o'clock I made my way to the Union Street corner of the Town Hall, where I was to meet the other three constables who had signed up for the extra hours. I was not surprised to see that one of them was George Swanney, who was wearing a cloak and carrying another one over his arm. He handed it to me.

"Another man with nothing better to do on a Sunday evening," I said lightly, swinging the cloak around my shoulders and then shaking his hand.

"Six shillings is six shillings," he replied. "And it means I can walk Kate home." He smiled at me. "Unless you want to take my place. It'll cost you a shilling."

"And it'll cost you two for me not to tell her that you're selling your sister to the highest bidder," I retorted.

Just then Mr Sedgwick appeared and we all stood up a little straighter. He looked us over. "Very smart, constables," he declared. "Mr Davy will be able to hold his own against Mr Purchas, which will put him in excellent humour. And as I am to sit near both of them, that puts me in excellent humour." He raised his hand in greeting and we all turned to see Mr Turnbull trotting towards us. "And now that the Junior Proctor is with us, we shall commence our patrol."

George Swanney and I took care to attach ourselves to each other and to Mr Turnbull; as a young man, the Junior Proctor was less of a stickler for formality on patrol and sometimes even joined us as we tarried just a bit too long in a tavern, checking for wayward gownsmen but also taking the opportunity to warm ourselves a little. When the bells tolled eight o'clock the proctors returned to the Town Hall for refreshments, and we constables were trusted to continue the patrol alone until ten o'clock. After that, we had been instructed to show ourselves in the vicinity of the Town Hall, to discourage any rogues who might have gathered in hopes of picking a pocket or stealing a fine hat. But the rogues, it seems, had chosen to stay warm in their beds. By half-past eleven my feet were aching and my fingers were numb with cold, and I was beginning to think that my extra six shillings had been very hard earned indeed.

"Thank goodness for that," said George, cocking his ear to the tolling bells of Great St Mary's. "Twelve o'clock. That's an end of it." Like me, he had been stamping his feet and swinging his arms to keep warm as we stood outside the Town Hall. A minute later the door opened and out came Mr Turnbull, red-faced and laughing over his shoulder at the man behind him. He stumbled a little and I put out my hand to steady him.

"Ah, constable," he said, none too clearly. "I now declare you," he raised his hand as though to bless me, "off duty."

His companion took hold of the Junior Proctor's elbow and smiled apologetically at me. "Come, now, Tom," he said, "let's get you home before the Vice-Chancellor sees you." And they walked carefully in the direction of Caius.

"That's me off too," said George. "You can keep that shilling." And he winked at me then strode off towards Bene't Street. He had just disappeared from sight when the door banged open again and the Vice-Chancellor, the Mayor and what must have been the remaining ball guests came out into the night air, gasping at the cold and quickly taking leave of each other. And at last out came the two seamstresses, each carrying a small workbag.

"Constable Hardiman," said Kate Swanney warmly. "This is Miss Franks," she said, and the other woman dipped her head at me.

"Miss Swanney's brother had to leave," I said, "and asked me to accompany her home. May I offer you an escort too, Miss Franks?"

"Thank you, but no," she said, pulling her shawl tighter about her shoulders. "I am just around the corner in Green Street, and if I turned up with a constable, my mother wouldn't stop asking questions for a week and wouldn't let me out of the house for a month." She smiled at Kate and set off across the market square.

I offered my arm to Kate, and to my delight she took it as we walked down Union Street. I was pleased to spot the green ribbon from Stourbridge Fair, fashioned into a sort of flower and pinned to the side of her hat. "Are you sure this is quite proper?" she asked. "While you're in uniform."

"If anyone asks, I shall say that I am doing my gallant duty to prevent you slipping on the ice," I said.

"Then I shall totter most becomingly if we are approached," she said. But just then she actually did slip a little, and tightened her grip on my arm.

"Here," I said, holding out my free hand. "Give me your workbag, and then you can hold on with two hands." This meant that she was pressed even closer to my side, which I can assure you was almost accidental on my part.

"Were you busy this evening?" I asked. "Mending all those..." I searched for the word, "trimmings."

"Trimmings," she repeated, a smile in her voice. "Well, yes, a few trimmings. Several fallen hems. One side seam split from over-indulgence at the table." Her voice became more serious. "And something I found a little disturbing."

"Disturbing? In what way?" I asked, checking right and left before we crossed Trumpington Street.

"A woman came into our room – they set aside a little cloakroom for us, with a table for our things and a couple of chairs where ladies could wait," she explained. "She had lost a button from her glove and asked me to replace it. When I asked her to give me the glove, she seemed reluctant. She asked if I could stitch it while she wore it, but I didn't want to prick her with my needle and get blood on the glove – it was a pale ivory colour. In the end she took it off – and her arm, from wrist to elbow, was a mass of bruises, Gregory. Small ones. As though someone had taken hold of her roughly." She gripped my arm with one of her hands to show me what she meant.

"What did you say?" I asked.

"What could I say?" she replied. "I passed the glove to Nancy – Miss Franks – to find a button, and I took the bottle of rose water that we offer to ladies and put a few drops on her arm and rubbed it in."

"Does rose water help with bruises?" I asked.

"No," admitted Kate, "but I thought a little gentleness might be welcome."

"Did you know who she was?" I asked.

Kate paused. "Well," she said carefully, "we could tell that she was not married – no ring. She was rouged." She glanced at me to see if I had taken her meaning. I nodded. "When she went back to the ball we peeped out to see who she was with, and Nancy recognised him: Mr Trew. An attorney, she said."

"Nicholas Trew," I said. "He is a member of my book club." I stopped dead and almost jerked Kate off her feet.

"What is it, Gregory?" she asked with concern.

"Nicholas Trew," I said again. "Initials NT."

Chapter Twenty-Seven

RUTHLESS

I f I had not had another reason for going, the grim weather would have put me off the meeting of the book club that Wednesday evening. The past couple of days had grown colder and colder. Remembering my father's teachings I had looked up at the pale sky and sniffed the air: snow was coming. And finally, on Wednesday afternoon, it arrived. Everyone who came into the yard seemed affronted by it arriving so early in the winter, but here it was. I was sorely tempted to head home to the stove in Mrs Chapman's kitchen, but a piece of good fortune had landed on me and I could not ignore it: George Fisher was serving as one of the librarians at tonight's meeting. And so I pulled my hat as far down as I could, turned my collar up as high as it would go, hunched my shoulders and walked through the swirling snow to Trumpington Street.

Usually there would be small groups of members chatting on the street outside the Black Bull Inn, but the snow had put paid to that. Like everyone else, I hurried inside as soon as I arrived and climbed the stairs to the top floor rooms where our book club held its weekly meetings. Whichever two members are taking their turn as librarians are expected to arrive early, so that people can return and take out items before the start of the meeting, and indeed George Fisher and another man – Richard Rowley, who ran a fellmonger's business on Magdalene Street – were hard at work. Rowley was re-shelving the books being returned while George was making a note in a large ledger of who was borrowing and returning which items. I walked over to him and handed over the copy of Hetrick's *Poems & Songs* that I had borrowed the previous week. George looked at the frontispiece and scratched out the title in the ledger next to my name.

"Any good?" he asked.

"Not really to my taste," I admitted. "I thought the one about Boney's death might be stirring, but it was rather trite. 'The pest of your pride and your pleasures', apparently."

"I shall not bother, then," said the banker, putting the book on the small pile waiting to be returned to the shelves.

I glanced behind me, and the three other men in the room were still selecting their books. "George," I said in a low voice. "I will explain later, but for now, would you permit me to look in the ledger?"

George smiled at Rowley, who had returned to the desk for another pile of books, and we both waited until he returned to the ladder and had his back to us. George quickly turned the ledger around so that I could see it. I paged back through it; at the start of each meeting, the names of both librarians were recorded. As these names changed only quarterly I was able to move rapidly through the months, and in June 1826 there it was: Nicholas Trew as one of the librarians. And as custom dictated that each librarian took his turn on the ladder and at the ledger, I had only two examples of handwriting to check. I reached into my pocket and pulled out the note that I had carefully kept, unfolded it and placed it alongside the ledger. The hand was the same.

"Your round, I think," said George as we found ourselves a small table in the cosy parlour on the ground floor of the Black Bull Inn. "And then you can explain your interest in the library ledger."

I signalled to the pot boy and two tankards were swiftly delivered to us. I took a drink and then wiped my mouth before saying plainly, "Nicholas Trew."

"The attorney?" asked George.

I nodded. "I had a concern about him. That he might be involved in something unpleasant. Illegal."

"Illegal?" repeated the banker. "You had better be sure of your ground, Gregory. From what I hear, Nicholas Trew is..." He paused.

"Nicholas Trew is what?" I asked.

"Good at his job," replied George. "He knows the law. Better than you, I daresay."

"Many people know the law better than I do," I said. "But that is not what you were going to say, George."

The banker sighed. "Ruthless. That is the word that came to my mind. Nicholas Trew is a good friend and a bad enemy. And if you move from the former to the latter, there's no coming back."

"Noted," I said, taking another drink.

"And how does our library ledger help with your concern?" asked George.

I reached into my pocket and took out the note that had been found in Charlie Booth's hand. I handed it to George, who read it and looked up at me. "Nasty," he said. "And the handwriting? I assume that's why you were checking the library records."

"Nicholas Trew," I said. George passed the note back to me and I carefully folded it and put it away. "I went to see the Howards earlier this month," I continued. "You remember: Major Howard's parents." George nodded. "And Mr Howard said that Trew had been asking him questions about me – where I was from, what they knew about me from their son. Now I think maybe..."

"He was trying to gather information to blackmail you as well," interrupted George. "He knew you were interested in the Bendall murder, and he wanted to have something to keep you under control."

"Perhaps," I allowed.

"You see: that is the danger of living a blameless life," he said, smiling at me before draining his tankard. He held it up and the pot boy nodded. "There would be no profit in trying to blackmail me, for instance. No-one expects me to behave well – indeed, my brother would be delighted to have written proof of my sins."

"You just need to find an occupation that suits you," I said. "Until then, you and your brother will continue to grate on each other."

"Perhaps I should become a university constable," suggested George, winking at me.

"Perhaps," I said, going along with the joke. In my pocket I could feel the small ledger that Sarah Booth and I had found in the tea caddy. "Let's see what you make of this then, Constable Fisher." I said. I took out the ledger and handed it to the banker. "I have marked the page."

"I remember," said George, looking at the ledger. "NT. Well, it certainly could be Nicholas Trew. Investment of £550 made on 21 September. And then there's that annotation: cave."

"Perhaps Gerard Bendall shared your view that Mr Trew is ruthless," I said.

George took a sip of his new drink then sat back in his seat, his hands clasped in his lap.

"What will you do now?" he asked. "Take the letter and that ledger to the town constables?"

I shook my head. "That may not be wise," I said. "As an attorney who has worked in Cambridge for many years – far more than I have been here – he will have friends. You know that the university constables and the town constables have, well, let us say an uneasy relationship." The banker nodded. "If I take this information to a town constable who is sympathetic to Mr Trew, he might warn him – and tell him who has been asking awkward questions and gathering even more awkward paperwork."

"I see your point," said George.

"What I need," I said, leaning forward, "is a witness. Someone equal to Mr Trew in the eyes of the town. A local, well-respected member of the business community. Someone whose impartial word will be believed." Something occurred to me. "Does Nicholas Trew bank with you?" I asked. George shook his head, a slow smile appearing on his face. "Impartial, as I say," I finished.

"If you drop those hints any more heavily," said the banker, "they will go right through this floor into the cellar."

Chapter Twenty-Eight

DECEPTION

The young clerk frowned slightly, his head to one side. "You are not quite as inconspicuous as you might be, Mr Hardiman," he said.

"He's right, Gregory," said George Fisher. "Can you press yourself closer to the wall? Breathe in?"

I did as instructed, and heard someone walking towards me and felt them twitch the long, heavy curtain over me.

"I think that might work, Mr Fisher," said the clerk, "if Mr Hardiman can stay silent, and if we sit Mr Trew with his back to the window."

"I agree, Stevens," said the banker. "Gregory, you can come out for the moment. We still have ten minutes before he arrives."

I stepped out from behind the curtain and looked around the small banking parlour. Thomas Stevens was lifting one of the chairs and positioning it right in front of me. When planning this meeting, George and I had quickly realised that the sharp-eyed clerk would miss nothing; it would be impossible for me to hide from him, and so we had taken him into our confidence. We hadn't told him the whole story, of course, but enough for him to understand that it was important for me to be able to overhear, undiscovered, whatever was said by the two men.

I made a quick visit to the privy and then returned to the parlour and took up my position behind the curtain. Stevens carefully arranged the fabric so that it draped over my boots. George was standing at the other side of the parlour, the furthest he could be from me, and said very quietly, "Can you hear me, Gregory?"

"Just about," I confirmed.

"Excellent," he replied in a normal voice. I heard the door open and close. "Stevens has gone to wait for Trew in the banking hall," said George. The small clock that stood on the desk in the parlour started to chime the hour. "Ready, Gregory?" asked the banker.

A moment later there was a smart knock on the parlour door. "Mr Nicholas Trew to see you, Mr Fisher," I heard Stevens say. "Will you be requiring any refreshments, sir?"

"A pot of coffee, if you please, Stevens," said the banker.

I heard footsteps walking towards me and then a creak as someone sat in the chair in front of me.

"Appalling weather today," said a voice very close to me, and I knew that George had managed to steer the attorney to that chair as we had planned. "Snow for three days, and we're only in November. I shudder when I remember how much my late wife would spend on coal during a bad winter. You're a bachelor, aren't you, Fisher?"

"I am, yes," said George.

"Well, if you'll take my advice on the matter," said Trew, "you won't be in too much of a hurry to change that."

"You don't recommend married life?" asked the banker.

"It has its compensations," conceded Trew, and I could imagine him smiling as he said it, "but a man is less agile with a wife in tow. If he takes it into his head to move on, to try a new adventure, well, it's that much harder with a wife. They do like to settle, women. And a household seems to cost so much more with a woman in residence. All the refinements of feminine life, I suppose." He laughed.

I heard the door open and the sound of Stevens setting a tray onto the table and pouring and handing cups of coffee to the two men. The door closed after him.

"Now then, Fisher," said Trew. I could hear him setting his cup down on the table. "Perhaps we should get to business. As you doubtless know, I have banked with your competitor round the corner for many years, but, as I said at the club, if you think that Fisher's can offer a better service at a more tempting fee I am always happy to consider moving."

"I feel I must be honest with you, Trew," said the banker, "about my real purpose in asking you here. Of course we would be very pleased if you were to move your business to our bank," he chuckled, "but more than your business, I need your help."

"My help?" asked Trew. "My help with what?"

"I know that you are a shrewd man," replied George. I heard his chair creak and guessed that he was leaning forward. "And as such, I am hoping that you will be able to advise me. One of the bank's customers has come to me with a problem and I am not sure where to turn to help him."

"I am happy to do what I can, Fisher," said the attorney, "but without knowing any of the particulars..."

"Of course, of course," said the banker. "More coffee?" I heard the cups moving again. "Our customer is an intelligent man but relatively, shall we say, unschooled in matters of finance."

The attorney chuckled. "So many of them are, Fisher."

"Indeed," agreed George. "Some weeks ago – in the middle of October – our customer was approached by a young man from London who was seeking investors for a scheme of his. A silver mine in Bolivia. Like me, this customer is a single man, with few outgoings, and the idea of taking part in such an exciting venture, even at a remove – well, he was tempted. To the tune of four hundred pounds."

I heard the attorney make a low whistle. "That is a pretty sum," he said.

"To be frank with you," said George, "it was more than our customer could afford to gamble, and had he asked me before investing, I should have counselled against it."

"Your man went ahead, then?" asked Trew.

"He did, yes," replied the banker. "And here is our problem. The man through whom he made the investment has since died. You may have read about it in the newspaper: Gerard Bendall, killed in a room at the Cap?"

"It's not a name I recall, no," said the attorney.

"No matter," said George. "As I say, the man died, and what our customer is wondering is: what has become of his investment? We – as his bank – paid over the money only the day before Mr Bendall was killed, so I doubt he had time to pay it on to anyone else. It will form part of Mr Bendall's estate, I suppose?"

"Indeed," confirmed the attorney. "And as to what happens to that estate, that depends on whether Mr Bendall had made a will. If so, the situation is simpler and clearer: the assets will be distributed according to the will. If not, a probate court may see fit to issue letters of administration, appointing people to distribute the estate according to fixed rules of inheritance. Once the estate is settled, your customer could throw himself on the mercy of the beneficiaries and ask them to return his money. It will doubtless come down to which they value more: Mr Bendall's posthumous reputation, or four hundred pounds."

"I see," said George. "In short, the money may be lost forever, or some or all of it may be returned but not for many months." He sighed heavily. "What a shame that Mr Bendall did not have time to invest the money as he had promised."

"In the silver mine, you mean?" asked Trew.

"Yes," said George. "The returns he was promised were gener-ous."

"Perhaps too generous," said the attorney.

"What do you mean?" asked George. I breathed as quietly as I could while straining to hear every word.

"It makes little difference now," said Trew, "but it may comfort you, Fisher, to know that your instinct – to warn your customer against the investment – was a good one. Now, it may not have been the same silver mine, of course, but some time ago I read a piece in a London newspaper about a failure in Bolivia. A mine being touted to investors in London and other European capitals turned out to be empty – just a hole in the ground, any silver long gone."

"When was this?" asked the banker.

"Let me see," replied Trew slowly. "Perhaps six weeks ago. But, as I say, it may have been a different mine entirely. Perhaps nothing at all to do with your Mr Bennett."

"Bendall," said George. "Quite possibly a different place entire-ly. But still, it shows the risks of such investments, of relying on reports and recommendations from the other side of the world."

The clock chimed. "That's a pretty little piece," said the attorney. "But I am afraid that it calls me to work, Fisher. If there is nothing else..."

"No, Trew," said the banker. "You have been more that generous with your time and your expertise. I shall pass on the rather dis-couraging news to our customer."

I heard both men getting to their feet.

"Discouraging, yes," said Trew, "but not entirely without hope. And if you will forgive me an ungenerous thought, at least this Bendall can no longer tempt people to invest their money in a worthless mine."

As we had agreed, and difficult though it was, I waited behind the curtain as I heard George and Trew leave the parlour and close the door behind them. Another minute passed as they said farewell, then another as George checked that all was well in the banking hall. Eventually I heard the parlour door open and close again, and at long last the banker walked up to me and pulled back the curtain. I took a deep breath; it had been stifling behind that heavy fabric.

"Quickly," he said, "before we forget. Sit down and we'll make notes of what he said. I have brought you some barley water."

I did as he suggested, taking my notebook out of my pocket and sitting in the chair that Trew had taken. George handed me the tumbler of barley water and I downed the drink in one. "Thirsty," I said.

"Write," he replied, gesturing at my notebook.

I wrote in silence for a couple of minutes, checking things with the banker as I needed to. "Six weeks, was it?" He nodded. "And Bennett, he called him?" Another nod. I read back over what I had written. "I think that's most of it." I handed the notebook to George and he read it.

"He was not at all rattled, was he?" he asked, closing my notebook and returning it to me.

I shook my head. "And he was very clear in what he said," I added. "And in what he did not say. He had every opportunity to admit to knowing all about Gerard Bendall – after all, he was the one who raised the subject with me, at the book club."

"And if he is the NT in the ledger," continued George, "then he more than knew about Bendall – he was in business with him."

"And..." I said slowly, taking out my pencil again and writing as I spoke, "if we assume that Trew met Bendall on his, Bendall's, first visit to Cambridge at about the time of the Stourbridge Fair – that's the middle of September – and invested with him straight away..."

"21 September," said the banker promptly. "That was the date against his initials in the ledger."

I wrote that down. "And then Trew said that he had read of the failure of the silver mine, what, six weeks ago." I reached into my other pocket and retrieved my diary, with the calendar printed at the front of it. I pointed at the dates and counted the weeks. "Let's say in the first two weeks of October. And Gerard Bendall was killed on 23 October." I looked up at George. "The dates work. Perhaps," I leaned forward and pointed my pencil at the banker, "perhaps Trew read of the collapse of the mine in which he had invested..."

"£550," said George, "on 21 September."

"And when he heard that Bendall was back in Cambridge," I continued, "he met with him and asked for his money to be returned. And Bendall refused."

CHAPTER TWENTY-NINE

POPES

The next day was a filthy morning, with slush underfoot and a dank fog clutching at me as I swept away the dirty melting snow. I helped a gentleman onto his horse and slowly led the animal out into Jesus Lane; after that, they were on their own, but I certainly did not want them slipping on the cobbles in the yard. My boots were mucky after all that, so I went into the stables and used a handful of straw to wipe them down, then called into the kitchen to tell Jamie that I would be out for a little while. He carefully wrote it down and I was pleased to see that his letters were becoming clearer.

"True?" he asked, when I said where I was going. "Like telling the truth? T R U E."

"It sounds the same," I agreed, "but you spell it T R E W." I watched as he printed the name. "If I am not back here by noon, you take that to Mr Bird and tell him where I have gone."

I did not really think that I was in danger, calling on an attorney at his office, but if my concerns were right and Nicholas Trew was involved in the death of Gerard Bendall, it was as well to be careful.

By the time I reached number 22 St Andrew's Street, my boots were as grubby as they had been before I cleaned them. I sighed and hoped the attorney would not notice. Turning my back to the elegant frontage of Emmanuel College, with its classical columns and large windows, I pulled the chain and heard a bell ring inside Mr Trew's premises. I had made a few enquiries, and I knew that his office was on the ground floor and that he lived alone in the rooms above; his wife had died some years earlier, and his only child was a married daughter living in Bedford. The door was opened by a maid, who looked curiously at my face and then ducked her chin.

"I would like to see Mr Trew," I said. "Tell him it's Constable Hardiman."

She stole another look at me and hesitated before opening the door wide. "Come in, sir," she said. "If you'd like to take a seat in there," she pointed at a door standing ajar, "I will tell Mr Trew that you are here."

I walked into a small parlour; tidy and clean, but without any personal touches, it had six identical chairs against the walls. I sat on one of them and looked down at my boots again. I heard the maid knock on another door, then open it and say something, then close it again and walk away to the rear of the house. About five minutes passed before I heard footsteps and Nicholas Trew stepped into the parlour.

"Mr Hardiman," he said, holding out his hand. I stood and shook hands with him, and then we both sat down. As before, I felt certain that his sharp eyes missed nothing. "Are you here as a constable, or as a fellow member of our book club?" He smiled tightly.

"Neither," I said. "A friend has made an unwise investment and we are exploring whether he has any recourse to the law. And I said that I knew an attorney who might be able to steer us in the right direction."

Trew's face relaxed a little. "Ah, but I am not that type of lawyer, Mr Hardiman," he said apologetically. "I am a country attorney – conveyancing, wills and the like."

"Ah, no, you misunderstand me," I said. "My friend invested money with Gerard Bendall – you remember, the man killed in the Cap last month."

A frown passed quickly across the attorney's face but he mastered himself again. "By a jealous husband, wasn't that it?" he said.

I shrugged, as though that was of little concern to me. "It turns out that Mr Bendall was encouraging people in Cambridge to invest in various schemes," I continued. "He kept a record of his investors in a ledger," I watched Trew carefully but he made no reaction. "And my friend was wondering whether, if several investors were to act together, pressure could be put on the scheme to repay their money – or some of it, at least."

"An interesting idea," he said. "What used to be called group litigation, I believe. Not so common nowadays, but popular in mediaeval times. If I am not mistaken, the Court of Chancery now has exclusive jurisdiction over such group actions – but I would have to check my Blackstone's. Would that be of assistance to your friend, Mr Hardiman?"

"I think he was wondering whether you might want to be more personally involved, Mr Trew," I said.

"Personally involved?" repeated the attorney. "Why would I want to be personally involved?"

"I have seen the ledger of investors," I said. "And one of the entries, well, to be blunt, we assumed it made reference to you."

"To me?" Trew gave a good impression of a man amused by a surprise.

"Only initials are used," I continued, "but NT is very clear."

"That is all?" asked the attorney. "No other identifying details? No address? No profession?"

I shook my head. "Only the date of the investment, the scheme invested in, and the amount," I said. "£550."

Trew laughed and spread his hands wide. "Well, there, you see," he said jovially. "That is an enormous sum of money, well beyond the resources of a country attorney. There must be another NT in Cambridge with much deeper pockets." He smiled at me. "Now, if that is all, Mr Hardiman, I do have other business to attend to." He stood and held out his hand again. "I am sorry for your friend, truly I am, but beyond recommending a London solicitor should he need one, there is nothing I can do."

I rose to my feet and shook his hand. "Thank you for your time, Mr Trew," I said. "Shall I see you on Wednesday at the Black Bull?"

We walked into the hallway and the attorney opened the front door for me. "Of course," he said easily. "By the way, Mr Hardiman. Your Christian name is Gregory, is it not?"

"That's right," I said. "My mother's choice, I am told. It means watchful, which she thought was apt for a farmer's son."

"It's not a name you hear very often in Cambridge," he mused. "In fact, the only people I can think of who share your name are popes." He looked sharply at me and I smiled mildly.

"Until Wednesday," I said, and turned away.

It was cleverly worded, to be sure, but I knew a threat when I heard one. Trew imagined that fear of exposure of my faith would shut my mouth. But Catholic or Protestant, we all read the same Bible. Have no fellowship with the unfruitful works of darkness, but rather reprove them. Ephesians, if I am not mistaken.

CHAPTER THIRTY

CAKE

"**M**r Lassiter," I said, leaning the broom against the wall and putting my hands to the small of my back to stretch it.

The message lad grinned. "Mr Hardiman," he replied, performing an elaborate bow.

"How are you today, Joe?" I asked. "And Sally?" I knew how diligently the boy took care of his younger sister, orphans as they were.

"Hungry," he said. "That's me. And pretty as a picture – that's Sally." He smiled determinedly, giving a sharp nod.

"When are you not hungry, Joe?" I asked, laughing. He shrugged. "Now, have you a message for me?"

"I do, sir," he said, suddenly professional. He reached into his coat pocket and pulled out a folded piece of paper. "I'm to take a reply if it's no, but not if it's yes."

"And you've been paid already?" I asked.

"It's from Mr Adeane," he said sternly. "He's a magistrate. He pays proper."

I bit my lip to stop a smile and unfolded the note. *Mr Hardiman,* it said, *I should be grateful if you could meet me in the parlour of the*

Blue Boar at three o'clock today, Monday. I have news from London. Your humble servant, Henry Adeane.

"It's yes," I said to Joe. "So no reply. But," I dug into my waistcoat pocket, "this is for your prompt and polite delivery." I handed him a coin, which he bit from habit and then shoved into his own pocket. I picked up my broom again. "And call into the kitchen on your way past," I said. "Tell Mr Young that I would be obliged if he could give you two hot rolls with meat. He can put them on my slate."

I made sure to be waiting at a small table in the parlour of the Blue Boar by ten minutes to the hour. It was an overcast day, with very little light coming through the windows overlooking Trinity Street, and the pot boy had already lit the lamps. Just as the bells of Great St Mary's started sounding the hour, the parlour door opened and in came Henry Adeane. I stood to shake his hand and he smiled warmly.

"Thank you for meeting me, Mr Hardiman," he said, signalling to the pot boy. "Tea? Wine? Ale?" he asked me.

"Tea, thank you," I said. "I am on patrol this evening."

"Tea, if you would," said the magistrate to the pot boy. "And cake – plenty of cake." After the lad had gone off to the kitchen, Adeane sat back in his chair and sighed. "I am exceeding fond of cake," he said.

"You are trim on it," I observed.

The magistrate raised an eyebrow at me and then laughed. "You have a keen eye – as a constable should," he said. He patted his stomach. "I have a good digestion," he observed. "I eat and eat, but I also walk and walk – they balance." The door opened again and the pot boy reversed into the parlour, carrying a large and apparently heavy tray, laden with a pot of tea, two cups, a jug of milk and what looked to be almost a third of a cake decorated with almonds, along with a knife and two small plates. The pot boy bent his knees slowly and carefully set the tray on the table between us.

"Dundee cake," he said. "Baked this morning."

"Excellent," said Adeane, reaching for the knife. "Cake, Mr Hardiman?" He served two generous slices and handed one to me. Then he poured the tea and added milk to both cups before giving his full attention to the cake. He took a large mouthful and chewed then swallowed. "Yes, excellent," he said happily. "Now we are fortified for our discussion." He took another bite of cake and a sip of tea, then wiped his mouth. "Mr Longman," he said, suddenly serious. "Selling the pills. Is it a crime, and if so, what crime? Not something we have seen often in Cambridge. But London, well, you yourself showed me that trial report. Longman lives in Whitechapel, and I know a magistrate at the Thames Police Office in Wapping. Will Broderip. Old friend from the Inner Temple. So I called on him last week." He paused for another mouthful of cake, licking his fingers to catch the crumbs. "Most interested in Mr Longman. You were right, Mr Hardiman." He leaned forward to put his plate on the table. "You were absolutely right. The London courts are taking this sort of thing much more seriously. In short," he looked longingly at the remaining cake, "Jeremiah Longman has been arrested. Now sitting in Coldbath Fields, awaiting his hearing."

I was genuinely surprised. "The house of correction?" I asked.

Adeane nodded; he had succumbed to temptation and taken another slice of cake and was now chewing it. He swallowed. "There may be no charge in the end, but Longman has been given a fright. Word may get out to others who ply the same trade." He looked at me, suddenly serious. "Magistrates – and constables – must protect those who may not be able to protect themselves."

John Lodge's warning that Nicholas Trew had many powerful men in his pocket had given me pause for thought, but the magistrate's fierce sincerity convinced me that I could trust him.

"And in the spirit of protecting others," I said, "may I ask for your assistance with another matter?"

"Of course, Mr Hardiman," said Adeane.

"It concerns a man you will know," I said carefully. "A man you may consider a friend." The magistrate said nothing. "I have concerns – no, suspicions – that he has something to do with the death of Gerard Bendall."

"The young man murdered in the Cap?" asked Adeane. "You think this man killed him?"

I shook my head. "No, but I think he was able to convince others to do the killing for him."

"Has he a motive?" asked the magistrate.

"I believe so," I said.

"And what can I do for you?" he asked.

"I wish you and your constables to detain him," I said. "You could do this right now. But I know that you will need more than my suspicions. You will need to hear something from his own lips."

"Ideally," said the magistrate grimly.

"I am meeting him tomorrow evening, at the Black Bull," I said. "We are members of the same book club. He has already dropped hints that he plans to blackmail me to keep my mouth shut, and I am sure he expects a response from me. If you were to come to our meeting and conceal yourself, I would make sure that you heard enough to convince you that he should be questioned. If you have a constable waiting outside, you can arrest him as we leave."

Adeane was silent, but I could see that he was thinking. "And now, Mr Hardiman," he said eventually, "I think you must give me the name of your quarry."

"Nicholas Trew," I said.

"The attorney?" asked the magistrate. "Premises on St Andrew's Street?" But he said it completely without surprise, simply to confirm the details.

After taking my leave of Henry Adeane, I decided to call on Mr Relhan to give him the news about Jeremiah Longman, and to buy some more pills of my own. In all honesty, the two matters had become linked in my mind, and I was uneasy about it.

The last streaks of watery light were disappearing from the sky as I walked to the apothecary's shop. The streetlights on Trinity Street and Bridge Street were already burning, but St Sepulchre's Passage was gloomy and I had to tread carefully. Thankfully light was spilling from the window of Mr Relhan's, and the man himself was at the counter, sitting on his stool and writing in a ledger. He looked up as I walked in and smiled in welcome. He closed the ledger.

"Mr Hardiman," he said. He looked behind him at his shelves and reached for the familiar jar.

I felt in my pocket for my little brown bottle and put it on the counter. There was still perhaps a half-dozen pills in it. The apothecary reached under the counter for his notebook and turned to the page where he noted information about me and my consumption of opium. He picked up a pencil and the calendar that he kept on the counter, and pointed at days as he calculated in his head.

He looked up at me with surprise. "You are overdue, Mr Hardiman," he said. He took hold of the bottle and shook it. "And you still have, what, two days' supply left." He indicated the stool on the shop side of the counter and I sat down.

"The incidents with the Morison's pills have unsettled me," I confessed.

"But they are an entirely different matter," he said. "You know that I am meticulous in preparing your opium. It is as pure as it can be. Whereas who knows what Morison is putting into his so-called universal remedy."

"I apologise, Mr Relhan," I said hastily. "I mean no criticism of you or your pills. I simply wonder whether I should still need them."

"Ah." The apothecary put down his pencil and leaned on his elbows. "The night terrors – they are lessening?"

"I think so," I said. "They come less frequently, and when they do come, they are less..."

"Vivid?" suggested Relhan. "Disturbing?"

"Both of those," I agreed. "But mainly less real. Less convincing. Like a child's nightmare rather than a..." I paused and shrugged.

"Rather than a revisiting," said the apothecary.

"Exactly," I said, pointing at him.

Relhan smiled. "That is excellent news," he said. "However, you must not simply stop taking your pills. That would be a terrible shock for your body and your mind. Rather, you must do as I suspect you have already been doing: you must gradually reduce the dose."

I nodded. "For the past six days, I have taken only one pill instead of two."

The apothecary shook his head. "That is still too sudden," he said. "I assume you have had some symptoms – agitation, perhaps, aching muscles, a runny nose?"

"Yes, yes, and yes," I said ruefully.

"As I say, too sudden," said Relhan. "I am glad you did not stop all at once, otherwise the symptoms would have been much worse – and probably obvious to other people. No: rather than missing a dose entirely, you should reduce the dose but maintain the frequency. Do that for a month. Then we can start reducing the frequency. Are we agreed?" I nodded. "I shall note it all later," he said, tapping his notebook. "For now, I shall cut these pills in half for you, as a reminder of the new dose." He took his black cloth from the drawer, laid it out and tipped my pills onto it. There were seven of them. He took out his pocketknife, opened it and carefully halved each pill before dropping the pieces back into the bottle. "Come back in a few days' time," he said, "and I will have some smaller pills made up for you. Unless you change your mind and want to return to the original dose." He put the cork into the bottle and handed it back to me.

I took it and shook my head. "I won't," I said. "I think I am ready." I slipped the bottle into my pocket. "And I have some interesting news for you. The man I met peddling Morison's pills at Stourbridge Fair has been arrested in London. He will be questioned about the pills he sold here in Cambridge, and may have to take some responsibility for the death of one of his customers."

"I am glad of it," said Relhan. "No matter what Mr Morison may say, we in the medical profession take our responsibilities very seriously. And you cannot have clickers touting remedies as if they were bootlaces."

Chapter Thirty-One

FILTHY

Given the nasty weather – frigid cold and punishing blasts of icy rain – town was surprisingly busy as I trudged along Trinity Street. As I passed Nicholson's, I saw Geoffrey Giles doing his final checks before closing the shop. I tapped on the window and he raised a hand in greeting, indicating that I should wait for him.

"Mrs Phipps?" I asked when he came out, turning from me to lock the door. The bookseller lived with his invalid father and usually had to tend to him in the evenings, but a kindly neighbour had taken to offering to help on Wednesdays, so that Giles could stay in town for our book club meeting.

"I thank my lucky stars for such kind neighbours," he said, dropping the key into his pocket and quickly pulling on his gloves.

"And their boy is doing well at the University press?" I asked as we started walking towards Trumpington Street. I knew that Giles had recommended the lad for his position.

"Better than we could have hoped," said Giles, turning to me with a happy smile. "He is in their printing house on Silver Street. Prayer books, apparently."

"Where can they all be going?" I said, as yet another group of well-dressed people crossed our path and we ducked out of the way of their dripping umbrellas.

"The Town Hall, I should imagine," said the bookseller. I must have looked blank. "The musical concerts," he continued. "A singer called Miss Paton, I believe, along with several others from the Royal Academy of Music. Two nights."

"Will you go tomorrow?" I asked.

"Oh no," said Giles. "Rather too rich for me – ten shillings a ticket, if you please."

"Plenty seem to be able to find it," I observed.

"Never mind, Mr Hardiman," said Giles, perhaps thinking that I was hankering after the music. "We will have entertainment aplenty ourselves at the Black Bull. Ah, here we are. I shall be glad to get out of this filthy weather."

Perhaps inspired by the musical event nearby, our lecturer at the book club that Wednesday evening spoke to us about the works of the German composer Beethoven, who died earlier this year. He even – to everyone's surprise – opened a black case, took out a trumpet and gave us a short concert of our own. This almost distracted me from my business that evening – almost, but not quite.

Before we had sat down for our concert-lecture, I had made sure to move freely around the two rooms used by our book club, to give Nicholas Trew every opportunity to catch my eye, touch my arm, pass me a note, or do whatever he wanted to continue our discussion. I was careful not to be drawn into other conversations which might put him off approaching me. But all this was in vain, as by the time we took our seats, there had been no sign of the attorney. I was not unduly worried, as the crowds in town, the foulness of the weather and even an unexpected client might easily have detained him. I took a seat towards the back of the room so that, should he arrive and signal me, I could slip out without disturbing anyone.

But when the lecture finished just before ten o'clock and Nicholas Trew still had not arrived, I began to fear the worst. I raised a hand in farewell to Giles, who was talking to our speaker, and hurried downstairs. Waiting in the parlour, as we had arranged, was Henry Adeane.

I looked around the room, just in case Trew had decided not to interrupt the lecture, but the magistrate beckoned me over. I sat down.

"I am sorry to have dragged you out on such an unpleasant night," I said. "And I sincerely hope you didn't have to give up your ticket to the concert at the Town Hall."

"Ha!" laughed Adeane. "As a widower, no-one expects me to attend that sort of thing. Cannot bear warbling. No, very happy here by the fire, with a newspaper and some surprisingly decent port." He looked at me. "But not such a pleasant evening for you, I fear. Drink?"

I shook my head, then changed my mind. "Something light – a barley water, perhaps. I have a sore head – the trumpet, I daresay."

Adeane looked surprised, but called over the pot boy and gave our order. My drink arrived quickly and I drained it almost in one.

"You may wish you had ordered something stronger," observed the magistrate. "No sign of Trew upstairs?" I shook my head. "Nor down here," he said, "and I have had a constable watching the door since seven o'clock. Just wish I'd started earlier."

"What do you mean?" I asked.

"Nicholas Trew is a clever man," he said. "You told me that he was planning to blackmail you. We can safely assume that he's on his guard." I nodded. I felt cold in the pit of my stomach. "With this in mind, I put another constable in St Andrew's Street, watching Trew's premises. Been there since four o'clock. And I have just had a message from him." He took a piece of paper from his pocket and unfolded it. "Trew arrived home at nearly five o'clock. The curtains were drawn. Lamps were lit and put out around the house in a manner suggesting dressing for dinner, dining and then readying to go out. But no-one left until the maid came out half an hour ago. The constable identified himself to her and she gave her name as Ellie Lodge. When asked where her master was, she said that he had packed two small bags and left from the back of the house. At about six o'clock."

"Blue Lion Yard," I said.

"Precisely," said Adeane.

"Where he could have had a horse waiting," I said. "Four hours ago."

As I lay in bed, sleep beyond my grasp, I wondered where Trew might have gone. His daughter was in Bedford – perhaps he had gone to stay with her, hoping to ride out the storm. I decided to call on the maid in the morning to ask if she had an address for Trew's daughter. And then my eyes shot open as I remembered the maid's name. It might be a simple coincidence, but the man I had spoken to in the gaol, the man who had been in the corridor the night Gerard Bendall was killed – his name was John Lodge.

Chapter Thirty-Two

DITCH

The next day I had fully intended to walk to St Andrew's Street after seeing off the *Star* to London and before welcoming the *Norfolk Regulator*, but events conspired against me. One of the horses meant for the London coach had kicked against its stall in the night and hurt its leg, so I had to send to the ostler at the Black Bull to ask if he had an animal we could use. I imagine you're thinking that the Sun, with its larger stable, would be the obvious place to try, but I happen to know that no coaches leave the Black Bull on a Thursday. And indeed, we were in luck: a horse was quickly trotted across town and the Star set off only twenty minutes late.

I turned my attention to the injured horse and bathed its bruise in my special mixture of myrrh and the oils of turpentine, swallows and pike before wrapping a bandage around it. I would do the same in the evening and twice the next day, and the animal would be ready to take up its duties again when the Star left on Saturday.

Unfortunately the change in routine upset Mrs Bird, and she then upset Seth Young in the kitchen, and he in turn upset Jamie doing the washing up, and what with one thing and another my morning disappeared in putting things to rights as best I could. By the time the *Norfolk Regulator* swung into the yard a half-hour late, with the driver grumbling about the mud and the poor state of the road between Bishop's Stortford and Great Chesterford, I was more than ready for my meal. But, as ever, my priority had to be the horses, which were hungry and filthy and unsettled by the smell of the injured animal and his embrocation. It took me quite some time to clean, feed and calm them. When the bells marked two o'clock, I was well and truly gut-foundered. I turned quietly from the horses and jumped a little when I saw Sarah Booth standing in the doorway of the stables.

"From Mr Young," she said, nodding at the tray she was carrying. "By way of apology, he said. For his bad temper this morning."

"Here," I said, "you'll never get that tray up the ladder. I'll take it piece by piece." I took the pot of coffee, carefully wrapped in a cloth, and put it on the lowest step of the ladder, then the covered dish ("Stew," said Sarah – she thought mutton) and finally the plate with two slices of damson loaf.

Sarah dropped the empty tray to her side and rolled her shoulders. She turned to go but I put a hand on her arm.

"May I ask you something, Sarah?"

"Of course, Mr Hardiman," she said.

"Your husband Charlie's friend, John Lodge," I started.

"I'm not sure they were friends exactly," she said. Then she blushed as she realised what I might think. "I don't mean not friends like, well, like he was friends with that other man. I just mean that I don't think they met before... before that night." She gathered herself. "Now, what did you want to ask me about John Lodge?"

"I was going to ask about his family," I said, "but if Charlie didn't know him well, you might well not know anything either. But I was wondering whether John Lodge has a sister. She'd be about your age, I imagine."

Sarah looked surprised. "There's a coincidence," she said.

"What do you mean?" I asked.

"Just that I hadn't seen Ellie for years," she replied, "and now here you are, asking about her." She stopped suddenly. "Oh dear – and Jamie asked me not to say anything to you."

I was befuddled – what had Jamie to do with it? "Sarah," I said, "this could be very important – much more important than upsetting Jamie. So start at the beginning, if you would. Who is Ellie?"

"Ellie Lodge," she said. "She was at school with me – a year younger, I think. Both her parents were dead, and her brother used to come to school to fetch her. I know he was called John because she used to tease him by singing that rhyme at him – the one about the dumpling."

"Diddle diddle dumpling?" I asked.

"My son John," completed Sarah, nodding.

"And you said you hadn't seen her for years, which means that you have seen her recently," I said. "When did you see her?" She hesitated again. "I will explain to Jamie that I made you tell me."

"He was only trying to protect you," she said.

"Protect me?" I repeated. "From what?"

"From being scared, I think," said Sarah. She took a deep breath. "Jamie was sweeping the yard on Monday afternoon – he said you were out and Mrs Bird would tell you off if the yard was mucky when the coach arrived from London. And Mr Trew came with something for you – a page torn out of the newspaper."

"Mr Trew the attorney?" I asked.

"That's him," Sarah agreed. "He told Jamie to give you the page. Then he looked around the yard and said it would be a pity if it all went up in smoke, and then he left. Jamie was scared. I was going past with a basket of linen and I heard him crying, in here." She indicated the stables. "So I asked him what was wrong and he told me about Mr Trew and the newspaper. And we looked at it together. Mr Trew had drawn a circle around one bit – a fire in a stables in Newmarket."

"Do you have the newspaper?" I asked.

Sarah shook her head. "Jamie kept it. I said he should tell you, but he didn't want to – said it would upset you, that you were frightened of fire."

"Musket fire," I said before I could stop myself. "I am frightened of musket fire." After much pestering by Jamie, who loved to read tales of adventure and heroism, I had once told him a very little of what a real battle feels like – the shrieks, the smoke, the stench, the terror – and I had mentioned, I was sure of it, how the flashes of musket fire would blind you for long moments.

Sarah put a hand on my arm. "As any sensible person would be," she said. I smiled palely and she took her hand back. "Jamie still has the newspaper – I caught him reading it again this morning."

"And Ellie Lodge?" I reminded her.

"When Jamie told me what Mr Trew had said, and how unpleasant he was, I remembered that another friend had told me that Ellie Lodge from school was working as a maid for a lawyer in town, for Mr Trew. And I wanted to warn her that he is not a nice man. If a maid is working in a man's house, well, you have to be careful. Not all men are as kind as you, Mr Hardiman. Quite a lot will..." She paused.

"Take advantage?" I suggested.

She nodded. "So during my dinner break I ran along to Mr Trew's house and had a quick word with Ellie." She smiled. "You know, she looked just like she did at school, only with her hair up now, of course. Just the same." Her hand went instinctively to her own face. "You can't say that of me."

"Sarah!" We both jumped when we heard the impatient voice of Mrs Bird. I peered around the door of the stables and there she was, standing in the yard with her hands on her hips. "Sarah is not your maid, Mr Hardiman," she said tartly. "Kindly release her to the duties for which I pay her."

I turned to Sarah and winked at her. "You'd better get back," I said. "I'll return the pot and plates to the kitchen when I've done. And thank you – you have been a great help. I'll make sure Jamie isn't cross with you."

The stew barely touched the sides I was that hungry, but I slowed down to enjoy the damson loaf, which was fresh and very flavoursome. With a coffee to wash it down, it was as good a meal as any I have had and I sat back in the ancient armchair and sighed. I could hear the rain on the roof and did not relish the idea of a damp walk to St Andrew's Street, but I had to speak to Ellie Lodge. I gathered the pot and plates and carefully went down the ladder. I kept under cover as much as I could, skirting the yard to the kitchen, and juggling everything into one hand I opened the door into the warm fug. I walked over to the sink and put my load down, gently touching Jamie on the shoulder so as not to startle him.

"Hello Jamie," I said, smiling. "Feeling better now?"

"Much better, Mr Hardiman," he said. He turned to look at me and dropped his voice. "Mr Young said sorry."

"I am glad to hear it," I replied.

"But no-one ever says sorry to me," said Jamie with wonder.

"Then they are wrong," I said. "Everyone should say sorry when they make a mistake – especially if they upset someone else when they do it."

Jamie paused, thinking, then nodded and reapplied himself to the pots in the sink.

"And I also need to say sorry to you," I continued. Jamie turned and stared at me. "I have made Sarah tell me something that you asked her not to," I said. "It was not Sarah's fault: she tried to keep your secret but I would not let her."

It would not have occurred to Jamie to try to hide his feelings, and I could see the anguish plain as day on his face.

"Dry your hands, Jamie," I said, "and come and sit with me for a minute."

Once we were both sitting on stools near the kitchen door, I spoke again. "Sarah told me that Mr Trew left a message for me – a story in a newspaper." Jamie said nothing, but his hand went to the pocket of his apron. "I know Mr Trew said some nasty things about a fire, and you didn't want me to be scared. And that is very kind of you, wanting to protect me."

"Friends look after each other," said Jamie.

"They do, yes," I agreed. "And now that I know about Mr Trew, I can be careful, can't I?"

Jamie nodded enthusiastically. "Very careful, Mr Hardiman," he said.

"And just so that I can be absolutely sure about what Mr Trew meant, could I read that newspaper, do you think?" I asked.

Jamie thought for a moment, then dug his hand into his apron pocket and pulled out a rather grubby and much-folded piece of newspaper and handed it to me. "He put a circle on it," he whispered loudly.

I unfolded the sheet; half of the name was missing, but from what was left I could see that it was from the *Cambridge Chronicle and Journal*. The date was Friday 9 November of this year. As Jamie had said, there was a thick circle drawn around one small piece, a single paragraph. *An alarming fire broke out in Newmarket, about six o'clock on Tuesday evening, I read, in the stables of the Five Bells, and it reached Mr Prince's stables before it was extinguished, having in its progress melted the lead and glass of the building to which it had extended. We are informed that it originated in the inebriety and carelessness of the ostler.*

"That's you," said Jamie, pointing. "It says ostler – that's you. And I know you are scared of fire. And the horses – they would be very scared."

"They would indeed," I said, "and that is why I am going to see Mr Trew to have a word with him about it. This fire was a long way from here, in Newmarket, Jamie – nothing to worry about." I smiled, but Jamie looked uncertain. I put my hand on his. "I promise you, Jamie: Mr Trew will not hurt either of us."

I had no idea how right I was.

I was walking back to the stables to fetch my coat when Joe Lassiter galloped into the yard before stopping and bending over with his hands on his knees to catch his breath. I beckoned him under cover.

"You again, Joe," I said lightly.

He looked up at me, his face serious. "You're to come now, Mr Hardiman," he said. "Mr Adeane is at the Shire House and wants to see you. Important, he said."

I reached into my pocket for a coin but Joe shook his head. "No time for that, Mr Hardiman – Mr Adeane said he would pay double if you came straight away." He was now hopping from foot to foot, glancing over his shoulder at the gate into Jesus Lane.

I grabbed my coat from the hook, put it on, turned up the collar and followed Joe out into the rain.

Joe kept up such a pace that only five minutes later we were at the Shire House, on the southern side of the Market Place. We ducked between the columns into the covered area, shook ourselves like dogs and then went into the building. Above us were the two courtrooms, but squeezed between them at the top of the stairs was a small room where lawyers could rest between trials. And standing outside this room, looking impatiently down the stairs, was Henry Adeane.

"Ah, Hardiman," he said as soon as he spotted me. "Come up, come up. Your money is on the ledge, there, by the window," he said to Joe, pointing.

"Thank you, Joe," I said. The lad took the coins that had been put out for him, pushed them firmly into his pocket and called, "Much obliged, sir," up the stairs before leaving us.

I climbed the stairs and the magistrate stood to one side to allow me into the room. It was a small, dark space, not the sort of room in which you would want to linger – which might have been the intention. A square table stood in the middle of the floor, four hard chairs around it, and against one wall was a tall bookcase crammed haphazardly with books. Legal ones, I guessed. Adeane gestured at one of the chairs and I sat, rain dripping from my coat onto the bare floorboards.

"Trew's dead," said the magistrate, dropping into the chair opposite me. "Found this morning in a ditch just this side of Hardwick."

"Hardwick?" I repeated. "That's west, isn't it, and not that far."

"About six miles," confirmed Adeane.

"Fallen from his horse, do you think?" I asked.

"Unless his horse had learned to use a skinning knife, I doubt it was responsible for his death," said the magistrate grimly. "Stabbed in the heart, apparently," he gestured to his own chest. "Nasty."

"Aye," I agreed.

"Found this morning by a farmer," continued Adeane. "The farmer sent word to town with a neighbour who was coming to the market, and the coroner rode out to look at the body. John Ingle. Recognised Trew immediately."

"No sign of the horse?" I asked.

"Standing nearby, uninjured," said Adeane. "The coroner brought it back and returned it to Blue Lion Yard."

"And the bags?" I asked. "The maid said he took two small bags with him."

"No mention of any bags," said Adeane.

"Could it have been a robbery, then?" I suggested.

"Unlikely," said Adeane, "given that this was pinned to Trew's chest with the skinning knife. Coroner thinks it might have been done after death, or there would have been more blood on it."

He took a piece of paper from his pocket and handed it to me. It had a tear in the middle of it from the knife, and bloodstains around that, but was still perfectly legible. The writing was neat but effortful. *We have not forgotten your arangement.*

"Mean anything to you?" asked Adeane, looking at me.

"Possibly," I said slowly. "I would need to check my notebook, at home." (You will know that I carry my notebook with me always, but I wanted time to think.)

The magistrate held out his hand and I gave him the blood-stained note. "I shall turn the matter over to the town constables," he said. "If you do think of anything..."

"Of course," I said.

We stood, shook hands and went our separate ways. As soon as Adeane was out of sight, I took out my notebook and wrote down the words that had been pinned to the attorney's body.

After supper that evening I went up to my room and sat in my armchair, a blanket on my knees like a square toes, mulling over what I had learned. The wording in the note found on Trew was an obvious – I would say a deliberate – echo of the message he himself had sent to Charlie Booth: *I trust you will not forget our arrange-*

ment. Whoever had written the note had known of the blackmail and had taken revenge for it, that much was clear. They had also known where to find Nicholas Trew. And the mis-spelling of the word *arrangement* suggested that they were not as educated as the attorney. I resolved to call on Ellie Lodge first thing in the morning.

Chapter Thirty-Three

MAID

With no coaches due until the London-bound *Norfolk Regulator* at midday, I was able to complete my morning duties in less than an hour. Thankfully the rain had stopped but the chill easterly wind for which Cambridge is famous was blowing straight along Jesus Lane and I was grateful to turn into Sidney Street and the lee of Sidney Sussex College. It was just before nine o'clock and the streets were busy with gownsmen and townsmen, all rushing to their appointments. In the summer months they would stroll and enjoy the morning air, but on this frigid day they drew their heads down between their shoulders and hurried along almost unseeing. I was one of them, and I soon found myself outside Nicholas Trew's premises.

I pulled the bell chain and waited. There was no reply, so I pulled it again. Surely Trew's daughter would be expected to deal with his affairs, and the maid would be preparing the house for her arrival. I stepped back and looked more carefully. The curtains were still closed at all the windows. I pulled the bell chain once more, and hammered on the door with my fist for good measure.

"You can batter the door down if you want," said a voice, "but there's no-one there."

I looked to my left, and standing in the doorway of the house adjacent was a stout woman of about fifty, her arms crossed over her apron.

"I'm looking for the maid here," I said. "Miss Lodge."

The woman looked me up and down. "You her sweetheart?" she asked.

"Hardly," I said, smiling. "I wanted to talk to her about her employer."

"Oh, him," she said, sniffing. "He'll be much missed, I don't think. As for Ellie, she hasn't been back since he left. And I don't blame her neither." She turned on her heel and slammed the door shut behind her.

I watched the house for a few moments, just to see if any of the curtains moved, but there was nothing. I walked on along St Andrew's Street, turned into Birdbolt Lane and then Downing Place, and hammered on another door – this time the heavy one belonging to the gaol. I shivered as I waited. After a few long minutes the door creaked open a little and the pinched face of Jones the turnkey peered out. Recognising me, he hauled the door fully open.

"Thought we'd be seeing you, Mr Hardiman," he said.

"Really?" I said as I stepped into the dank prison yard and helped him shoulder the door closed. "Why is that?"

"Now that Mr Trew has met his end, well, those who had their mouths stopped by him might feel a bit more talkative, I should imagine," he said. "Mr Lodge, for example. He's the one you want to see, isn't he?"

"He is, yes," I agreed.

"Well, you know where he is." The turnkey handed me a key.

I walked towards the stone steps leading down to the cells, then stopped and turned. "How on earth did you hear about Mr Trew?" I asked.

"There's plenty in this town happy to share that news, Mr Hardiman," he said, disappearing back into his little room next to the gate.

I walked down to the basement of the gaol, feeling the air growing colder with each step I took. I unlocked the door to John Lodge's cell and, unlike on my previous visit, he rose from his stool to greet me.

"Mr Hardiman," he said, ducking his head.

"Mr Lodge," I said in turn. "You don't seem surprised to see me."

"Mr Jones said things might be different now," he said. "Now that Trew is dead."

"Yes," I said. "It has worked out well for you, him dying."

The prisoner shrugged. "I know I might still hang," he said without emotion, "but at least now I can tell people why I did what I did. That I wasn't wicked. That I never meant harm to that poor man. I'm a thief, Mr Hardiman: not a murderer."

"Are you sure?" I asked. "You can murder a man without holding the weapon yourself."

Lodge looked anguished. "I told you," he said. "I was only waiting in the corridor..."

I interrupted him. "I'm not talking about Mr Bendall. I mean Mr Trew."

"Mr Trew?" he repeated. "You think I am responsible for the death of Mr Trew? But how could I be, when I am in here?" He indicated his surroundings.

"You have a sister, I believe, Mr Lodge," I said.

The prisoner frowned a little at the change of subject. "I do, yes. Ellie. Eleanor."

"Working as a maid for Nicholas Trew," I continued.

"What?" said the prisoner. "No." He shook his head and sat down on his stool, confusion on his face. "No. She is a maid, yes, but not for him. She works in one of the big houses on Newnham Road. She's saving to be married."

I took out my notebook and made a note of what he said.

"Married?" I said.

He nodded. "To James Burgess," he said. "He's a farmer – oats and peas, mainly. She met him at the market. Big lad, built like an ox. Dotes on Ellie." He looked up at me. "What on earth made you think she was working for Nicholas Trew?" he asked.

"When did you last see Ellie?" I asked in turn.

"The day before yesterday," said Lodge. "She brought me a clean shirt and some food and a flagon. She said she was going away for a few days."

"Did she say where?" I asked.

"To visit James and his family," he said. "I think she likes being with his mother and sisters – female company, I suppose. And with a wedding to talk about, well, you know." He smiled sadly. "Not that I'll see it, of course."

"And where does this James Burgess live?" I asked.

Lodge thought for a moment. "One of the villages out west," he said. "Not as far as Bourn. Hardwick, that's it."

Chapter Thirty-Four

HARDWICK

"Well, he's no rum prancer, I'll grant you that," said Benjamin, "but he's a steady, comfortable ride, and he could have been made to fit you."

Benjamin Jordan's livery yard was the best-regarded in Cambridge, and whenever I had had cause to visit I had been impressed by the kind manner with which he and his men treated the animals. And indeed, as we spoke he was gently stroking the muzzle of the chestnut horse, which in turn was leaning against him.

"You get up," continued Benjamin, leading the animal to the mounting block, "and I'll check the girth – you don't want to end up underneath him. His name's Copper."

I mounted Copper and Benjamin led him into the middle of the yard and walked around us, pulling on bits of tack and harness to check that all was well.

"You'll do," he said. "Two gentlemen of middle years out for a stroll on the Lord's Day." He smiled, raising a hand in farewell as we walked out of the yard and onto Bridge Street just as the church bells marked eight o'clock.

We crossed the Great Bridge, which was mercifully quiet, and I wondered whether Copper was relieved when we turned left into Northampton Street rather than going up the hill towards the castle. Minutes later we had left the town behind us and were heading due west on the St Neots road. Now buildings were few and far between; sometimes a long lane would suggest a farmhouse at the end of it, and to our right an elegant tree-lined avenue led to the new observatory. As the winter sky lightened I enjoyed its vastness, reminding me of my boyhood in Norfolk. Benjamin had been right: Copper was a comfortable mount, and whenever I spoke to him he would blow out gently and shake his head in his harness. He was good company.

I know that our journey took two hours because the bells of the small grey church in Hardwick were ringing as we approached. An old woman carrying a basket on her arm stopped and stared at me.

I pulled Copper to a halt. "Good morning, missus," I said.

"Morning to you, sir," she said, not taking her eyes from my face.

"I am here to call on Mr James Burgess," I said. "Could you kindly tell me where he lives?"

"You'll be from town," she said, coming a little closer and jerking her head in the general direction of Cambridge.

"My name is Hardiman," I said, smiling pleasantly.

She did not smile in return, but apparently decided that I was no threat to the good people of Hardwick. "Down there," she pointed, "and turn left at the bend – there's an oak with an owl hole in it."

"Thank you, missus," I said, urging Copper into a walk. When I reached the bend she had described, I looked back and she was where I had left her, staring after me.

The lane was pitted and rutted with winter mud set hard, and I let Copper pick his own way along it. I slumped into the saddle so that I was not fighting him and I left the strings loose, holding instead to the pommel. Perhaps three hundred yards along the lane we reached the farmhouse. It was one of those buildings that look as though they have grown out of the ground around them, with stone walls the same colour as the earth. Not that it was grubby in any way; on the contrary, the path leading from the lane to the front door was swept clear and I could see a pale glow of lamplight coming through the small windows. As we stopped, a dog started barking.

I dismounted and tied the strings to a nearby tree. Copper sighed heavily. I walked up to the door and knocked.

"Quiet, Jess," said a woman's voice and the dog was silenced.

The door opened and there stood a woman of about forty, who had obviously once been very pretty. From her rolled-up sleeves and the flour on her apron, I guessed I had interrupted her at her baking.

I took off my hat and inclined my head. "Good morning, missus," I said. "My name is Gregory Hardiman and I have come from Cambridge to have a word with Ellie Lodge, if I may."

"She's not here," said the woman, putting her hand on the head of the brown dog that had appeared at her side.

"Not here for now, or not here at all?" I asked. "It is very important that I see her."

"Let him in, ma," said a man's voice. "There's no harm now."

The woman hesitated but opened the door and stood to one side to let me pass. The dog sniffed at me as I did so. The woman closed the door and my eyes took a moment to adjust. As I had guessed, the table was covered with flour and rolled-out pastry and part-lined pie trays. Standing by the fire, wearing trousers and a shirt and holding a coat in front of the flames – drying it or warming it, I could not say – was a young man. He still had a year or two of growing left in him, to my eye, but he was already broad and sturdy. He reminded me of the workers on my father's farm. He shrugged on the coat.

"Hardman, you said?" he asked.

"Hardiman," I replied. "Gregory Hardiman. I'm the ostler at the Hoop Inn in Cambridge."

"Thomas Burgess," he said.

"May I trouble you for a drink, Mrs Burgess?" I asked the woman. "It's a long ride from town."

She fetched a jug from her larder and poured two tumblers of small beer, handing one to me and one to her son.

"This is good," I said. "Thank you." I gave the empty tumbler back to the woman.

"You wanted to know about Ellie," said Thomas.

"I spoke to her brother," I said, "and he told me that Ellie is to be married to James Burgess, and that she had come out here to stay for a few days."

"James is my older brother," said Thomas. "There's six of us, and ma. Our pa died last year."

"I am sorry to hear it," I said. "My condolences to you, Mrs Burgess." She had returned to her table and was thumping a ball of dough, but she inclined her head to show that she had heard me.

"We all like Ellie," continued Thomas. "She's teaching my sisters to read, to help with the farm accounts. She was teaching them to read," he corrected himself. "You'd better sit." He pointed at the two chairs by the fireplace and we sat down. "Ellie arrived from town a few days ago – Thursday, was it, ma?"

"Wednesday," she said. "Late – gone nine o'clock."

"Were you expecting her?" I asked.

Thomas shook his head. "Not me," he replied. "She said that her employer had shut up the house for a while – going to London or some such. She didn't like being there by herself, I know that. So she came here a few days early, to help about the place. And they were going to read the banns in church for the first time today."

Mrs Burgess attacked the dough with her rolling pin.

"You said 'not me'," I said. "Did your brother know she was coming?"

Thomas frowned. "I can't be sure," he said. "A letter arrived for him on Tuesday. It might have been from Ellie – he didn't show me, just threw it into the fire and said nothing."

"Your brother can read?" I asked.

"All my boys can read," said Mrs Burgess, the pride obvious in her voice. "Our sexton here, at St Mary's, he teaches them."

"We can read well enough," confirmed Thomas.

I took out my notebook and pencil. "A letter arrived for James on Tuesday," I said, writing it down. "And Ellie herself arrived on Wednesday, late in the evening." I looked up at Thomas. "And the banns were to be read today, Sunday – but Ellie and James are not here. Is that right?" He nodded. "So where are they?" I asked.

Thomas Burgess sighed.

"Liverpool," said his mother.

"Liverpool?" I repeated, surprised.

Thomas nodded. "I tried to talk him out of it, but they were determined. More opportunities, he said. They talked of working for a couple of years to save for their passage to the Americas. With James knowing about farming and Ellie, well, Ellie could turn her hand to anything, I reckon. They said they could get a decent parcel of land over there, and I daresay it's true. Like I said, we're six – four of us brothers – and not much land to go around. And with a kiddy on the way, they have to think of their future."

"Ellie is expecting a baby?" I asked.

"Due in May," said Mrs Burgess. "Not that I'll see it, my first grandbabby." The poor dough took another thump.

Thomas rolled his eyes at me.

"When did they leave?" I asked.

"Thursday," he said. "About midday. Seth Peters was taking a delivery to the mill in Great Gransden and took them on his cart."

"And you think they have gone for good?" I asked.

"They took as much as they could carry," said Thomas. "Two leather bags and two canvas ones. Good job Ellie's a strong girl."

I closed my notebook. "It seems I'm too late, then," I said. I stood and put the notebook and pencil into my pocket and then held out my hand. Thomas Burgess shook it. "Thank you for your hospitality," I said. "And to you, Mrs Burgess."

Mrs Burgess wrapped something in a cloth and brought it over to me. "For your midday meal," she said.

"That is very kind of you," I said.

She took hold of my wrist and spoke urgently. "He's a good man, my James. A good, decent man. Always looking out for those weaker than him, ever since he could walk."

"Standing up to bullies, you mean?" I asked.

She nodded. "I like to think of him and Ellie and the little one, somewhere new. Making a good life for themselves. Away from all that." She let go of my wrist and gave a flick of her hand. "All that nastiness."

Her son put a hand on her shoulder. "That's right, ma," he said. "All that nastiness." But he looked at me as he said it. "I'll see you to your horse, Mr Hardiman," he said.

Copper was slowing down by the time we turned back into Jordan's yard at nearly three o'clock. The weak winter light was fading even more, and despite my thick coat I was chilled. I dismounted stiffly and stroked the side of the horse's head. He huffed out through his nostrils and started to walk himself to the stables. One of Benjamin's lads darted out and took the strings from me. I put up a hand to halt him, then dug around in my coat pocket for a coin –

my hands were cold and it took me a moment to find one. I handed it to the lad.

"Dry him carefully," I said. "He feels cold to the touch, but he's worked up a sweat nonetheless."

"Yes, sir," said the lad, grinning quickly as he shoved the coin into his own pocket. He clicked his tongue and led Copper away.

At the entrance to the yard I turned left into Bridge Street and walked a few steps before stopping, turning around and heading towards St Clement's. I knew that if I did not discuss what I had learned with someone it would keep me awake all night. And having seen the confusion and uncertainty of Francis Vaughan over his recent investment error, I guessed that he would have some sympathy for my dilemma.

"Show him in quickly, Wells," said the Master, "and then go to the kitchen for a pot of coffee, if you please."

Vaughan's footman held the door open for me then slipped out quickly; I could hear him trotting down the steps.

"Come, come, Gregory," said the Master, beckoning to me from his armchair. "It's bitter out there – come and thaw yourself here by the fire." I sat gratefully and held out my hands to the warmth.

"I am trying to gather as much heat as I can before I have to go to chapel," he said. "I have no idea why worship has to be so very uncomfortable, but there it is. And where have you been today?" He glanced down at my boots and I realised just how muddy they were.

"Hardwick," I said.

"I don't think I know..." said the Master.

"A hamlet about six miles west of Cambridge, on the road to St Neots," I clarified.

"Ah," said Vaughan. The door opened and Wells came in, balancing a pot of coffee, two cups and a covered plate on a tray.

"Apologies from the kitchen," he said, "but there is no cake left. There is some buttered block gingerbread." He put the tray on the sideboard, then cleared several books and a pile of papers from the small table near the Master's chair. "Shall I serve, sir?"

"If you would, Wells," said the Master, nodding.

After Wells had poured our coffee, taken the cloth from the plate of gingerbread and wrapped it around the pot to keep the coffee warm, he bowed and left us.

I held my cup in both hands and sniffed. "This is good," I said.

"Don't tell anyone," said Vaughan, reaching for a piece of gingerbread, "but I prefer this to almost any fancy cake. Reminds me of being a boy, putting two slices together with the butter in the middle, stuffing it into my pocket and setting off on adventures. Now," he stood, "I must go to chapel. Might I suggest that you wait here and warm yourself – drink all the coffee and eat all the gingerbread. I will be back in half an hour."

The next thing I knew, someone was shaking me gently by the shoulder. I looked up, blinking, and Francis Vaughan smiled at me.

"You were worn out, Mr Hardiman," he said. He turned and bent towards the fire, warming first his hands and then his backside. "Chapel was every bit as cold as I had feared," he said. "Thankfully it made the chaplain very efficient with his prayers." He sat down. "And while I was praying, I remembered where I had heard of Hardwick before. Isn't that where they found Nicholas Trew's body?"

"It is, yes," I replied.

"Hence your visit today," said Vaughan.

"Hence my visit today," I confirmed. "I went to see the man who may well have killed him."

"Ah," said the Master. "And have you sent word to the town constables to arrest him? Or is Hardwick beyond their reach?"

"Liverpool certainly is," I replied. And I told Francis Vaughan all that I knew of Ellie Lodge and her brother John and her husband-to-be James Burgess. "If I took the matter to the town constables and the magistrates," I added, "I would have to tell them about Sarah Booth, and maybe even Matthew Gibbs." Vaughan nodded. "And Ellie Lodge is expecting a baby," I finished, "so even if she went on trial she would plead the belly."

"I see," said the Master. "It certainly is a moral conundrum." My hand went to my coat pocket and Vaughan laughed. "Not too tired to enjoy a new word, I see." He waited until I had opened my vocabulary notebook and then spelled the word out for me. "A riddle – a puzzle," he explained.

"From Latin?" I asked.

"Ha – you would think so, wouldn't you?" he replied. "But no: it was made up by gownsmen in Oxford, as a sort of mock Latin. Perhaps we should ban it here in Cambridge – but it is such a useful word." I closed my notebook and slipped it back into my pocket. "As I understand it," he continued, "Nicholas Trew was a man with many enemies and not many redeeming qualities. But his daughter will mourn him nonetheless. And to repay the wrong done to her brother – and to Charlie Booth, and to who knows how many others – a pregnant young woman has persuaded her betrothed to kill Mr Trew. The two have then fled to Liverpool, with plans to start afresh in the Americas. Is that it?"

I nodded. "I believe so, yes," I said.

"And you are wondering," said Vaughan, "what purpose would be served in hunting down Miss Lodge and Mr Burgess, when the latter would surely hang for his actions, leaving the former to struggle alone with their child. And," he held up a hand to silence me as I opened my mouth, "with the story of Sarah Booth and her marriage coming under scrutiny as part of the enquiry. Do I have it, Mr Hardiman?"

"You do, sir, yes," I said miserably. "I know what the law requires, but in my heart, I cannot see how the death of a good man will remedy the death of a bad one. Not that I wished Nicholas Trew dead, but might it not be seen as, well, natural justice?"

"It is not for me to say, Mr Hardiman," said the Master, but gently. "Neither the victim – any of the victims – nor the perpetrator is a member of the University. If questioned, I should have to say simply that I heard rumours and tittle-tattle which I ignored – after all, I am a dusty old mathematician living a quiet life with my books. But you." He paused and looked keenly at me. "You are a constable, yes, but more importantly, you are a man who has seen more of the world than I ever shall. You have been to war, Mr Hardiman – you have seen killing in all its guises. And you know better than anyone that a killing always exacts a price from someone. If you choose not to take this matter to the law, thereby letting the judge and jury take the burden from you, it will remain your burden. Can you carry it, Mr Hardiman, for the rest of your days?"

Chapter Thirty-Five

Heart

Three days later, I was still considering Francis Vaughan's question, and the distraction was making me careless. I shut my thumb in the door of one of the stalls at work, which made me shout in pain and startle two horses. As my hand was sore, I dropped a plate that Mrs Chapman was handing to me, spilling my dinner all over her clean floor. And as she knew that I was not a clumsy man, this made her look at me closely and ask all sorts of questions. It was clear that she thought my inattention was down to a romantic entanglement with, as she put it, that nice Miss Swanney, and she kept winking at her husband and giving me knowing smiles.

"Good heavens, woman," said George Chapman in the end. "Leave the man alone. If he was thinking of marriage, seeing what I have to put up with will soon change his mind."

"Well, really," said his wife, pouting. "It's come to something if we can't take a caring interest in each other's lives." She turned her back on us and clattered the pots into the sink.

George Chapman caught my eye and jerked his head towards the door. I took the hint and made good my escape while he stayed, martyr that he was, to absorb whatever was coming.

I stepped out into a bitter, crisp winter night, the inky sky bright with stars. I stood for a moment looking upwards until the depth of it all made me dizzy. Ahead of me a small group of gownsmen tumbled out of Jesus College, laughing and shoving each other as they walked towards town. At the end of Jesus Lane they turned right, while I headed in the other direction, skirting the empty marketplace and walking along Bene't Street to the welcome lights of the Black Bull Inn. In another half-hour it would be busy with men arriving for the meeting of the Bull Book Club, but as one of the two librarians for this quarter I was obliged to be at my desk by a quarter past seven. I walked up the stairs to the top floor of the building and went into the room that had been set aside for our library. My fellow librarian was already there, and looked up as I walked in.

"Mr Hardiman?" he asked, standing to shake my hand. He was tall and spare, with fine curling hair. "My name is Robert Sadd."

"Mr Sadd," I said.

"Robert," he suggested. "We are to work together for some months – it may as well be friendly."

"Gregory," I offered.

"The university constable," he said, smiling.

"You have the advantage of me," I replied, smiling in return.

"Hairdresser," he said. "Our premises are just over the road from here."

"Ah yes," I said. "I recall the name." I put a hand to my head. "I am afraid I rely on my landlady and her kitchen scissors."

"Not your wife?" he asked.

"No-one in Cambridge has taken me on," I replied.

"Well, if someone catches your eye and you want to impress her," he said, "we can tidy you up."

I laughed; I had fallen into that trap too easily.

"Ledger or shelves?" asked Robert. "We can take turn and turn about each week."

"I'll do shelves," I said, and for the next thirty minutes I was kept busy, returning books to their places as Robert ticked them off in the ledger, and helping members to find titles that they had hoped to read. If any member had to pay a fine for returning a book late, Robert would note it in the ledger and I would put my initials next to it as witness. At a quarter to the hour we could hear a bell being rung in the meeting room next door, which was our signal to hurry along those who were still choosing, in readiness for a prompt start to the meeting at eight o'clock.

At a third, more insistent ringing of the bell, we closed the door to the library and took our seats at the back of the room. It was a good showing and nearly every chair was taken. The president – a man I did not know, but Robert whispered "John Clay, a teacher" in my ear – stood and welcomed us.

"Gentlemen," said Mr Clay. "Before we embark on the formal business of our meeting this evening, we should pause for a moment to honour the memory of a recently departed member of this book club, Mr Nicholas Trew. Mr Trew was a respected attorney and a valued member of our group, and we shall miss his lively contributions to our debates." He stopped and bowed his head. We all did likewise. A minute passed. "Thank you, gentlemen," said the president at last. "And now our speaker for this evening is Mr Charles Caesar, solicitor, who is here to tell us about the," he glanced down at the piece of paper in his hand, "the Cambridge and Cambridgeshire Association for the Prosecution of Felons and Thieves of Every Denomination, which held its annual meeting recently and of which he is a founding member. Mr Caesar, if you please."

Mr Caesar's talk, dwelling as it did on the application of the law to miscreants, did nothing to settle my mind and after the meeting had finished I decided to take a walk around the town before going home. I knew that sleep would not come easily, and I would be tempted to take one more of Mr Relhan's small pills, and I thought that walking myself to exhaustion might help. I said goodbye to George Fisher as he turned into Bene't Street while I continued southwards along Trumpington Street. I was just approaching Lensfield Road when I heard someone call my name. I stopped and peered into the darkness, and a man on a horse – both looking weary – plodded towards me.

"Ingle," he called. Ah, the coroner. He pulled his horse to a halt alongside me and bent down to shake my hand. "I thought it was you, Hardiman. Not on patrol, surely?"

"No, sir," I said. "I have been at a meeting and wanted to clear my head before bed. And you?"

"Attending a death in Grantchester," he said. "A young farmer in a cart accident – very sad. His wife will have a hard time of it now."

"It is worse for those left behind, I always think," I said. "Like Trew's daughter." The words were out of my mouth before I could stop them – Nicholas Trew was much on my mind.

"Indeed." John Ingle sighed. "But she was not unprepared, I think. His heart had troubled him for years."

"His heart?" I echoed.

The coroner's horse shook its head, jingling the harness, and Ingle leaned forward to pat its neck comfortingly. "Angina," he said, yawning widely. "Forgive me – I missed my supper and I am dog-tired."

"Of course," I said, "but if I may just ask. I heard that Mr Trew was attacked with something sharp – waylaid, pulled from his horse, and left with a note attached to him. That is what I was told by Mr Adeane." I added that last bit in case the coroner should think I had been listening to idle gossip.

"And so it seemed, Mr Hardiman," agreed the coroner. "But when the body was brought to town and I spoke to Trew's physician, he seemed certain that the heart would be at fault. At his request I conducted an autopsy and he was right. Plain as day. All heart valves were severely enlarged. Hence no need for an inquest – no doubt in my mind as to cause of death."

I frowned and shook my head. "But the wound on the back of the head – the note pinned to the body?"

"All very dramatic, but – from a medical point of view – purely coincidental," said the coroner. "Not nearly enough blood, you see. Not on the ground around him, not on the knife in his chest. Blood had stopped moving around the body some time before all of that happened. My guess is that his heart stopped, he fell from his horse – and whoever it was came across him, thought he was sleeping and decided to finish him off." He yawned again. "Could have saved themselves the trouble. And now, Mr Hardiman, my bed is calling." He urged his horse onwards and raised a hand in farewell as they walked slowly into town.

As you can imagine, this encounter with the coroner did nothing to aid my sleep. I lay in bed, eyes wide open. The best laid schemes, I thought, imagining Ellie Lodge and James Burgess planning to waylay Trew to take their revenge, and then happening upon him and thinking that fate was smiling on them to deliver him so easily into their hands. If only they had thought to check that he was still alive – but then perhaps they would not have felt that justice had been served. Either way, they were now running from a punishment that would never be exacted, and would live with a guilt that was unnecessary.

I sat up and swung my legs out of bed, reaching for my dressing gown and pulling it on. We were only a couple of days past the full moon, and there was enough light falling into my room for me to make my way to my little table without bumping into anything. I quickly lit the Argand lamp (a gift to myself some months before, as it made reading in the evenings so much easier) and waited for the flame to settle. I opened my box of writing materials and took out a fresh piece of paper, and then dipped my pen in the ink. I paused. *Dear Mr Burgess,* I wrote in my clearest hand. *The coroner has found that the attorney died of natural causes. There was no inquest. There is no charge to answer. You may wish to get word to your brother.* I paused again – I would find a way to have this delivered to Thomas Burgess in Hardwick, but if the carrier were curious and read what I had written, I did not want to cause difficulty for the Burgess family by suggesting any link to me. *From your caller from Cambridge,* I finished.

I folded the note, extinguished the lamp, took off my gown, shuffled under the covers again, and – at long last – fell asleep.

CHAPTER THIRTY-SIX

FARMER

The next day, before heading home for an early supper and then going out on patrol, I decided to call in on Francis Vaughan to tell him what I had learned about the death of Nicholas Trew. When I arrived at St Clement's, I saw George Chapman huddling over the small stove in his lodge. He lifted a gloved hand in greeting.

"Is the Master in?" I mouthed through the window.

He nodded and I set off across the court. As I trudged up the stone stairs I wondered, and not for the first time, why no-one had thought to put doors at the foot of these staircases. The wind, trapped in the corners of the court, forced its way past me and all but hammered on the doors of the rooms above.

At the Master's door, I knocked smartly and entered when he called. It was often said that colleges spent half their money on drink and the other half on coal because both were essential to survive the Cambridge winter, and I was relieved to see that Francis Vaughan had not stinted on his fire today. The man himself was sitting in an armchair pulled as close as he dared to the flames, and he waved me over.

"Come, Mr Hardiman," he said, indicating the other armchair. "Sit and warm yourself." He shuddered. "I do hate December."

I sat and stretched my hands towards the warmth. "Drear nighted December," I said.

"Shelley?" asked the Master.

"Close," I said, smiling. "Keats."

Vaughan chuckled. "There cannot be many constables as fond as you are of poetry," he said.

"You would be surprised," I replied. "Perhaps not poetry, no, but most of us like to improve ourselves."

"And very laudable it is too," said the Master. "Would that all our undergraduates were as determined. But some of them are ill-suited to their studies."

"Like Edwin Bendall?" I asked.

The Master considered for a moment. "I suspect he would have stuck it out, for his brother's sake," he decided, "but he would have been miserable. Cold comfort to him, I am sure, but his brother's death does mean that Edwin is back where he belongs. He will be much happier as a farmer than as a scholar, I am sure."

"Talking of farmers," I said, "I have been told something that may interest you. Information from John Ingle – the coroner."

"The coroner?" asked Vaughan. "Concerning whom?"

"The attorney Nicholas Trew," I replied.

To my surprise, the Master gasped and put one hand to his mouth, clutching tightly at the arm of his chair with the other. "That wretched man," he whispered. Then he looked at me. "Forgive me, Mr Hardiman – it is wicked of me to speak ill of the dead."

"And most unlike you, if I may say so, Mr Vaughan," I said. I leaned forward. "I have had a suspicion for a little while, and I must put it to you. Were you being blackmailed by Nicholas Trew?"

The Master's eyes widened. "I... you...," he spluttered. Then he said quietly, "How did you know?"

"You were far from his only victim," I said. "Will you tell me about it?" I reached for my notebook.

Vaughan hesitated and then nodded. He sat back in his chair, sighed and then began. "As you know, I made an unwise investment on behalf of the college, with Mr Bendall." He held up a hand as I opened my mouth. "I know what you will say – that no investment was made. But that was only because poor Mr Bendall died and you were able to stop the money being paid out. The fact remains that my judgement was poor. And Nicholas Trew found out about it."

I thought about the entry I had seen in Bendall's ledger, identifying Francis Vaughan. If I had guessed who it was, anyone else reading the ledger with even a small knowledge of Cambridge would be able to make the same guess. What if Bendall, seeking to allay Trew's fears about his money, had shown him the ledger to demonstrate that others had put their faith in him and his silver mine?

The Master continued. "The first demand arrived the day we had the balloon in Cambridge – what was that, the middle of October?" I nodded. "It said that he was aware of my investment, and that I was playing fast and loose with college money. That was his exact phrase: 'playing fast and loose'. It stuck in my mind."

I looked up from my notebook. "You did not keep the demand?" I asked.

"Good heavens, no," said Vaughan, shaking his head. "It went straight onto the fire. A man of my age, Mr Hardiman – I could die at any moment, and if someone found that amongst my papers... No, I kept none of them."

"How many did he send?" I asked.

"Three," replied the Master promptly. He ticked them off on his fingers. "The first, then another one two days later, and a final one just before he died. Although I doubt he intended it to be the final one. True to form, as I believe is the nature of blackmail, the amount being demanded was increased each time." He shook his head. "I am such a fool, Mr Hardiman."

"You are no fool, Mr Vaughan," I said stoutly. "You have acted foolishly, perhaps – tricked by someone cunning, taking advantage of your inexperience in commerce. But no-one who has guided hundreds of undergraduates through their studies and launched them into the world as good, productive men could ever be judged a fool."

The Master was silent for a few seconds. "You are kind, Mr Hardiman. Very kind."

I cleared my throat. "The three notes you received – were they signed?"

"The first one, yes," he replied. "The other two, no. I assume he knew that I would know who had sent them."

"And where did you take the money?" I asked.

"Oh, I didn't pay him anything," said the Master, surprised.

"You didn't pay?" I asked.

He shook his head. "I thought about it – I considered paying," he admitted. "Fifteen pounds, he asked for. It was a good deal of money, but I could have laid my hands on it. And I had almost made up my mind to, and then the second letter arrived, this time demanding double that – thirty pounds! And that brought me to my senses. What was it John the Baptist said? Exact no more than that which is appointed you."

"Excellent advice," I said. "And what did the third letter say?"

"He wrote that he would be taking the matter to the Vice-Chancellor unless I paid a hundred pounds," said Vaughan. "And at that point I decided that I would go to Mr Davy myself and confess everything – and tell him about Mr Trew. And then of course..." he shrugged. Then he looked at me, horror on his face. "Mr Hardiman, surely you don't – surely the coroner doesn't... Do you think that I killed Mr Trew?"

I couldn't help myself – I laughed. "No, no," I said, shaking my head. "Not for one moment. In fact, that is what I came to tell you: no-one killed Mr Trew." And I told him what John Ingle had told me.

"And what of the poor man who thinks himself responsible?" asked the Master once I had finished. "The farmer from Hardwick? He may have intended to kill a man, but I am sure it will be a great relief to his conscience to find that he did not."

"I have sent word to his brother, who will be almost as relieved," I said. The long-case clock chimed. "And now I must leave – it will not go well for me if I keep Mr Sedgwick waiting." I stood, and Vaughan reached up and took one of my hands in both of his.

"Thank you, Mr Hardiman," he said earnestly. "Tonight will be my first good night's sleep since this all began."

⌒ell⌒

I had to run the last hundred yards or so, and I burst into the Proctors' Court just as the Senior Proctor was glancing at the clock.

"Mr Hardiman," he said, "it is not like you to be so tardy."

"I apologise, sir," I said, reaching for my cloak. "I was talking to Mr Vaughan at St Clement's and the time slipped away from me."

"Hmmm," said Mr Sedgwick. "You're with Mr Turnbull, you and Swanney. Gilbert and Wilson, you're with me."

As we sorted ourselves into pairs and followed the proctors down Senate House Passage, George Swanney whispered to me. "I have news," he said.

"Wait until Turnbull goes into a tavern to check the back room," I said quietly.

George smiled impishly; we knew that the Junior Proctor often used this excuse on cold or wet nights to stay a little longer indoors. And indeed, when we were passing the Eagle on Bene't Street, he used exactly those words and disappeared into the warm fug of the tavern. George and I drew close to the wall.

"What's this news of yours, then?" I asked.

He looked at me with a broad grin. "I'm to be married," he said.

"At last," I said, shaking his hand. "I wish you and Miss Warwick every happiness."

"We are already very happy," he said. "Left to our own devices, we would have wed long ago, but Ann's aunt – her late mother's sister – hoped that someone better would come along and kept asking Ann to delay."

"Then more fool Ann's aunt," I said robustly.

"Thank you, Gregory," said George. "The wedding is the second week of January. And I was hoping, Gregory, that you would be my best man."

I was astonished. "Me?" I asked.

"I can think of no-one better," said George. "Do you accept?"

"I do," I said. "Thank you."

"Kate will be pleased," said George. "At least she cannot complain about it being a dull affair if you are there. And who knows? It might give you both a taste for marriage."

I was about to protest when the Junior Proctor reappeared.

"Come, come, gentlemen," he said, as though we had been the ones keeping him waiting. "We can't stand around here all night."

George Swanney raised an eyebrow at me. "The proctors may change," he said to me out of the side of his mouth, "but their excuses stay the same."

CHAPTER THIRTY-SEVEN

ASPARAGUS

The following Tuesday evening, I was waiting outside the door of the Town Hall at five minutes to the hour. Exactly as the bells started to ring, I saw Kate Swanney hurrying across the market towards me and I raised my hand in greeting.

"Mr Hardiman," she said, smiling. I noticed that her cheeks were pink with the cold and that it suited her.

"Miss Swanney," I replied, taking off my hat. I opened the door for her and paid a sixpence for each of us to the stern-looking woman sitting at a table just inside.

"Flowers to the left, fruit and vegetables to the right," said the woman. "Prize-winners have rosettes on them."

"Did your husband's asparagus do well, Mrs Widnall?" asked Kate.

The woman's face was transformed as she smiled broadly. "It did, Miss Swanney, yes," she said happily. "Best in class."

"We shall look out for it," said Kate, taking my arm, and we walked into the main hall.

"Asparagus?" I said. "In December?"

"He grows it under glass," she explained, "and covers it in straw when the nights grow colder. Takes his asparagus very seriously indeed, does Mr Widnall." And she smiled impishly at me.

The Cambridge Horticultural Society may sound like a polite and proper organisation, but their annual competition was hard fought. I had even heard rumours of foul play, with flowers dug up in the middle of the night and snails slipped into vegetable patches. But the end result was always a sight to see, with every entry displayed to best advantage. Kate led me over to a short, scrubbed-face man with a large grey moustache, standing proudly behind a bunch of asparagus with a red rosette tied to it.

"Mr Widnall," she said, "this is my friend Mr Hardiman. Your wife said you had done well, and we wanted to congratulate you." She turned to me. "Mr Hardiman, Mr Widnall was our neighbour in Newnham, and there is no-one better at growing asparagus."

I leaned across the table and shook Widnall's hand.

"Thank you, miss," he said. "And second prize for me chrysanthemums too – the superb white have done wonders this year." He pointed across the hall to the flower display.

"Congratulations, Mr Widnall," I said.

"Are you a grower yourself, Mr Hardiman?" he asked.

I shook my head. "I'm an ostler," I said.

"And a university constable," added Kate. There was a note of pride in her voice and both Widnall and I caught it. He looked at me a little more keenly.

"I hear your brother's to be wed, Miss Swanney" he said after a moment. "About time."

Kate laughed. "Yes: no-one could accuse George of being hasty in his choice. But they will be happy together, I think."

"And you, miss?" asked Widnall. He looked from Kate to me and back again.

"Well, it will be a little more crowded when Ann – Miss Warwick – moves into our rooms on Silver Street with us, but we shall manage," she said brightly. "And now we must look at the other displays, Mr Widnall. It was lovely to see you, and congratulations again."

We moved off to look at the impressive presentation of apples on the next table; a sign alongside it said "150 varieties of apple grown by Mr Ronald of Brentford".

"I don't think he was asking about your living arrangements, Kate," I said quietly.

"I know perfectly well what he was asking," she replied. I expected her to smile flirtatiously at me or squeeze my arm, but she did neither. "If I marry," she said, "it will be because I cannot tolerate the thought of not marrying that man."

"I see," I said seriously. We walked to the next table and admired a large blue bowl of prize-winning pears. For some reason it was easier to have this significant conversation without looking directly at each other. "And what is most important in a marriage, do you think?" I asked.

Without a second of hesitation, she answered. "Honesty," she said. "Secrets, lies, any sort of dishonesty – I cannot bear them." And now she did squeeze my arm. "It is something I value greatly in our friendship, Gregory. I know that you are always honest with me."

And my heart sank as I thought of everything that I had not told her.

CONCLUSION

"I will confess that I am slightly uneasy about this evening's talk," I said to Robert Sadd as we once again worked together in the library room at the top of the Black Bull.

"The giant?" he said, taking a book from me for re-shelving.

"It seems... unfair of me to stare at someone for their physical state when I myself..." I could not quite find the words, but I gestured at my face.

"Hypocritical, you mean?" said Robert.

I reached quickly for my vocabulary book. "I collect words," I explained as I opened it. "I have heard that word a few times but the spelling is tricky." I looked up at him. "Do you know the origins of the word?"

"Meaning, yes, origins, no," said Robert. "Shall we check?" He walked over to the reference bookcase and pulled out Johnson's *Dictionary*. He carried it to the desk, opened it and turned the pages until he found the word he wanted. "'Hypocritical'," he read aloud. "'Dissembling, insincere. From hypocrite.' Hold on," he moved his finger down and then across the page. "Hypocrite, here we are. Ah, it only says that it is French, which is not much help, is it? From the sound of it, I would guess at a Greek origin."

I stood and looked where he was pointing and copied the spelling of the word into my notebook. "Thank you," I said. "I shall ask Mr Giles from Nicholson's – he is bound to know."

"Undoubtedly," agreed Robert. He closed the dictionary and returned it to the shelf. "But regardless of the origin of the word, I do not think it applies. Yes, people have paid to stare at Monsieur Frenz for his stature, but that is not our purpose this evening. He has been invited to talk to us about his life, and to discuss the medical implications of his condition."

And indeed, so it proved. Monsieur Louis Frenz was, so he told us, seven feet and four inches in height, and although only a young man of twenty-seven, he was already suffering from pain in his hips and his knees. The expense of having to alter his clothing and furniture was considerable, he explained, and for this reason he had agreed to be exhibited in England in order to make his fortune before returning to France. His two sisters, he said, were nearly as tall as he was – and his brother even taller, but much shyer. At the end of the talk, Monsieur Frenz was applauded very warmly, and I hope that we made him welcome as a man rather than as a spectacle.

As it would be our last book club meeting of the year, George Fisher and I had arranged to meet in the parlour downstairs for a drink after the meeting. I had to make sure that the library was tidy and secure after the talk and so George went on ahead. And when I joined him, I was pleased to see that he was sharing a table with Henry Adeane, with a third chair waiting for me.

"Allow me, gentlemen," said the magistrate, once I had shaken hands with each of them and taken my seat. He beckoned to the pot boy and ordered drinks. "Interesting fellow, the giant," he said as we waited. "Did you see his hands and feet? Huge." He held his own hands out in front of him to inspect them. "Dashed awkward for writing." The pot boy returned and put three tankards on the table. "And drinking," added the magistrate. He lifted his tankard. "Your good health."

George and I did likewise. We all drank deeply.

"Ah," said George, leaning back in his chair. "I often complain about it, I know, but I am glad to be back in Cambridge."

"Been away?" asked Adeane, then put his tankard down with a thump. "O'course," he said eagerly. "The tolls case, Fisher – what's the outcome?"

George sighed. "Inconclusive, I am afraid."

I cannot remember whether I have mentioned this to you before. For many years, a toll of tuppence has been levied on every laden cart entering or leaving the town. The year I arrived in Cambridge, a coal and corn merchant called Samuel Beales objected to paying the toll any longer and withheld his payments. The Corporation was forced to go to law to recover the money from Beales's account at Fisher's bank. Last year the court finally found in favour of Beales, and the Corporation immediately appealed. This appeal was heard just this week in Westminster, before Lord Tenterden and a special jury, with George required to attend to represent the bank.

"Inconclusive?" asked Adeane, draining his tankard and waving it at the pot boy. "How so?"

"The jury found in favour of the Corporation," said George, "but Beales's lawyer jumped up and said that a new case was being brought against Joseph Brett, the tollgate keeper in Barnwell. Lord Tenterden ruled that no payment should be made by Beales until this new case is resolved."

"Infuriating," said the magistrate. "Thank you." (This was to the pot boy, who had brought three more tankards.) "Waste of time, waste of money. Already cost the Corporation £3,000 in legal fees, I hear – and the tuppence toll brings in only £750 a year." He shook his head.

"And it means I shall have to go down to London again," grumbled George.

"I thought you would enjoy London," I said. "A whipster like you."

George snorted into his tankard. "Whipster? Me? I am too old to be a whipster, even had I the boldness. No: a whipster is still wet behind the ears and thinks the world an exciting place. Like poor Gerard Bendall – he was a whipster if ever I saw one." He shook his head sadly. "As for me, I shall be thirty before too long, and so I enjoy a quieter life, sitting in the tavern with you two square toes."

"And I may be a square toes," said Adeane, "but I could not do without my visits to the capital. Let me know when you have the date for the next trial, Fisher, and I'll come with you and we can kick up our heels, two bachelors together. Now I must be off." He tipped the last of his drink into his mouth and stood. "Nearly forgot. Jeremiah Longman, Mr Hardiman. Interesting development. Turns out he was not paying the required stamp duty on those pills he was hawking. Fined twenty pounds and his stock confiscated. Goodnight, gentlemen." And he left.

I yawned. "I should turn in too," I said. "Early start tomorrow, with the Star. Did you manage to get the notebook, George?"

"I did," he said, reaching into his coat pocket and pulling out a flat, rectangular package. He handed it to me. I carefully unwrapped it to find a slim notebook with *Lett's of London* stamped in gold on the dark red cover. I opened it; the blank pages were made of thick paper, neatly finished. "Is that right?" he asked.

"Perfect," I said. "Now that Jamie is doing so well with his letters, I thought a proper notebook all the way from London might encourage him to practise more often. Thank you, George. How much do I owe you?"

"Four shillings," he replied. I pulled some coins out of my pocket and paid him. "And while I was in the shop I found this for you. A Christmas gift, if you will permit me." He pulled another, smaller package out of his pocket and gave it to me.

I unwrapped it. It was a small diary, the twin of the one I had in my pocket, except for the date on the front: this new one said *DIARY 1828*. I turned it over in my hands.

"It seemed a fitting way to mark the end of one year and the start of another," said George. He smiled at me. "It's not often that you are lost for words, Gregory."

I cleared my throat. "Indeed not," I agreed. I looked again at the little diary.

George lifted his tankard. "To 1828," he said.

"And to friends," I said, raising my own drink. "To very good friends."

GLOSSARY

Money

In the 1820s, nearly all money that Gregory would have encountered was in coin form. There were banknotes, but these were for large denominations and would not have been in common usage for people of his class and limited wealth.

The coins that Gregory would have handled are these (in ascending order of value):

- Farthing (a quarter of a penny)

- Halfpenny

- Penny

- Sixpence

- Shilling (twelve pence)

- Half crown (two shillings and sixpence)

- Crown (five shillings)

- Sovereign (a gold coin worth a pound, or 240 pennies)

You may also have heard of a guinea – this is one pound (i.e. a sovereign) and one shilling.

As for the actual spending value of these denominations, of course that changes as our modern currency values fluctuate. But at the time of writing – summer 2025 – here are some approximate exchange rates:

- A penny in Gregory's time would buy what would cost us about 30p today

- A shilling would buy about £3-worth of goods today

- A sovereign would buy about £60-worth of goods today.

So when Gregory buys a month's worth of opium for two shillings, he is paying about £6.

Definitions

Apoplexy – paralysis caused by a stroke

Argand lamp – a type of oil lamp, invented in 1780 by Frenchman Aimé Argand and popular as it gave off a light equivalent to about eight candles

Assizes – a session in a law court, and used especially to describe the sessions held periodically in each county of England as judges toured their circuit to administer civil and criminal justice

Belly timber – meal, food of any sort

Blackstone's – more completely, Commentaries on the Laws of England by William Blackstone; a treatise on the common law of England, first published in four volumes between 1765 and 1769

Block gingerbread – a dense, dark, treacle-flavoured gingerbread made using wooden moulds and very popular in the nineteenth century

Cagged – to be sulky or out of humour

Clicker – a person employed by a shopkeeper to stand at the door and solicit customers

Cobweb morning – an old Norfolk term for a morning when the mist hangs so thick that it looks like a spider's web

Conventicle – a gathering or assembly

Curricle – a smart, lightweight, two-wheeled, two-seated chariot drawn by two horses and designed for speed – the sports car of the Regency period

Dropsy – swelling caused by the accumulation of large amounts of fluid, mostly caused by kidney disease or congestive heart failure

Fall onto the parish – in the nineteenth century, before workhouses were widespread, care for paupers fell to individual parishes, which taxed wealthier citizens in order to provide basic food, shelter and clothing for the poorer members of the community

Fellmonger – a dealer in hides or skins, particularly sheepskins, who might also prepare skins for tanning

Freaking – (in this context, as origin is uncertain) wild and unpredictable movement and dancing

Gut-foundered – exceedingly hungry

Hostel ale – cheap, poorer quality beer

In the suds – in trouble, in a disagreeable or difficult situation

Joskin – a country bumpkin, an unsophisticated person

Livery yard – nowadays a livery yard is a stable where a horse owner pays a weekly or monthly fee to keep their horse, but in Gregory's day they also served as places to hire a horse (not unlike our modern car rental companies)

Maltster – a maker of (or dealer in) malt, which is used to make beer

Nettled – made uneasy or provoked by something

Nib – a self-important person (today, people still talk of His Nibs)

Ostry – a room set aside for the ostler to live or rest in, often a loft above the stables

Parish – see *Fall on the parish*

Piece – wench, young woman, usually used in a positive sense (fine piece, comely piece, etc.)

Plead the belly – a woman who was (or who claimed to be) pregnant when sentenced to death could "plead the belly"; they would then be examined by a jury of matrons and if movement of the baby could be detected, the execution was respited until after the baby was born. In principle they could then be executed, but in practice sympathy for the newborn child (or concern over the cost of caring for it) meant that the mother was often pardoned.

Pottle – a now obsolete unit of volume, which was two quarts, or half a gallon

Registrary – the senior administrative officer of the University (first appointed in 1504 to compile and maintain the records of the University)

Rum prancer – a fine, elegant, beautiful horse

Scrub – a low, mean man, employed in all sorts of dirty work

Small beer – because water was often unsafe to drink, many people (including children) drank small beer, which was a weak alcoholic beverage made with boiled water

Square toes – an old man, as they are fond of wearing comfortable shoes with room around the toes

Squib – a small firework that burns with a hissing noise

Strings – the reins used to control a horse

Stump bed – a bed without posts (most of our modern beds would have been considered stump beds)

Suds – see *In the suds*

Tanner – slang for sixpence (worth about £1.50 in today's money)

Tas – from Middle English for a heap or pile, with 'in tas' coming to mean in a crowd or en masse

Turnkey – a gaoler, being a description of one of his main responsibilities

Unfortunate woman – a person considered immoral or lacking in religious faith or instruction, often used to suggest a prostitute

Whig – in the 1820s, the two main political parties were the Tories (who took a more conservative stance) and the Whigs (who were more liberal-minded – and indeed eventually became known as the Liberals)

Whipster – a young man of energy, confidence and some mischief, along the lines of a whippersnapper but perhaps a few years older

Yeoman Bedell – one of the group of bedells appointed to assist with University ceremonies and duties (the Yeoman Bedell, for instance, was responsible for collecting fines from undergraduates)

UNIVERSITY STRUCTURE

For readers who are not familiar with the organisational and command structure of Cambridge University in the 1820s, here is a very brief overview.

The ceremonial head of the University was the **Chancellor** – chosen for his ability to bring fortune and favour to the University. He did not reside in Cambridge or exercise day-to-day power, and so the head of the University for all practical purposes was in fact the **Vice-Chancellor**. He was one of the "head of houses" – heads of the colleges, who might be known as masters or principals – and was chosen by them from their own number every 4 November, to serve for a year. In 1827 – the year in which this book takes place – the Vice-Chancellor was Christopher Wordsworth (a theologian and Master of Trinity College) until 4 November, and after that Martin Davy (a physician and Master of Gonville and Caius College). The duties of the Vice-Chancellor included managing university finances and estates, deciding on prizes, holding authority in Cambridge city government, granting licences, deciding in matters of discipline, and opening Stourbridge Fair each September, as a prelude to the academic year. The principal administrative officer of the University was the **Registrary**, and his main role was to compile and maintain the records of the University.

Each college had its own command structure. At the top of the tree was the head of house, usually known as the **master**. He had oversight of all college affairs – administering its property, seeing to the learning and good conduct of its members and presiding over meetings of college fellows – but he left most financial concerns to the **bursar**. The master received a good income and was provided with a gracious lodge in college grounds. He would also receive a dividend from the profits of college estates. Crucially, heads of houses were the only senior members of the University who were permitted to marry. In the 1820s, this small number of dignitaries and their wives formed Cambridge's upper class society of mixed-gender dinner parties and morning calls.

Attached to each college were academics known as **fellows**. They had rooms assigned to them within the college and lived and dined within its walls. They were generally appointed for life, and spent their time on their own academic research and writing. The teaching staff within a college were known as **tutors**, who might themselves employ **assistant tutors** to help with the teaching workload. The students were known as **undergraduates** or **gownsmen**. Some lived in college – often in a "set" composed of a bedroom and a sitting room – and some lived out in lodgings. If a student was particularly ambitious, he might employ a private tutor (often a young, recently-appointed fellow) to help him cram for his exams.

The undergraduates themselves were divided into categories according to how much they paid to attend the University. The most select were **noblemen** (peers and their sons, baronets, knights, those close to the King and their eldest sons) who paid £10 [about £600 today] a quarter. **Fellow commoners** were sometimes titled and/or landed but were always wealthy, and they paid £5 a quarter. Most undergraduates were **scholars** or **pensioners** who came from gentle and professional but not wealthy families and paid £2 and ten shillings a quarter: scholars had financial help from their colleges, while pensioners paid their own way. (Charles Darwin was accepted as a pensioner at Christ's College in 1827.) And finally there were the **sizars**, who paid £15 shillings a quarter and performed duties in college to earn their keep.

One of the fellows would serve as the college **bursar**. It was often a thankless task, and finding a fellow willing to do it was sometimes tricky. The job of the bursar was to oversee college finances, with money coming in from leases and rents on college properties (buildings and extensive agricultural land), and money going out to maintain the college and its inhabitants. In the time period covered by the Gregory Hardiman books – 1825-1830 – college finances, and therefore the job of the bursar, were becoming more complicated. Bursars were expected not simply to take in college income and make payment for college expenses, but also to make sound investments to secure the future of the college. Many of them were not up to the task.

AFTERWORD

Thank you for reading this book.

If you liked what you read, please would you leave a short review on the site where you purchased it, or recommend it to others?

Reviews and recommendations are not only the highest compliment you can pay to an author; they also help other readers to make more informed choices about purchasing books.

ACKNOWLEDGEMENTS

As always, I am astonished by the generosity of people who are willing to share with me their time and their expertise as I work on my books. For their help with *Whipster*, particular thanks are given to the following wonderful individuals...

Richard Reynolds, crime fiction expert (and now proud part-owner of Cambridge's newest independent bookshop, Bodies in the Bookshop) – for suggesting a Cambridge series in the first place

Jon Harris, artist – for creating the beautiful map of Gregory Hardiman's Cambridge

Lucy Lewis (University Marshal), **Tim Milner** (Pro-Proctor for Ceremonial) and **Seb Falk** (Senior Proctor) – for their expert insight into the role of the university constable, past and present

Jacqueline Cox (Keeper of University Archives) – for helping me to untangle knotty bits of University history

Mary Burgess (Local Studies Librarian at the Cambridgeshire Collection) – for answering every single daft question I have ever asked about the history of Cambridge

Kuladipa (Cambridge Buddhist Centre) – for showing me around what was once the Barnwell Theatre

Roy McCarthy – for being, as always, a simply sterling beta reader

I am extremely grateful to you all for knowing so much and then agreeing to share that knowledge and your time with me. Thank you.

And if despite this wealth of world-class assistance I have made errors, they are entirely my own.

REVIEWS

and the pace well fitted to this genre. The novel shows excellent research and writing ability – a recommended read." *Barbara Goldie, The Kindle Book Review*

"Regency police constable Sam Plank, so well established in the first book, continues to develop here, with an interesting back story emerging about his boyhood, which shapes his attitude to crime as an adult. This is not so much a whodunit as a whydunit, and Grossey skilfully unfolds a complex tale of financial crime and corruption. There are fascinating details about daily life in the criminal world woven into the story, leaving the reader much more knowledgeable without feeling that he's had a history lesson." *Debbie Young, author and book blogger*

Praise for *Worm in the Blossom*

"Ever since I was introduced to Constable Sam Plank and his intrepid wife Martha, I have followed his exploits with great interest. There is something so entirely dependable about Sam: to walk in his footsteps through nineteenth century London is rather like being in possession of a superior time travelling machine... The writing is, as ever, crisp and clear, no superfluous waffle, just good old-fashioned storytelling, with a tantalising beginning, an adventurous middle, and a wonderfully dramatic ending." *Jo at Jaffareadstoo*

"Susan Grossey not only paints a meticulous portrait of London in this era, she also makes the reader see it on its own terms, for example recognising which style of carriage is the equivalent to a 21st century sports-car, and what possessing one would say about its owner... In short, a very satisfying and agreeable read in an addictive series that would make a terrific Sunday evening television drama series." *Debbie Young, author and book blogger*

Praise for *Portraits of Pretence*

"There is no doubt that the author has created a plausible and comprehensive Regency world and with each successive novel I feel as if I am returning into the bosom of a well-loved family. Sam and Martha's thoughtful care and supervision of the ever-vulnerable Constable Wilson, and of course, Martha's marvellous ability, in moments of extreme worry, to be her husband's still small voice of calm is, as always, written with such thoughtful attention to detail." *Jo at Jaffareadstoo*

"Do you want to know what a puff guts is or a square toes or how you would feel if you were jug-bitten? Well, you'll find out in this beautifully researched and written Regency crime novel. And best of all you will be in the good company of Constable Sam Plank, his wife Martha and his assistant Constable Wilson. These books have immense charm and it comes from the tenderness of the depiction of Sam's marriage and his own decency." *Victoria Blake, author*

Praise for *Faith, Hope and Trickery*

"What I like about the delightful law enforcement characters in this series is their ordinariness. They are not superheroes, they do not crack the case in a matter of a quick fortnight, but weeks, months, pass with the crime in hand on-going with other, everyday things, happening in the background. This inclusion of reality easily takes the reader to trudge alongside Constable Plank as he threads his way through the London streets of the 1820s, his steady tread always on the trail of bringing the lawbreakers to justice." *Helen Hollick of Discovering Diamonds book reviews*

"The mystery at the heart of the novel is, as ever, beautifully explained and so meticulously detailed that nothing is ever left to chance and everything flows like the wheels of a well-oiled machine. There's an inherent dependability about Constable Plank which shines through in every novel and yet, I think that in *Faith,*

Hope and Trickery we see an altogether more vulnerable Sam which is centred on Martha's unusual susceptibility and on his unerring need to protect her." *Jo at Jaffareadstoo*

Praise for *Heir Apparent*

"*Heir Apparent* is possibly my favourite Sam Plank book yet, with great twists and turns to the plot and meticulous research. This author really gets the historical detail just right, but what stands out for me is the captivating character development the author has honed throughout the series, and I will own that for me the crime element is almost superfluous, as it is the characters who keep me coming back to these books." *Peggy-Dorothea Beydon, author*

"There's an authenticity to the characters, particularly Sam and his wife Martha, which not only makes these stories such a joy to read, but which also gives such an imagined insight into life in the capital in the early 1800s so that it really does feel as though you are moving in tandem with Plank, Martha and the intrepid Wilson as they go about their business, forever trying, and usually succeeding, to live their lives in the full glare of the criminal fraternity." *Jo at Jaffareadstoo*

Praise for *Notes of Change*

"I have followed this series from the start, and thoroughly enjoyed each and every one. Once again, the book immerses us in the streets of 1820s London, in the excellent company of constable Sam Plank and his wife Martha. This latest standalone case takes a number of well crafted turns, not least the reappearance of an old adversary in some unexpected circumstances, and all of which ties in nicely to the very apt title. A very worthy addition to the series and a very fitting finale." *Graham T, Amazon reviewer*

"This well-written and thoroughly researched series strikes a balance between historical correctness and feel-good fiction –

there's no hiding the harshness of life in Sam's era, but the warmth and depth of the central characters ensures they are comfort reads all the same." *Debbie, Amazon reviewer*

Praise for *Ostler*

"A first-rate historical crime novel, with a sympathetic hero, a good plot and convincing language and atmosphere. It's the first of a new series, and already I'm looking forward to the sequel." *Promoting Crime Fiction*

"Beautifully written by an author whose knowledge of Cambridge, and impeccable research, brings this nineteenth century world alive in such a way that place and people bound into life. The story wraps around you with ease and at each step of the mystery a little bit more is revealed, not just about Hardiman, who I am sure we will discover more about as the series progresses, but also about the intricacies of nineteenth century life in a bustling collegiate town." *Jo at Jaffareadstoo*

Praise for *Sizar*

"The beautifully meticulous detail with which the period (the 1820s) is reconstructed is one of the pleasures of this excellent series." *Mrs A C Koning, Amazon reviewer*

"The sign of a good read is to want to know what happens next so you keep turning the pages, to totally believe that what you are reading is fact not fiction, the characters are 100% believable in what they say, do and act, and to reach the last page thoroughly satisfied and having learned something new along the way. Without hesitation, *Sizar* ticks all the boxes and is a very good read indeed." *Helen Hollick, Amazon reviewer*

LEARN MORE ABOUT GREGORY'S TIMES

Every month I produce a free e-newsletter featuring some of the research I have done on Regency times – from food and celebrations, to money and policing. Like most authors of historical fiction, I do far more research than I can ever use in my books, and it's all fascinating!

If you'd like to receive my free e-newsletter each month, please sign up at www.susangrossey.com/insider-updates

And as a little thank-you, you will receive **a FREE complete e-book of *Fatal Forgery* (the first book in the Sam Plank Mysteries series)** – and the chance to take part in occasional giveaways and competitions. See you there!